Jun 2017

Beasts Head for Home

WEATHERHEAD BOOKS ON ASIA

WEATHERHEAD BOOKS ON ASIA

WEATHERHEAD EAST ASIAN INSTITUTE,
COLUMBIA UNIVERSITY

Literature

DAVID DER-WEI WANG, EDITOR

Ye Zhaoyan, *Nanjing 1937: A Love Story*, translated by Michael Berry (2003)
Oda Makato, *The Breaking Jewel*, translated by Donald Keene (2003)
Han Shaogong, *A Dictionary of Maqiao*, translated by Julia Lovell (2003)
Takahashi Takako, *Lonely Woman*, translated by Maryellen Toman Mori (2004)
Chen Ran, *A Private Life*, translated by John Howard-Gibbon (2004)
Eileen Chang, *Written on Water*, translated by Andrew F. Jones (2004)
Writing Women in Modern China: The Revolutionary Years, 1936–1976, edited by Amy
    D. Dooling (2005)
Han Bangqing, *The Sing-song Girls of Shanghai*, first translated by Eileen Chang, revised
    and edited by Eva Hung (2005)
Loud Sparrows: Contemporary Chinese Short-Shorts, translated and edited by Aili Mu,
    Julie Chiu, and Howard Goldblatt (2006)
Hiratsuka Raichō, *In the Beginning, Woman Was the Sun*, translated by Teruko Craig
    (2006)
Zhu Wen, *I Love Dollars and Other Stories of China*, translated by Julia Lovell (2007)
Kim Sowŏl, *Azaleas: A Book of Poems*, translated by David McCann (2007)
Wang Anyi, *The Song of Everlasting Sorrow: A Novel of Shanghai*, translated by Michael
    Berry with Susan Chan Egan (2008)
Ch'oe Yun, *There a Petal Silently Falls: Three Stories by Ch'oe Yun*, translated by Bruce and
    Ju-Chan Fulton (2008)
Inoue Yasushi, *The Blue Wolf: A Novel of the Life of Chinggis Khan*, translated by Joshua
    A. Fogel (2009)
Anonymous, *Courtesans and Opium: Romantic Illusions of the Fool of Yangzhou*, translated
    by Patrick Hanan (2009)
Cao Naiqian, *There's Nothing I Can Do When I Think of You Late at Night*, translated by
    John Balcom (2009)
Park Wan-suh, *Who Ate Up All the Shinga? An Autobiographical Novel*, translated by Yu
    Young-nan and Stephen J. Epstein (2009)
Yi T'aejun, *Eastern Sentiments*, translated by Janet Poole (2009)
Hwang Sunwŏn, *Lost Souls: Stories*, translated by Bruce and Ju-Chan Fulton (2009)

For a complete list, see page 193.

Abe Kōbō

Beasts Head for Home

A NOVEL

Translated by Richard F. Calichman

COLUMBIA UNIVERSITY PRESS   NEW YORK

COLUMBIA
UNIVERSITY
PRESS

Columbia University Press gratefully acknowledges the generous support
for this book provided by Publisher's Circle member Donald Keene.

This publication has been supported by the Richard W. Weatherhead
Publication Fund of the Weatherhead East Asian Institute,
Columbia University.

Columbia University Press
Publishers Since 1893
New York   Chichester, West Sussex
cup.columbia.edu
Kemono tachi wa Kokyou wo Mezasu
Copyright © 1957 by Kobo Abe
English translation rights arranged with the Estate of Kobo Abe through Japan
UNI Agency Inc., Tokyo
Translation copyright © 2017 Columbia University Press

Library of Congress Cataloging-in-Publication Data

Names: Abe, Kōbō, 1924–1993, author. | Calichman, Richard, translator.
Title: Beasts head for home: a novel / Abe Kōbō; translated by
Richard F. Calichman.
Other titles: Kemonotachi wa kokyō mezasu. English
Description: New York: Columbia University Press, 2017. |
Series: Weatherhead books on Asia | First published in Japanese as
Kemonotachi wa kokyō mezasu.
Identifiers: LCCN 2016041666 (print) | LCCN 2017001595 (ebook) |
ISBN 9780231177047 (cloth: alk. paper) | ISBN 9780231177054 (pbk.) |
ISBN 9780231544665 (electronic)
Subjects: LCSH: Japanese—Manchuria—Fiction. | Identity (Psychology)—
Fiction. | Manchuria (China)—History—1945—Fiction. | Psychological
fiction. | GSAFD: Historical fiction.
Classification: LCC PL845.B4 K413 2017 (print) | LCC PL845.B4
(ebook) | DDC 895.63/5—dc23
LC record available at https://lccn.loc.gov/2016041666

∞

Columbia University Press books are printed on permanent
and durable acid-free paper.
Printed in the United States of America

Cover design: Lisa Hamm
Cover image: [composite] Shutterstock

Contents

Introduction

A be Kōbō's novel *Kemonotachi ha kokyō wo mezasu* (Beasts head for home, 1957) occupies a rare place among his fictional writings. Abe's most famous works typically provide a bare minimum of proper nouns as indicators of people and place, as he seeks to present situations whose meaning, in its generality, goes beyond the limits of any particular context. Indeed, as he once remarked in an interview, "In my fiction, proper nouns are insignificant; they don't need to be there."[1] And yet *Kemonotachi ha kokyō wo mezasu* is inconceivable without the specificity of its references, for these mark the concrete place and time of postwar Manchuria. Abe possessed firsthand knowledge of Manchuria, having been raised in the city of Shenyang within the confines of the Japanese colony that had been established there. Certainly the attention to historical detail that punctuates the novel can be traced back to Abe's own experiences in Manchuria, but it must be remembered that *Kemonotachi ha kokyō wo mezasu* is neither Abe's only novel set in Manchuria (*Owarishimichi no shirube ni* [The signpost at the road's end, 1948] is also set there) nor his only "historical" novel (in Japan, it is rather *Enomoto Buyō*, published in 1965, that is regarded as Abe's most properly historical work). In the present novel, Abe grounds fictional characters and situations in a concrete historical setting in such a way as to provoke among his readers a reconsideration of the relation between historical specificity and those more general elements that remain irreducible to any particular historical event.

Historically, *Kemonotachi ha kokyō wo mezasu* depicts one of the over-looked casualties of Japan's transition from empire to nation-state following the end of the Pacific War. As part of the terms of its surrender in 1945, Japan was forced to relinquish control of its extensive colonial holdings throughout Asia. This transfer of territory brought about a drastic reorganization of populations on at least three levels: (1) Japanese soldiers and civilians residing overseas began to return en masse to the Japanese islands; (2) a large majority of those colonized peoples first brought to Japan for the purpose of slave labor gradually returned to their countries of origin; and (3) the collapse of the various institutions supporting the colonial framework brought an end to the ideological identification among the colonized as members of the Japanese Empire, resulting in the emergence of new forms of subjective affiliation. It is against this background of dislocation among peoples, for whom the shift from the war-time to postwar periods effectively invalidated previous modes of identification and belonging, that Abe describes Kuki Kyūzō's tortuous journey from Manchuria to Japan.

Abe is intent on re-creating the specific historical context in which Kyūzō finds himself. In a chronology of global events from 1946 to 1948, the narrator informs us that "the Foreign Affairs Office reports that a total number of 4,039,447 Japanese remain unrepatriated."[2] In envisioning the figure of a Japanese youth abandoned in what was previously the Japanese puppet state of Manchukuo, Abe provides a layer of fictional representation to the Soviet occupation of Manchuria and the final years of the Chinese civil war between the Nationalist and Communist (Eighth Route Army) forces. If the narrative present of the novel focuses on the Soviets and Chinese as the central collective agents in postwar Manchuria, however, we must not fail to note how Abe continually refers back to the wartime figure of Japan. This he does not simply through the technique of flashback, significantly, but also by alluding to the surviving traces of that otherwise vanished past. Just as, at the very opening of the novel, Kyūzō's room is described as in a sense haunted by the remnants of an absent past—"On the wall, pale traces remained of such long ago objects as a dresser and picture frame, adding to the sense of emptiness"[3]—so, too, is the former presence of wartime Japan signaled throughout Abe's text in terms of such things as a Chinese Nationalist military truck expropriated from the Japanese army, the Residence of Overseas Japanese Retainers, the discontinued Japanese repatriation ships, and the red roofs of "the Japanese residential district from long ago,"[4] as well as of course the lingering hatred toward the Japanese that prevents the characters from freely speaking the Japanese language in public.

Yet if Abe is committed to the task of recalling this history of Japanese militarism, we should nevertheless not be led to reduce the complexity of his ideas as introduced in the work to mere empirical history. This would be to fall into the trap of historicism, understood here as the reduction to a strictly empirical event of what are rather general conditions of possibility. Such a trap can be seen, for example, in the literary critic Isoda Kōichi's "Commentary" (kaisetsu) on the novel that is appended to the original paperback edition. Isoda writes as follows regarding the issue of man's historical situatedness:

Moreover, how effective can it possibly be for an individual to assert his autonomy [*jishusei*] when encountering a reality in which even his personal safety cannot be guaranteed without passing through the mesh of politics? When reality is enmeshed in political relations, even the escape of the individual cannot take place by ignoring the political power of the outside world. Even such questions as "What is an enemy?" and "What is an ally?" are determined by external reality and its contingencies. An autonomous individual is nothing; rather, it is only the "relations" with the outside world that determine the raison d'être of the "individual."[5]

Isoda forcefully argues that the individual is to be seen in the essential context of his relations with the world. Taking issue with a liberalist x ℥ INTRODUCTION

conception of the individual as existing, in his freedom, originally distinct from others, inhabiting a personal zone of integrity and autonomy,
Isoda insists that no autonomy can be achieved without first negotiating
the multiple bonds that determine the individual as inherently social.
Indeed, *Kemonotachi ha kokyō wo mezasu* can be read as a particularly
vital illustration of this point in showing how Kyūzō's desire to return to
Japan is consistently thwarted by forces over which he ultimately has no
control, forces that expose the limits of his freedom and so ground him
in the complex reality that is postwar Manchuria. Nevertheless, the
notion of "reality" (*genjitsu*) to which Isoda appeals in order to disclose
the restrictions placed upon personal autonomy derives quite clearly
from the empirical context that surrounds Abe's protagonist. The "political relations" that threaten an individual's "personal safety," as he writes,
refer in this instance to a postcolonial Manchuria in which the vacuum
created by Japan's defeat has given rise to a violent, lawless society that is
temporarily under Soviet occupation but where a protracted battle for
national sovereignty is being waged between the Chinese Nationalist
and Communist forces. It is this larger political reality that Isoda regards
as the foremost restraint upon individual autonomy. In attributing the
impossibility of such autonomy to empirical circumstances, however,
Isoda disregards the possibility that individuality can *never* be formed or
fully achieve itself under any circumstances whatsoever—and this for
essential rather than merely empirical reasons. What is required here, in
other words, is a shift of perspective from the discourse of historiography
to that of philosophy. Isoda provides a crucial insight into Abe's text by
reminding us that the "autonomous individual is nothing," but the explanation for this failure of autonomy—without which, in all rigor, the
individual is incapable of ever forming himself qua individual—is to be
sought less in particular historical phenomena than in the general, or
essential, exposure of individual propriety or identity to worldly alterity.
In Abe's novel, such exposure cannot be limited to the *specific* site of
Manchuria or to the *specific* time of the postwar period. On the contrary,
the protagonist Kuki Kyūzō's inability to achieve a sphere of selfsame

identity marks itself from the very moment he originally appears in the world as such.

How then can we as readers recognize this force of alterity operating throughout the novel? I would like to argue that, in the particular context of *Kemonotachi ha kokyō wo mezasu*, Abe elaborates what might be called a notion of *homelines* that serves to call into question the fixity or givenness of all borders, and above all those borders that delineate the space of the home. Here the concept of home that appears in the very title of the novel would refer not only to the "hometown" or "native place" typically designated by the word *kokyō*. On the contrary, an attentive reading of the novel reveals that Abe seeks to generalize this concept by reconceiving the notion of border. The traditional understanding of home requires the functioning of borders, but Abe implies that this use of the border paradoxically dissimulates or disavows its force. Whereas the boundary that allows a home to appear in its identity is seen to mark its difference from the nonhome, or that which exists outside this privileged domestic space, Abe suggests instead that borders can at any moment potentially be drawn *within* that internal space itself, thereby disrupting its putative unity. In the novel, Kyūzō learns this lesson from Kō, who emphasizes the precarious and strangely proliferating nature of the border:

"I wonder where we are now."

"We're probably about twelve miles outside of Taonan."

"Will we go into town there?"

"No, we won't be able to. We're still at the border between friend and enemy. When all is said and done, I think, the most dangerous thing is a border. They're more dangerous than being in the midst of enemies. At least in my experience, they certainly are."

"Then how about the next town?"

"The next town is Shuanggang. That's also on the border. The towns after that, Kaitong, Bianzhao, Tanyu, Taipingchuan, as well as the towns thereafter, are all on the border. In times such as these, the border definitely expands."[6]

In these lines the border is narrowly determined as that between friend and enemy, but Abe's reconceptualization of the notion of home leads him to define this space more broadly as referring to *any* privileged site of interiority whose enclosure appears to provide security or a sense of refuge vis-à-vis the threat of external difference. The home territory that Kyūzō and Kō seek, therefore, would in principle safeguard them from the outer force of the enemy by consolidating their bonds with the friends or allies whom they identify as in some sense similar to themselves. Here the relation between the notions of border and home comes clearly into view: the borderline that demarcates the home establishes the nonhome, or the *foreign*, in that same gesture, thereby determining the home as the site of identity, interiority, and security, while simultaneously projecting the qualities of difference, exteriority, and danger onto the alien nonhome. It is in order to disturb or in some way unsettle this bounded oppositionality that Abe is led to conceive of a proliferating homelines, in which the presence of fixed or given borders comes to be desedimented and traced back to the *instituting act* that first allows these borders to appear as themselves. No home is possible without this act of bordering, and yet the maintenance, or continued recognition, of the home as such demands that this border be constantly redrawn in order to confirm the distinction between friend and enemy, inside and outside, security and danger. For Abe, the disclosure of the border as in truth an act, continually repeated, of redrawing borders effectively threatens the security and self-identity of the home, since this latter is incessantly redetermined at each and every moment homelines are marked.[7]

In *Kemonotachi ha kokyō wo mezasu*, Abe presents a variety of homes whose delineation introduces an essential instability to this concept, one that the reader is tasked with recognizing. I would like to identify four such instances of homelines, where Abe both sets forth what appears to be a space of interiority and security and demonstrates how this space is *from the beginning*—that is to say, beyond the limits of historicism— violated from within: (1) the home qua individual subject, (2) the home qua family, (3) the home qua nation-state, and (4) the home qua human.

It is these four levels of home, Abe suggests, that provide in their overlapping mediations the major framework by which to understand the modern world as depicted in the novel.

1. Given the nearly exclusive focus throughout the novel on the figure of Kuki Kyūzō, it may be tempting to read Abe's work as an example of bildungsroman, a novel of formation or education in which the main character's development is reflected in his changing ideas about Japan and himself as Japanese. In the sense that the other characters in the novel are viewed largely from Kyūzō's subjective standpoint and that the otherwise neutral third-person narrative comes frequently to be breached by his own narrative voice, there can be no question that Kyūzō occupies the very center of this text. Yet it is precisely this centrality that Abe calls into question by attending to the particular borders that establish the protagonist's unique identity and thus distinction from others. By the very name Kuki Kyūzō, for example, in which the initial character of the youth's last name is doubled in the initial character of his first name, Abe hints at the repetition and internal divisibility that mark all instances of identity. This theme of duplicity can in fact be found scattered throughout the work, from the appearance of Kō, whose theft of Kyūzō's travel certificate allows him to fraudulently represent himself to others as Kyūzō, to the occasional references to the Japanese mainland (or "Japan proper": *naichi*), which comes in the course of colonial expansion to be duplicated by the *gaichi*, or "external territories," where Kyūzō was born and raised and where the novel is first set, to finally the conspicuous date of 2.22 that appears in the ship's log toward the end of the work. These instances draw attention to the manner in which the sphere of oneness, whose boundaries function to maintain the self in the unity of its home, finds itself continually exposed, drawn outside itself into other iterations.

For Abe, it is important to unearth the conceptual prejudice involved in the literary convention whereby characters must be presented as ultimately unified. By absorbing the variety of differences manifested by characters as strictly instances of *internal difference*, the discourse of literature in effect reveals its debt to the most classical notions of subjectivity.

In the character of Kyūzō, one can see Abe respond to this domestication of alterity in the particular language of his descriptions, and above all in his use of the word *tanin*, or "other(s)," which typically signifies those people *outside of* or *in addition to* one. Let me cite three instances of this term so as to emphasize the unusual status with which Abe endows Kyūzō: (1) After having been viciously beaten by Kō: "I might die now, he felt at last, as if referring to someone else [*taningoto/hitogoto*]." (2) Upon arriving both physically and mentally exhausted at the Residence of Overseas Japanese Retainers: "He felt absolutely no sense of reality. He could not even distinguish whether he felt happy or sad. Only his long journey ran through his mind, as if it were someone else's [*tanin*] story." (3) Finally, in a profoundly ironic sense given that Kō has illicitly claimed Kyūzō's identity for himself, Kyūzō considers that "Kō's fate could no longer be someone else's [*taningoto/hitogoto*] problem."⁸

In these passages, Abe attempts to underscore the elusive nature of difference by focusing on the divisibility that marks the subject in the entirety of his relations with the world. This would represent a radicalization of the traditional literary device of the doppelgänger, in which an already existent self is merely doubled on the outside. On the contrary, Abe's intent here is to show that the root of such duplicity is to be found in the essential insufficiency of identity. Much like his novel *Tanin no kao* (The face of another, 1964), the subject-protagonist discovers that the appearance of the double must be traced back to a difference that lies at the very heart of the one, thereby preventing the one from ever fully encapsulating—or, as it were, *homing in on*—itself. At the end of the novel, Kyūzō finds himself to be doubled twice: first by Kō, who in his insanity now believes himself to actually be Kyūzō, and then by himself, as he dreams of two distinct Kyūzōs, one safely inside the walls of the home and the other outside, excluded, unable to do anything but look in. Regardless of whether Kyūzō is doubled by another character or by himself, or indeed whether such doubling divides his actual self from a dream self or a dream self from a second dream self, Abe's overriding concern is to examine the fault, or cut, that inhabits all forms of unicity. Once doubled—and again, there can be no appearance of identity without this doubling—the home that is the individual subject finds itself to be internally violated.

2. In the novel, the appearance of the family is signified primarily by the figure of Kyūzō's mother. Let me now cite in full Kyūzō's dream of the two Kyūzōs, since his mother in fact plays a pivotal role in this dream:

> For an instant, Kyūzō dreamt a sparklike dream. He dreamt of Baharin when he was very little. His mother was doing laundry behind a high wall. Crouching at her side, he played with the bubbles from the washbasin, popping them with his fingers one after another. No matter how many bubbles he popped, the infinite sky and sun whirled around in radiant gold. From over the wall, another Kyūzō, this one exhausted, peeped timidly in at the sight of them. He was utterly unable to cross over. Why must I spend my whole life wandering outside the wall?[9]

Here the difference between the two Kyūzōs is depicted as starkly asymmetrical. The "exhausted" Kyūzō positioned outside the wall of the home peers in at the Kyūzō located within the home's interior, the comfort and security of which are indicated by the presence of the mother. It is significant that this image of the mother appears on the very final page of the novel, since it was the mother's convalescence and eventual death much earlier in the narrative that were initially responsible for Kyūzō's separation from the Japanese community in Baharin,[10] thereby paving the way for his encounter with the Soviet officer Alexandrov and subsequent escape across the Manchurian plains with Kō. That is to say, if the mother's death originally set in motion a series of events that led to Kyūzō's "return" journey to Japan, then the ultimate failure of that journey comes to be mitigated by her appearance in the dream. For Abe, Kyūzō's desire for Japan is seen as strangely paralleling his desire for the absent mother. Here the circularity of his desire comes into view: the loss of an original presence as manifested in Kyūzō's belonging to a Japanese community, emblematized by his proximity to the live mother, must upon her death now be negated by returning to Japan. The return fails, let us note, not simply for the external or contingent reason that Kyūzō has come to be imprisoned in the ship's hold (i.e., this painful event either may or may not take place) but rather for the internal, logical reason that he has in fact never previously been in Japan, and that such a return would therefore mark less a repetition than a first-time occurrence (i.e., the return in principle cannot take place). Given the mother's intimate association with Japan, the frustration of his desire to return there finds compensation in the dream of her return, or of his return back in time, prior to her death, to her. Only in this way can the circle of Kyūzō's relations with Japan come to be closed.

It is noteworthy in this regard that the figure of Kyūzō's Japanese mother finds itself repeated in the three other mothers that appear in the novel, all of whom are similarly described as Japanese: Kō's mother (whose father, Abe carefully notes, is Korean), the mother behind the walls of the Residence of Overseas Japanese Retainers, and the female mummy whose remains Kyūzō horrifyingly discovers after having finally escaped the wasteland. From Kyūzō's perspective, this repetition results in an increased presence of the mother, for now there are four such maternal figures rather than one, but also—and by that same token—a strange dilution of his mother's original force, since such multiplication requires that the maternal presence now be redistributed beyond the borders of her own individual life. This double movement of expansion and diminution is emphasized by Abe through the overlapping notions of repetition and substitution. Here the term *kurikaeshi* comes to the fore in scenes that describe the mother's death:

After 4:00, the dormitory had become completely silent. "It's shameful, it's shameful," his mother droned on repeatedly [*kurikaeshite*].

Leaving the room, Kyūzō began walking furtively around the empty
dormitory...
"Where have you been?" his mother demanded. Her face appeared
larger with swelling.
"There are mice everywhere," [Kyūzō] replied. His voice was flabby
and weak.
"It's shameful, it's shameful," his mother repeated [*kurikaeshita*].[11]

The meaning of such repetition comes to be grasped only when Kyūzō
discovers that his mother's presence uncannily resists confinement to her
proper identity. This he learns primarily (although not exclusively) in
dreams, where the particular image of the mother comes to be caught up
within the more general logic of substitution. Here we touch upon the
structure of metonymy, understood in the particular sense of a "veering
off of signification" that produces a potentially endless chain of replace-
ments without ever reaching fulfillment.[12] Kyūzō, that is to say, desires to
return to his Japanese mother following her death but finds that this
recovered image constantly slips outside itself onto others that are *not*
her but are nevertheless somehow *like* her. In appearing, he observes, the
mother irrevocably repeats herself otherwise. Abe is insistent in demon-
strating this point, and first of all by describing how the distinction between
Kyūzō's mother and Kyūzō himself comes to be blurred.

Removing Kyūzō's mother from the stretcher, they placed the body
and bedding at the bottom of the hole. Taking a bottle from his pocket,
Punsha sprinkled several drops into the grave. It smelled of alcohol.
He began filling the grave with dirt. Kyūzō had the uncanny feeling
that it was he himself who was being buried.[13]

Paradoxically, the desire to keep the mother is satisfied only on the
condition that the mother *herself* not be kept, that she rather give herself
in exchange to a proxy or agent through which alone she may reveal herself as elusively other to herself. Just as the mother comes to metonymically

displace herself onto Kyūzō, so, too, will her image now slip and transform itself into the Soviet officer Alexandrov. As Kyūzō dreams,

A man with a dog stood up in the shadow of the smokestack. It was Lieutenant Alexandrov. As Alexandrov turned around, his face changed into that of Kyūzō's dead mother, in whose eyes soup was simmering. Ladling some of the soup with his hands, he poured it into the hole of some black bread. The many men gathered around him then dipped their hands into the soup.[14]

In his dreams, the *place* of Kyūzō's mother will also come in the course of the novel to be replaced or displaced onto the mummies, the Soviet medic Dania, and finally Sachiko, the attractive daughter of the chief clerk who lived during the war years in the same Japanese dormitory in Baharin as Kyūzō. We can observe in this metonymical chain that the notion of identity—that is, the *is* or *and* that comes to bind Kyūzō's Japanese mother with a host of other characters—is essentially plastic. The borders that determine such accepted categories as gender and race or ethnicity, for example, are routinely violated, their parameters redrawn by a vastly more general force of identification that at any time potentially places apparently disparate things together while also differentiating those things that are typically seen to be similar. In this way, the unit of the family must, in order to present itself, cede power to a movement of repetition and substitution that effectively withdraws that presence from itself, demanding that it be remarked outside its proper limits.

3. As in so many other works by Abe, the figure of the nation-state occupies a central position in *Kemonotachi ha kokyō wo mezasu*. It should be recalled that Kyūzō's very presence in Baharin is to be explained by the historical path of Japanese imperial expansion, which led to the creation in 1932 of the puppet state of Manchukuo. This hometown of Baharin appears consistently as the nostalgic object of Kyūzō's dreams, and yet the novel clearly suggests that the fixity and stability of this childhood environment in fact originated in an act of territorial dispossession, an act

that will be repeated in 1945 following Japan's defeat and the gradual reordering of the postwar world. Again we see here Abe's attentiveness to the shifting of borders, from the transition of Japan from nation-state to colonial empire to a Manchuria whose violent appropriation by the Japanese will be followed by the no less violent disappropriation and subsequent reappropriation by the Soviet Union before then becoming a crucial battleground over national sovereignty between the Chinese Nationalists and Communists. While it is important to distinguish between various instances of border appropriation—for example, the Japanese colonization of Manchuria can in no way be immediately equated with the Chinese civil war as mere examples subsumed within an abstract concept of territorial arrogation[15]—one must nevertheless acknowledge that *any* claiming of land is already an act of violence. In other words, the violent appropriation of territory does not begin through an act of invasion of land that has previously been settled or domesticated, since this earlier institution of borders that effectively establishes an interiority (home) in its distinction from an exteriority (the nonhome, foreign) is in and of itself violent. In, for instance, the scene in which Kyūzō encounters a group of Chinese youths erecting a sign that reads, "Dongbeiren de Dongbei"—northeast China (i.e., Manchuria) for the northeast Chinese—it is imperative to recognize as necessarily violent this act by which land is claimed on the part of a collective self that tautologically takes its name from that land. For Abe, the modern nation-state both inherits and substantially refines a long tradition by which such violence comes to be concealed in a political gesture of legitimation.

Abe's intervention in this desire for appropriation takes place partly in the domain of language, for he wishes to interrupt the modern logic of the nation-state in which, for example, what is retroactively identified as Japanese land is seen to be populated by Japanese people who speak the Japanese language and contribute in their individual ways to the totality that is Japanese culture (which in turn, it must be remembered, comes to be presented as a particular object of knowledge to individuals of other nation-states within the academic discipline of Japan studies).[16] The protagonist Kuki Kyūzō reveals himself to be especially sensitive to this series of mediations by which the quality of Japaneseness is established, for he hopes to identify Japanese people through the specific medium of the Japanese language in order to achieve his goal of "returning" to land that is properly Japanese (*naichi*). An early expression of Kyūzō's desire can be glimpsed when he receives his travel certificate from an Eighth Route Army officer, who addresses him in fluent Japanese.

> This was the first Japanese that Kyūzō had heard in two years. "Are you Japanese?" he blurted out.
>
> "Korean," the officer replied curtly.

For Kyūzō, the language that he regards quite literally as his mother tongue appears as an object of desire because it seems to promise the formation of communal bonds with other Japanese individuals, and yet he discovers that this linguistic mediation can always lead outside this chain of Japaneseness. Indeed, it is precisely through Kō's recognition of Kyūzō's desire for Japanese communality through that particular linguistic medium that he first initiates contact with him, cunningly allowing Kyūzō to glimpse the Japanese title of his book. Kyūzō's failure to grasp the naïveté of his desire for a sense of Japanese community through the Japanese language finally leads, at the end of the novel, to his deception and imprisonment on board the ship. Hearing the men around him speaking in fluent Japanese, Kyūzō can hardly conceal his pleasure. "How about it? Look! Everyone's Japanese!" he thinks to himself.[17] Yet if his understanding of the link between national language and national identity happens to be accurate in this case, he will eventually learn that it is this same Japanese community of Japanese speakers who will forcibly prevent him from arriving on Japanese land.

In addition to his insight that language appears in modernity as a privileged articulation of the nation-state, Abe will also adroitly direct the reader's attention to the importance of race or ethnicity in the project of national identity. Just as Kyūzō's attunement to the Japanese language functions as a tool by which to identify other Japanese individuals, the category of race or ethnicity will play a similar role. In the following passage, for example, the desire for an established link between the Japanese language and Japanese nationality leads Kyūzō to actively project what he believes to be specifically Japanese racial or ethnic features onto Kō:

> "So you're Japanese. I thought you might be," [Kō] whispered in a low, dry voice while shooting a glance outside. He spoke Japanese easily. When Kyūzō looked at him again, the features of a Japanese person rose to the surface on the man's face [*aratamete minaosu to, otoko no kao ni Nihonjin no rinkaku ga ukabideru*].
> "Are you Japanese, too?" Kyūzō couldn't help but whisper back.
> "No, I'm Chinese."[18]

Abe carefully notes the strange temporality involved in Kyūzō's identification of Kō as a fellow Japanese. It is only *after* this stranger first addresses him in the Japanese language that Kyūzō retroactively determines him as possessing the distinct physical appearance of a Japanese person. Such attribution of racial or ethnic features derives entirely from Kyūzō's subjective desire, but we would be mistaken to assume that Abe regards this issue as merely one of individual psychology. On the contrary, Abe's point is that such racism must be seen as constitutive of the project of national identity. In order to reinforce this insight, Abe will later describe Kyūzō himself as a victim of the same prejudice. This scene, the most explicitly racist in the novel, takes place at the Residence of Overseas Japanese Retainers, where from behind a wall Kyūzō surreptitiously observes two Japanese children at play.

> One of the boys suddenly looked up and yelled. "Hey, there's a beggar spying on us!"
> With that, he threw a lump of mud at Kyūzō. Covering his face with his arms, Kyūzō yelled back. "I'm Japanese, you idiot. I'm Japanese!"

"There's a beggar!" cried out the other boy toward the house. "As if Japanese people would have such dark faces!"[19]

The specific term for skin color Abe uses here is *kuroi*, meaning not only "dark" but also "black." This determination of darkness or blackness as non-Japanese refers both to an imagined difference in skin pigmentation among Asians and a classical trope of civilizational progress, according to which proximity to whiteness signifies a decisive overcoming of primitivism and backwardness in favor of cultural advancement. In this scale that correlates skin color with the relative degree of modernization among peoples, one can discern during the war years a pronounced "tendency among Japanese to try to distance themselves physically from the 'darker' peoples of Asia," as the historian John W. Dower writes.[20] It is in this particular context that we must understand Abe's response to the history of Japanese racism, which of course adopted many of the tenets of "Western" racism. Not only is Kyūzō identified by his compatriots as non-Japanese on account of his darkened skin (owing to his prolonged exposure to the elements while crossing the Manchurian plains); Abe also represents other Asians as possessing lighter skin relative to the Japanese characters in the novel. We can see this in the figure of Zhao, the Shenyang broker and business associate of Ōkane's whose complexion is described as "whitish" (*iro ga shirokute*), as well as in the Chinese Nationalist officer General Bai, whose face is "shaven clean and white" (*shiroku*) and whose very name means "white" in Chinese.[21] Here Abe's strategy consists in effectuating a certain historical reversal *not* in order to argue that Chinese are in fact empirically lighter than Japanese but rather so as to call attention to the underlying presence of the category of race in the discursive formation of the nation-state.

4. By its very title, *Kemonotachi ha kokyō wo mezasu* alerts us to the presence of the animal in Abe's work. What precisely is accomplished in referring to Kyūzō and Kō as "beasts," as seems to be the intention here? First of all, it is important to note the centrality of the figure of the animal in the history of racist discourse. In this novel about the modern primacy

of the nation-state, Abe suggests that the home afforded by the security of national affiliation has come to define the human in its distinction from the animal. Once again it is a question of borders, the lines by which the opposition between the self (interiority, identity) and other (exteriority, difference) comes to be fixed. "Outside the wall people are lonely," Kyūzō reflects at the end of the novel, "forced to bare their teeth like apes in order to live. They can only live like beasts."[22] Beyond the boundary of the particular nation-state can be found not only the foreigner, then, but also the animal, broadly defined. The animal is the beast or brute whose brutality condemns it to exist outside the limits of civilization. The quality of whiteness that determines the human includes within it those faculties that are believed to be the sole property of humanity in its essence, such as reason, consciousness, language, and moral sensibility. Given the internally mediating notion of humanity, however, the concretization of this otherwise abstract universal (in Hegelian language) can take place only through a movement of particularization. That is to say, humanity must concretely instantiate itself in a *particular form* that in some way embodies or incarnates the essence of humanity in general. And this, precisely, is the historical meaning of whiteness. Let me insist that this term must be lifted from all empirical content in order to grasp its significance in modernity as the privileged exemplar of reason, consciousness, language, and moral sensibility. Following this framework in its pure duality, to be human is to be white while darkness or blackness resides strictly on the side of the animal.

Once excluded from the interiority of the home—regardless of whether the space of domesticity is defined here in terms of the mother or of the Japanese community in Baharin—Kyūzō is reduced to a beastlike existence. This is primarily what binds him to Kō, whose lack of any fixed national identity (he identifies himself over the course of the novel as alternately Chinese, Japanese, and Korean) appears to permanently condemn him to the status of outsider. In their wandering through the wasteland,[23] their regression from human to animal is marked by a gradual departure from the mediation of reason to the immediate or bare instinct for survival. As Abe writes, "Since their confrontation, what had sustained the two was not rational will [*riseiteki na ishi*] but merely fear, phantoms, and a beastlike [*kedamono jimita*] visceral impulse."[24] By the end of the novel, Kō indeed appears to have lost all semblance of reason in his lunatic ravings, while Kyūzō, who is consistently described in bestial imagery— for example, panting like a dog, eating like a dog, potentially being killed like a dog, and so forth—seems to have surrendered all traces of humanity in being transformed into a howling, enraged beast. The pain that these two men suffer is extreme, and yet Abe steadfastly resists any notion that salvation is to be found through an ideal return to humanity. As Abe realized, such a return can, in the specific terms of the novel, be effected only by passing through the various mediations of national identity.

NOTES

1. "Kokka kara no shissō: 'Nihon dokusho shinbun' no intabyū ni kotaete" [Disappearance from the state: In response to an interview with the "Japan Readers Newspaper"], in *Abe Kōbō zenshū* [The complete works of Abe Kōbō] (Tokyo: Shinchōsha, 1997–2000), 21:428.

2. *Kemonotachi ha kokyō wo mezasu*, in *Abe Kōbō zenshū*, 6:324.

3. Ibid., 303.

4. Ibid., 414.

5. Abe Kōbō, *Kemonotachi ha kokyō wo mezasu* (Tokyo: Shinchō bunko, 1957), 245.

6. *Abe Kōbō zenshū*, 347–48.

7. In the language of Heidegger, whose influence on Abe is widely recognized, it is a question of thinking the Greek notion of *peras*: "A space is something that has been made room for, something that is cleared and free, namely within a boundary, Greek *peras*. A boundary is not that at which something stops but, as the Greeks recognized, the boundary is that from which something *begins its presencing*" ("Building Dwelling Thinking," in *Poetry, Language, Thought*, trans. Albert Hofstadter [New York: Harper and Row, 1971], 154).

   For Abe's reflections on Heidegger, and particularly Heidegger's notion of "being-in-the-world," see, for example, Abe's essay "Shi to shijin (ishiki to muishiki)" [Poetry and poets (Consciousness and the unconscious), 1944], in *The Frontier Within: Essays by Abe Kōbō*, trans. and ed. Richard F. Calichman (New York: Columbia University Press, 2013), 1–17.

8. *Abe Kōbō zenshū*, 422, 426, 447.

9. Ibid., 451.

10. In *Abe Kōbō no toshi* [The "city" in Abe Kōbō] (Tokyo: Kōdansha, 2012), 177–78, Karube Tadashi interprets this dream as emblematic of Kyūzō's desire for his lost hometown of Baharin.

11. *Abe Kōbō zenshū*, 319–20.

12. Jacques Lacan, *Écrits: A Selection*, trans. Alan Sheridan (New York: Norton, 1977), 160.

13. *Abe Kōbō zenshū*, 322. This image of Kyūzō being buried in place of his mother will reappear in one of his dreams (393).

14. Ibid., 393. While this dream cannot be read as a mere reflection of earlier events, it is nonetheless important to note that Alexandrov had in fact given Kyūzō a meal of soup and black bread immediately prior to his mother's death.

15. Throughout his work, and particularly in his essays, Abe repeatedly sought to explore the inherent tension between the necessity and danger of conceptual abstraction. See, for example, "Eizō wa gengo no kabe wo hakai suru ka" [Does the visual image destroy the walls of language?, 1960], in *The Frontier Within*, 61–65.

16. Here one understands more broadly how the formation of area studies, with its articulation of particular difference along explicitly national lines, remains essentially indebted to the modern system of nation-states. For Abe's resistance to this framework, see his series of dialogues with Donald Keene titled *Hangekiteki ningen* [The antitheater person] (Tokyo: Chūkō shinsho, 1973). I undertake a reading of this text in *Beyond Nation: Time, Writing, and Community in the Work of Abe Kōbō* (Stanford, Calif.: Stanford University Press, 2016), 171–201.

17. *Abe Kōbō zenshū*, 438.

18. Ibid., 329–30. Mark Laurent Gibeau also refers to these lines in his fine analysis of the novel. "Nomadic Communities: The Literature and Philosophy of Abe Kōbō" (Ph.D. diss., Stanford University, 2005), 77.

19. *Abe Kōbō zenshū*, 428.

20. John W. Dower, *War Without Mercy: Race and Power in the Pacific War* (New York: Pantheon, 1986), 209.

21. *Abe Kōbō zenshū*, 434, 408.

22. Ibid., 451.

23. The great importance of this notion of the wasteland as a key to understanding Abe is underlined by Miyanishi Tadamasa, whose *Abe Kōbō: Kōya no hito* [Abe Kōbō: Man of the wasteland] (Tokyo: Seishidō, 2009) is instructive in a biographical sense.

24. *Abe Kōbō zenshū*, 374.

Beasts Head for Home

Chapter 1

The Rusted Tracks

I

"It's finally set for tomorrow. I heard that's when the southbound train will depart," said First Lieutenant Bear upon entering. The snowflakes clinging to the shoulders of his overcoat grew smaller, heading into water.

"Tomorrow, you say?" First Lieutenant Alexandrov looked at him questioningly, partly raising his face from the soup bowl he was hunched over. "Then what about the Chinese Nationalist troops at the number twelve railway bridge zone?"

"It seems they've disappeared."

"Disappeared?"

"I bet they ran off. That's why the departure time is set for tomorrow morning at 9:00."

("In that case," thought Kuki Kyūzō as he stirred the ashes in the stove, "I can finally escape tonight.") His hand suddenly trembled, upsetting the grille. A red ball of flame fell to the floor, emitting smoke as it gave off a hissing sound.

"Careful!" said Alexandrov in a businesslike tone, lightly striking the edge of his bowl with his spoon.

"It seems to be a direct train to Tieling." Bear squinted as he peered into

2 ❤ BEASTS HEAD FOR HOME

the soup pot on the stove. "If everything goes well, by this time next year we'll be over the Ural Mountains."

"Want to try some of that soup?"

"No, Second Lieutenant Shiver is waiting at the office."

"Then we'll certainly be drinking tonight." Removing from his pants pocket an absurdly large green handkerchief nearly a meter in length, Alexandrov wiped his mouth briskly while rising to his feet.

("That's a good sign," Kyūzō thought to himself as he went to get Alexandrov's overcoat.) Bear flicked his Adam's apple, smiling at Kyūzō. Kyūzō tried to smile back, but his heart stuck in his throat, and he could only grin feebly.

After the men left, Kyūzō jumped on his bed, made of empty boxes and old newspapers. Swinging his feet, one after the other, he opened his mouth wide and, without making a sound, laughed heartily. He then went out back to fetch some coal. The frozen wind struck his cheeks like a damp cloth. Still he could not seem to stop laughing.

After washing the dishes, there was not a thing left for him to do. He looked around the room once again, thinking how utterly forbidding it was. On the wall, pale traces remained of such long ago objects as a dresser and picture frame, adding to the sense of emptiness. Even the built-in Russian-style oven was cracked and useless, the ventilation hole covered by a photograph of Stalin. This meant that the stove had to be brought in separately. His escape finally set, however, he realized that he would never again see this room and felt a twinge of regret for those things with which he could never reconcile himself. The room was in every way peaceful. Particularly at times like this, such thick, solid walls were in and of themselves already a rare treasure.

With a sense of stillness, Kyūzō pulled out from under his bed the waterproof blanket that he had prepared just for this moment. He then took some clothes as well as food supplies that he had gathered at every opportunity—salt, two hunks of cheese, a dozen packets of dry bread, a smoked sausage, and a bottle of vodka—and bundled everything together with some hemp rope. There was nothing else to take. After considering a while, it occurred to him to bring matches. From the large box of yellow phosphorous matches, about half still remained. Making three piles of twenty matches each, he put these in three separate places.

II

Two hours later, at about 4:00, Alexandrov and Bear returned with two guests, Second Lieutenant Shiver and Dania, a female army medic.

Bear and Shiver were both Alexandrov's drinking companions, and Kyūzō knew them well. However, it was a bit difficult to understand why they had been given these nicknames. Bear received his nickname because his habit of swinging his head around while speaking made him resemble a bear in the zoo, while it seemed that Shiver's body was always trembling. With his bloated, hairy face and small, round eyes that seemed as if soaked in water, however, Shiver was the one who looked much more like a bear. Compared with him, First Lieutenant Bear was slim like an actor. In terms of body size, Bear was the smallest, followed by Alexandrov and Shiver. If such bears actually exist, they must be a rather unusual type. For a long time, Kyūzō had mistakenly believed that the word *medved'* [bear] meant something like a squirrel. As for Dania the medic, she was physically the largest of the group. Her facial features were rather childlike, but she was utterly imposing. Doubtless she was also the strongest. The men always treated her with respect, and this was not simply because of their consideration for her.

Kyūzō felt chilled as he took the overcoat that Dania had tossed to him, as if he were clutching the frozen wind.

"How many are there now?" asked Dania, gazing at the mountain of empty vodka bottles piled up by the front wall.

"Twenty-eight more than the last time," replied Alexandrov playfully.

The mountain of empty bottles was his pyramid. If he were asked how many there were in total, he would have been able to answer immediately at any time. At that moment, there were perhaps 1,283 bottles.

Dania would then make a serious face and launch into a long speech about the harmful effects of alcohol. Today, however, she merely shook her head and emitted a small laugh of amazement.

The table was now ready. Five cups and five plates, a jar of salt and bread, as well as sliced onions, cheese, and sausage . . . But there was enough for everyone. There were three hunks of cheese, each the size of a child's head; several types of sausage, from fatty meat to liver paste; and on the stove a rich soup was boiling. For the next several years, in fact, Kyūzō would always be forced to remember this meal with a sense of despair. He would think of it as his last meal that was humane and satisfying . . .

Vodka was poured to the brim in each cup. Alexandrov and Bear added to theirs a pinch of salt. Shiver put some salt on a slice of onion and took a bite. Dania and Kyūzō quickly swallowed pieces of liver paste. As if by mutual arrangement, they all then grabbed their cups and downed the first shot. "But this is our last time together," exclaimed Dania, putting her cup down.

Only Kyūzō took a small sip. When he tried to stand up to take down the soup cans, both Dania and Alexandrov, sitting on each side of him, grabbed his arms, pulling him back. Today was a special day, they said, and so he of course had an obligation to drink like everyone else. Even Dania was firm in her insistence, asking Kyūzō if she herself had not downed this poison. He declined, explaining that he was underage and had never drunk like this before, but his excuses seemed merely to incite the others. "There can be no end without a beginning," Shiver stated loudly, for some reason constantly flicking his Adam's apple with his index finger. "Among friends, only fools and traitors would speak of the law," declared Alexandrov, looking strangely serious. The atmosphere stiffened and it appeared that the mood would be spoiled, so Kyūzō relented, grabbing his cup. Everyone now issued random orders: "Take a bite of an onion!" "Lick some salt!" "Hold your nose!" It's just like a ritual, Kyūzō thought as he held his breath, downing the shot. His chest burned hotly. Inside his mouth there was a rough feeling, as if he were tasting a peppery lye.

Upon seeing his expression, the others laughed with amusement.

Shiver poured everyone a second cup. When the first bottle was empty, Alexandrov stood up and placed it atop the pyramid.

III

Bear took out the folded military map, spreading it out casually atop the sausage and onions. Everyone gazed in silence, as if admiring a piece of art. Grease from the meat seeped through near Vladivostok.

("All right, I'll steal this map," thought Kyūzō.)

"It's exactly midnight in Moscow," Alexandrov groaned.

"I've been in the Gobi Desert ever since I was twenty-three," Shiver declared as if in retort.

"You're always exaggerating," interrupted Dania, quickly pouring more vodka for herself. The edges of her eyes were red, and she seemed to be on the verge of crying.

Alexandrov turned on the radio. Switching to shortwave, there was first some gibberish before they heard syrupy light music.

"It's Domino!" exclaimed Alexandrov.

"Yes, it's Domino," repeated Dania in a coarse voice.

For a while they all stared at the map silently, reaching for the sausage and cheese underneath, eating as they emptied their cups. When the bottle was finished, Alexandrov rose and placed it atop the pyramid. Bear swung his head around again and again. Shiver took out his cherished sheathed knife and began carving the cheese. The knife was quite rare, a specialty of the Gobi region.

("Things would be easier if I took that as well," Kyūzō reflected, stealing a sidelong glance at the knife.) He had borrowed and used the knife once before. When unsheathed, its lightly oiled smoothness made it seem alive. The widely curved blade shone as if transparent, and the sight of it alone gave off a sense of sharpness. The knife was twenty-five centimeters long and heavy in the hand, with both handle and sheath wrapped in a patterned cowhide.

Alexandrov and Dania began dancing.

"As for me, though . . ." muttered Shiver.

"You're different," replied Bear, brusquely folding up the map. Putting it away, he added, "Everyone who has a place to return to has no choice but to return there. That's called 'instinct.'"

"Don't use such bourgeois language as 'instinct,'" growled Alexandrov.

"Even Dr. Pavlov uses that word," said Dania, irritably turning around and waving her hand.

"It makes no difference to me one way or the other," murmured Shiver, looking down as he carved the cheese into small pieces.

Someone made a movement and a cup fell to the floor, broken. Alexandrov and Dania laughingly returned to their seats.

("Get drunk, get drunk!")

Four people suddenly began speaking all at once. Twenty-five tons . . . gauge . . . train [*poyezd*] . . . absolutely not! [*chto tvoy*] . . . mandolin . . . quickly [*bystro*] . . . because [*potomu chto*] . . . continuation [*prodolzheniye*] . . . freight car roof [*krysha vagon*]. It sounds like they're talking about the train tomorrow. Yet Kyūzō was utterly unable to grasp the relationship between their return to the north and tomorrow's southbound train. After all, words used for work are different from those involving food and laundry.

Suddenly everything changed color. The burning soup and third cup of vodka that Kyūzō was alternately taking sips from suddenly became a black curtain, unfurling from his head down over his face. His heart was like an iron rodent, scurrying around his body, as his blood vessels swore. Alexandrov stood up and switched on the light. On the window glass, now darkened to a deep blue, ice crystals rose up in a floral pattern. In Kyūzō's narrowing vision, Second Lieutenant Shiver's pale, watery chin floated up and disappeared.

Kyūzō slid down from the chair and pressed his forehead to the floor.

IV

He awoke to the sound of Bear singing. ("Damn! Why are you still awake?") Suddenly, Alexandrov began sobbing quite violently. His overly large shoulders heaved, beastlike, as he wailed away, sounding like a windbreak forest in a gale. Second Lieutenant Shiver lowered his face to the table directly in front of him, peering up from beneath lowered brows. On the floor lay three empty bottles, overturned. I wonder if Alexandrov grew tired of carrying these over to the pyramid . . . Glancing at the clock, Kyūzō saw that it was past 1:00. He was now completely sobered up and shaking with cold. On Alexandrov's bed, huddled in a blanket fast asleep, lay Dania. Three months ago she had passed out in exactly the same manner, and the men had received a good scolding from her the next day. She compelled them to sign a joint statement of apology that read, "We offer our sincere self-criticism for ignoring Comrade Dania's wishes and forcing her to drink more than 200 cc of vodka, resulting in her loss of consciousness. In the name of our homeland, we vow to never again engage in such misconduct." Kyūzō was rather amused wondering what would happen this time, although he also felt sorry for them. Since they all liked Dania, however, there was nothing to be done about it.

Bear stopped singing and looked around. He stared at Kyūzō, who was unable to avert his eyes in time. "So it's you!" he nodded, making his way over as if swimming toward him. Kyūzō gave a start.

"You're a pathetic fool! Utterly pathetic! I heard that your mother was killed by fascists. Idiot [*glupaya mat'*], that's horrible! And what do you plan on doing about it? Tell me . . . Well then, tell me . . ."

Bear gradually pressed down on his body as if lying on him, making a strange sound in his ear. Perhaps he was laughing.

Kyūzō lay petrified, unable to move. He should calmly do what he usually does, asking, "Bear, isn't this a little embarrassing?" while poking him in the ribs. Bear gave another snort. ("Maybe he's discovered my secret!")

Bear pulled out a card from the back of his collar. "This is my daughter in Kiev." It was a card-sized photograph. Frayed and edgeless, it revealed the laughing figure of a young, white-haired girl. Bear continued muttering, spraying saliva on the back of Kyūzō's neck. Son of a bitch!

With a sudden realization, Kyūzō took the photograph, pretending to look at it while extricating himself. Bear then collapsed to his hands and knees, falling to his side fast asleep.

("This will be useful when I steal the map.")

It was 2:30. Everyone was already half-asleep, but not yet fully so. Every two or three minutes, someone closed their eyes, stared, snored, or hummed. It must be too cold. I'll stoke the fire a bit and make them drowsy...

The red flames had merged together, stifling the air. Removing the ashes, Kyūzō gently added some coal, and before long the fire was burning with a crackling sound. The soup boiled as the window glass sweated. Everyone quieted down.

Before making his move, Kyūzō decided to wait and see for thirty minutes. The weather strip on the window screeched like a grass whistle. Wild dogs barked to one another from afar as red patches began forming on the surface of the stove. ("Damn, I want to sleep too!") He hurried to the window, pressing his forehead against the pane. Between the double frame of glass, the wood grain appeared like the cleft of a seashell, its thin film of snow and smoke intricately overlaid. The sharp smell of winter filled his nostrils.

Pretending to go to bed, he circled behind Shiver and confirmed that his knife handle stuck out some five centimeters from his pants pocket. "Water, water," groaned Alexandrov, thrashing about on the table. Kyūzō hurried over and brought him a cup before then closing the ventilation hole of the stove. Once again he circled behind Shiver, making sure that he was fast asleep. There was a very long interval between his exhaling and inhaling, which Kyūzō had heard was proof that someone was sleeping deeply. At times he would suddenly stop breathing, making Kyūzō wonder if he were dead. Standing diagonally behind him on his left, Kyūzō planted his right knee, using it to support his weight as he turned Shiver around, repositioning him. With his right hand he lightly grasped the knife handle, feeling for the edge of the grip with his left index finger, and then slowly pushed up. Shiver was sitting in such a way that the opening of his pocket was now closed tightly, the knife digging into his buttocks. When half the knife was drawn out, he forcefully shifted his body. This altered his position, shifting his weight such that the pocket became slack. Kyūzō was now able to extricate the knife without difficulty by simply pulling the handle. Tucking it into his belt underneath the jacket, he suddenly felt his courage rise.

He then walked around the table over to Bear, who with his left side raised clutched the table leg with his right hand. Bear's bent left leg pressed against his chest as he extended his right leg around Alexandrov's chair. Kyūzō leaned down behind his back, the knife handle slightly restricting his movement.

The map should be in his right coat pocket. For precaution's sake, Kyūzō first took out the photograph, holding it in his right hand. Grabbing Bear's shoulder with his left hand, he boldly pushed his upper body over so as to force him faceup. Clawing the air, Bear lay back with his limbs sprawled out beside him. Kyūzō then slipped his right hand with the photograph into Bear's pocket, removing the map. Folding the map tightly in four, he placed it in his inside pocket.

Kyūzō suddenly noticed that Second Lieutenant Shiver was looking up from under his brows, staring right in his direction. He felt rooted to the spot. The pores all over his body immediately opened up. His tongue, dry in his mouth, began twitching, blocking his throat. It seemed to him that the second lieutenant was slowly raising his head . . . With a sinking feeling, Kyūzō waited for his first words. The time of danger seemed to leap past. It was brief, but felt much too long.

Yet nothing happened. When Kyūzō looked again at Second Lieutenant Shiver, he was sleeping, eyes closed, the same as before. Kyūzō uttered a sigh of relief. The storm had passed, and yet blood rang in his ears like the raging sea. He returned to his bed, clutching his knees to his chest as he leaned against the wall.

By his head stood the Russian-style oven, beyond which could be seen the bed on which Dania was sleeping at a right angle. The front of the oven was illuminated, and while he couldn't glimpse the photograph of Stalin inside, he was able to see Shiver's sleeping figure.

It was now 3:40. Kyūzō unconsciously kept staring under Alexandrov's bed. If possible, he didn't want to think about what was there. This was where Alexandrov kept his possessions, although he didn't particularly try to conceal this fact. On numerous occasions, he had fumbled with his collection right in front of Kyūzō. Of course these things were not worth much money. There were some imitation old coins, a woman's comb set in a gaudy pattern, a cracked ceramic pipe, and some other unusual odds and ends. Alongside these things, however, Alexandrov had also casually tossed in several wads of red military currency.

Kyūzō fully understood that he needed to be determined in order to make his escape. Both the knife and map were excellent weapons. Unless he were traveling in a savage land, however, the most effective weapon would be money.

He glanced at the clock. Only five minutes had passed. Best to leave slightly before dawn. He might be seen and questioned if he left after it was light, whereas if he went too early, he might end up giving them that much more time to come and search for him.

The sleepy rumbling of the earth slowly approached and then slowly receded.

("Right! I should take Alexandrov's silver spoon!")

The spoon was large and rather heavy, with a naked woman engraved on the handle. Alexandrov used it often, calling it Dania. Whenever the real Dania visited, however, he would rush to hide the spoon in the box underneath the bed. Something like that would probably fetch a good price. Kyūzō suddenly felt heartened if he could avoid stealing money. Upon straining his ears to confirm that everyone was still breathing deeply, he quickly crawled out of bed. As he touched the floor, the board underneath his buttocks suddenly snapped, ringing out sharply. Second Lieutenant Shiver rolled over, his face turned in Kyūzō's direction. Nevertheless, his eyes remained closed. That bastard!

The box, which had originally been made to hold apples, was turned over on its side, its opening facing in his direction. Inside was stuffed various types of junk. The box was small, made of tin, and had been made rust-proof by coal tar. The lid contained a hinge, which groaned unpleasantly when opened. He moistened it with saliva, slowly and carefully detaching the lid. Still, a piercing sound echoed from within. For a moment, Dania interrupted her breathing.

The silver Dania was piled on the very top together with the military currency. Kyūzō quickly grabbed it, putting it in his pocket. Keeping the lid slightly ajar, he hurriedly returned the box to its original place. He then tiptoed back to the bed. All the preparations were now complete. In order to avoid making his pocket too bulky, he jammed the spoon into the bundle holding the waterproof blanket.

V

6:10—one more hour until dawn . . .

Wrapping himself in a scarf as if buried to the chin, Kyūzō slipped on his coat, put on a pair of skating earmuffs, and donned a student's cap whose emblem had been removed. Making sure that his gloves were in his pocket, he slowly left the bed. He made a loop with the rope holding his belongings together and placed it over his shoulder. Time to set off!

("But what will they say later when they discover I'm gone? No doubt they'll call me an ingrate. But that's not true. I really liked all of them.")

Kyūzō passed between the stove and Alexandrov's bed. The fire pan gave off a clanking sound. ("But if they had known of my plans, they would never have let me leave. At one time, Bear had told Alexandrov about an orphan home run by the Eighth Route Army in the city of T.")

A loud sound of scurrying mice could be heard above the ceiling. The bed creaked as Dania rolled over. Kyūzō found his way to the door that led to the kitchen. He could not help but feel that someone was watching him. Gently he turned around, but nothing seemed unusual. He felt that Shiver had stirred slightly, but that was surely his imagination.

Turning the knob, Kyūzō pushed open the door. Frigid air pushed back at him from the other side. With trembling hands, he held the door ajar and turned his body so as to exit by his side, allowing his belongings to pass through first. The door closed naturally from the force of the wind, emitting a low but distinct sound of metal. Kyūzō held his breath, petrified, his entire body at attention. There was the sound of a light tap, as if someone had placed the heel of a shoe on the floor. Then there was silence. Only the northern wind that hovered around the house could be heard groaning in fits and starts.

Quickly reaching under the sink, he drew out the large vodka bottle that he had spied during the day. Planning to fill it with water, Kyūzō peered inside the barrel to discover that a thick layer of ice had formed there. He pressed firmly down against it with his palms for a while, but this served only to increase the trembling of his own body, as the ice showed no sign of melting. He remembered that there was a hammer on the shelf above the sink. Using the sink as a foothold, he began searching. Together with the hammer he found something hard and shaggy, like a scrub brush. It appeared to be the remains of a mouse. He quickly pulled his hand away, and the hammer fell. Fortunately it landed on his shoe, making some noise but not as much as he had feared. Still, the sound was quite loud. A sharp pain coursed through his toe, infuriating him.

Bit by bit, Kyūzō began striking the corner of the ice with the hammer's edge. After several strikes, however, the dull, heavy echoing caused his courage to falter. Listening intently, he again continued when suddenly he noticed that his fourth and fifth strikes were already producing an effect. The ice broke in two, a part of which separated from the barrel. Kyūzō dipped the bottle inside, filling it with water, and then crumpled up some scrap paper lying about, stuffing it inside the bottle in place of a cork. He applied another layer of scrap paper on top of that before placing the bottle in his coat pocket. His hands, now soaked, began to throb as if they had gone numb. He rubbed each hand one after the other under his armpits, and then put on his gloves.

Stepping down onto the earthen floor, Kyūzō silently turned the spring lock of the back door. He went outside, pushing his way through the wind that swooped down upon him as if locating prey. The snow had already stopped, but flakes whirled up from the ground, covering him. At this rate, his footprints would soon disappear. His blinking was sticky. It had to be twenty-five degrees below freezing.

Kyūzō felt nervous, fearing that at any moment the door would open and he'd be called back by Alexandrov and the others. He climbed up the coal bunker and scaled the wall. A remarkable alley wedged between two walls twisted and turned for some fifty meters all the way to the embankment at the edge of town. It was so dark that the ground and sky were indistinguishable. Kyūzō had lived in this town for nineteen years, however, and knew the alley so well that he could immediately recall each scribbling on the wall.

This place was once a marvelous playground for children. It was a fantasy land that could be transformed into anything—a jungle, waterway, or tunnel. Now that it had become a barracks for Russian engineer officers, however, only hordes of field mice would occasionally run through. During the three years that had passed since the war's end, nobody had come to clear away the dirt, and so it came to be used indiscriminately as a garbage dump. The garbage had frozen over, becoming as hard as a rock, and gave the appearance of fresh lava.

Kyūzō continued on, slipping several times as he carried his belongings in his left hand while feeling his way along the wall with his right. At one point he almost sprained his ankle.

The wall ended. There were no longer any houses here. He climbed up the embankment and began walking toward the station. The wind blew directly against him, roiling the ground at his feet. His face stiffened and felt numb.

After fifteen minutes, the river turned toward the center of town. Kyūzō spent some time cutting across the sorghum field that ran alongside the river. The plant stubble became entangled in his legs, making the ground reverberate with bone-crunching sounds.

Up ahead there appeared a lone night-light. This was the bridge he was looking for, the bridge that connected the old part of town with the new part as built by the Japanese on account of the pulp factory. Kyūzō could cross the river, which was frozen so thickly that even trucks were able to pass on it, but the low water surface and steep bank made it difficult to climb back up. Stone steps could be found only all the way upstream, where rafts that came down from the Stanovoy Range would dock. He needed to cross the bridge in order to arrive at the station. Martial law remained in effect until 7:00, which meant that all would be lost if he were discovered by the soldiers on patrol.

6:10—patrolling soldiers would appear every hour from each side of the bridge, identify one another with their flashlights, and then return to their respective areas. At 7:00, when martial law ended, they would go back to their stations, which meant that their final stop at the bridge would be roughly between 6:30 and 6:40. Now was the safest time.

Kyūzō made a dash across the bridge. His arid footsteps echoed all around. He sensed that a whistle rang out from somewhere in the distance. In the wind, however, such sounds could always be heard. Once across, he quickly turned left. There was a lumberyard here. He could relax having made it this far. The streets in the old part of town were a maze. In the back of his throat he tasted blood.

Crossing the lumberyard, he turned right, passing behind a small foundry, and then cut across a garbage facility before entering a side street that contained a cheap lodging house, which stood in front of a row of coffin makers. On his left there was a drainage ditch, and beyond that several willow stumps and a mound of low-grade coke, on top of which soared an even larger gas tank. It seemed that long ago this road functioned as a main artery linking north and south. This was the oldest part of town, and yet at the same time it was now the most desolate part. A stray dog stared at him.

After walking a bit down the street by the cheap lodging house, Kyūzō crossed the ditch and emerged on the far side. He found himself in a run-down vacant lot. Beyond were the railroad tracks, situated on top of the high embankment. The station was three hundred meters on the right.

From the opposite side, footsteps approached from the soldiers on patrol. The Eighth Route Army soldiers mainly wore boots with rubber soles. They were nearly upon Kyūzō by the time he heard them. He crouched down, completely burying himself in the snowdrift. The flashlights lightly caressed the edge of the embankment before slowly vanishing.

His path was soon obstructed by a barbed wire fence. Slipping through it, Kyūzō emerged in a courtyard in front of a warehouse. Before him stood a building illuminated in red, and in the window, thickly covered with ice, several figures could be seen moving about.

There was a sudden clearing in the western sky near the horizon, and the moon broke through, distorted in blue light. Kyūzō gave a start. Inside the station there was only white, with several rails stretching empty and black. No trains could be seen anywhere. Could it be that the trains departed not here but rather further north, merely passing through this station? He could not hide somewhere until 9:00. Why hadn't he thought of this possibility beforehand!

The moon passed swiftly through the torn clouds before plunging back into darkness. This darkness descended upon Kyūzō, battering him as he staggered to the hollow gaps in the warehouse. Soon it would be dawn, and he could no longer turn back. What had he done?

Gradually the pale light of dawn appeared. The wind began to die down, but the cold became even more intense. After relieving himself, he started to shiver uncontrollably. An idea suddenly struck him in desperation: perhaps the train is not leaving from the station but from somewhere else, such as near the siding of the pulp factory.

As the wind died, the fog began to rise. On the railroad tracks, the blurred shadows of the patrolling soldiers turned back in the opposite direction. As soon as they disappeared, Kyūzō crawled out from the hollow space of the warehouse, cut across the tracks, and slid down the far side of the embankment. Here there were fields as far as the eye could see. On his right one kilometer away there appeared an iron bridge, directly in front of which the railway siding split off from the main line.

He rushed down the slope of the bank, jumping in short steps so as to avoid slipping. The milky white mass of fog gradually came into view.

Kyūzō soon detected the heavy echo of iron striking together. He then heard the jumbled sounds of footsteps and people speaking.

In the fog, it was best to stay low. He ventured to get as close as possible. A train! Just as he had thought.

One of the men standing there was a soldier, while the other seemed to be some type of maintenance worker. Suddenly a red light appeared in the cab of the train. It's about to depart, Kyūzō thought, and he hurriedly slid down the embankment and ran toward the back of the vehicle. The train was surprisingly compact. There were two open freight cars, three large boxcars, two small boxcars, an additional three open freight cars, and finally two linked passenger cars in the rear. The passenger cars were of course out of the question, and the open freight cars would also prove difficult. He would thus need to choose from among the five boxcars in the middle. The small ones, with their many gaps and open glassless windows, seemed to be used for livestock transport. Yet they contained burlap sacks rather than livestock. The windowed cars would be more convenient in various ways, but the larger boxcars appeared best on account of the blowing wind.

In order to get a better sense of things, Kyūzō ducked under the train and emerged on its eastern side. It was already quite bright. The surface of the freight cars shone with a chalky texture. The first two cars were bolted tightly with wire, but the third car's bolt had been removed, so he decided upon that one. The door was iced over, making it difficult to open. As soon as he exerted strength, his chilled body began to creak with pain. He changed position. Now the door opened easily. It was smooth, sliding back and forth properly.

Laughter could be heard near the train. It sounded very close, and Kyūzō hurriedly crawled inside. The car reeked of oil and mouse urine. It was dark and he could barely see anything, but it was empty inside, with apparently no cargo. He closed the door and struck a match. The front contained several machine parts wrapped in straw mats, while in the back there were casually tossed a number of wooden boxes of various sizes.

Kyūzō sat down on one of the boxes. Burying his face in the frigid gloves on his lap, he began panting like a dog.

Along the tracks, footsteps approached of someone stepping on the railway ballast. Kyūzō shifted his body, lying flat against the wall. The footsteps hammered something a few times underneath the freight car and then disappeared. Kyūzō's anxiety, however, suddenly returned. Was it really possible that something so vital as a freight car could be left empty? At any moment now a truck or carriage would certainly arrive and workers would begin loading its cargo onto the train. If so, it would be impossible to conceal himself. It might be safer to stow away in a car where the cargo was already loaded, even if it were one used to transport livestock.

Raising his head, Kyūzō saw light dimly shining in above the door. There was a hole about the size of his thumb, and a dusty light could be seen whirling about. Peeking through the hole, he noted that the fog had nearly disappeared, and that several sheets of mist that had failed to escape hovered close to the ground, moving south. By the horizon a milky white light had begun to shine.

On his left, a large patch of fog was burning off in swirls, exposing the lowland that stretched from the northwest to the southeast. This was Xinghe. Here and there the snow had become bare, revealing a surface of ice that gleamed like new sheets of zinc. Further to the right, the town of Baharin stretched out like a stockyard of black brick.

In such light, however, it would no longer be easy to change cars. Suddenly the train emitted a burst of steam. Kyūzō stood motionless, vacillating, when again he heard the sound of approaching footsteps. They stopped directly in front of him. Someone rapped on the door with a stick and spoke in Chinese, with a provincial Shandong accent, "What happened to the cargo that was supposed to have been loaded here?"

Kyūzō pulled back, unconsciously grabbing the knife handle under his jacket. The other man replied in beautiful standard Chinese, "I hear that it was cancelled because it didn't make it on time."

The man with the Shandong accent followed up. "I'll need certification for that. I'm an honest man, and it would be trouble if they thought I was cheating them."

The two men set off, laughing.

Kyūzō leaned against the door. His shoulders heaved painfully. He told himself that things would work out, but his legs would not stop trembling. He pulled out the bottle and took a sip. The liquid flowed around his teeth.

He moved one of the wooden boxes in the corner, piling it up on the outside so as to create a small hiding place. Putting his belongings down, he returned to the peephole. It was now completely bright out. This flat town that was typically colorless and filled with smoke was now fresh and vibrant, illuminated by a pale backlight. The shantytown roofs beyond the mill tank ran on one after the other. For Kyūzō, they looked like dried fish skins. In the center, the upswept roof of a tall, many-walled Lama Buddhist temple glittered with a faint green light. Straight ahead past the river lay the alley through which he had just escaped. On his right, part of the bridge could be seen, and the smokestack of the pulp factory appeared especially high. Slightly in front of that stood the factory dormitory where Kyūzō was born and raised. A single red flag fluttered softly.

("It seems I'm finally leaving.")

The corner of an eroded sand dune could be seen where the river sharply diverged to again touch the edge of town. A few slanting Korean pine trees stood there, under which lay the unknown grave of his mother. When Kyūzō was in middle school, he had examined the sand dune's movement as part of science class. He discovered that as the dune eroded with the annual spring floods, it moved northward by twenty or thirty centimeters. Before long it would overtake his mother's grave, swallowing it up. After several hundred years, in the sandy plains created after the sand dune had swept through, what would someone think if they came across those crumbled, yellow bones?

The siren began its whine. It was 7:00. Martial law was now over.

It felt a bit strange to think that in two hours he would finally say good-bye to this town. It was difficult for Kyūzō to grasp that the town would still continue its life after he had gone. All his memories lived in this town. Now, however, those memories must depart together with him.

Just as today exists within yesterday, so, too, does tomorrow exist within today; and just as today exists within tomorrow, so, too, does yesterday live within today. He had been taught that this was how man lived, and he had come to believe it. Because of the war, however, this convention had disintegrated, becoming something scattered and unrelated. For Kyūzō now, yesterday and tomorrow were no longer linked together.

In two hours, this place here would become another's land, one that could no longer be called "yesterday." And as for tomorrow, nothing yet could truly be known about it. What he knew about Japan was only what he had imagined from the textbooks at school. (Mount Fuji, the Three Views of Japan, a smiling island of green surrounded by the sea, where the wind was gentle, birds sang, and fish swam. In the autumn, leaves fell in the forest and then the sun would shine, ripening the red seeds. A land of diligence, with diligent people.) A lost lover has a face, but this lover was still faceless.

Given that yesterday would never return and tomorrow could not yet be glimpsed, how could one conceive of the meaning of today, which existed between them? ("Am I happy? Perhaps I am, but I can't really be sure.")

Kyūzō felt a pain deep in his eyes. He returned to the darkness of his hiding place and lay down atop his belongings. Tears ran from his eyes and froze, itching his eyelids. Suddenly he fell into a deep sleep.

VI

Both of Kyūzō's parents came from obscure backgrounds. In particular, almost nothing was known about his father, Kyūjirō.

His father had apparently been a woodcrafter who came over from Kitakyūshū together with the engineers about twenty years ago when the pulp factory was built in this town. His mother had followed him here to Manchuria six months later. Kyūzō was born that winter, but his father died soon thereafter. The cause of death was unclear. With no home to which to return, his mother was allowed by the plant manager to stay on as the housemother. When Kyūzō was thirteen, a Japanese school was built in the city of T, and his mother promptly enrolled him there. This was a period of hope, however modest. It seemed that there would still be time before the disturbance of the war came to affect this remote area.

It was in the afternoon of August 9, 1945, in the summer of Kyūzō's sixteenth year, when news suddenly came that the Soviet Union had entered the war.

Like exotic horseflies, black fighter planes flew south overhead. In the evening, a Kwantung Army battalion began heading east, just outside of town. Yet nobody seemed particularly concerned about these developments.

On the next day, however, someone was refused when they tried to buy tickets at the station. All trains were requisitioned by the military, and even the passenger cars were occupied by evacuating soldiers and their families. It was then discovered that the troops based in town had suddenly disappeared. The peasants nearby attacked what remained, smashing everything to pieces. The military police at the station received word of this attack, but for some reason did nothing. Finally, people became anxious.

Early on the morning of the twelfth, the sound of gunshots rang out from across the river. A power outage broke out thirty minutes later. One hour thereafter a Red Army officer suddenly appeared at the dormitory as if from nowhere. Accompanied by several soldiers and a Chinese interpreter, he had shoulders like a wall and wore gray fatigues from which dangled three covered medals.

With a curt manner, the officer asked if this were a barracks, school, or private residence. Upon being told that it was a residence, he cocked his head skeptically, ordered that the building be entirely vacated within two days, and then hurried out with no change of expression. That was Alexandrov.

Who could possibly imagine that this is how wars begin and end? It had just been announced on the 9:00 news that fighting was taking place in eastern Manchuria. Some people declared that this was doubtless the Soviet Fifth Army staging a rear attack. Others claimed that it was not the main unit but probably just a small number of paratroop forces. In any event, the general consensus was that the mop-up campaign against Japanese troops would certainly begin soon. Sharp-edged wooden bayonets and quarterstaffs were distributed to the twenty households, which numbered (excluding infants) forty-eight people.

Calls to Qiqihar were made in order to learn more about the situation, but the lines had already been cut. Around noon a military policeman fled to the dormitory, asking to be concealed. Taking off his uniform, he dug a hole in the garden in which to bury himself. "Just you wait and see!" he repeated with great bravado, but the fear on his face was even more palpable. Shortly thereafter a group of disarmed Japanese soldiers was led dispiritedly to the front of the dormitory.

An endless mass of heavy tanks eventually appeared on the silent prefectural road, their massive guns pointed skyward, raising white sand clouds as they rolled past. The entire town shook from the ground up.

Some people cried aloud while others merely wandered aimlessly about. Kita, the plant manager, was the first to come to his senses. "Hey! We must all place red ribbons on our chest. The Russkies like red. But don't use the word 'Russki' in front of them! Say 'Sovet' instead. 'Sovet'! And all you women must go cut your hair!"

From that moment onward, Kita naturally became the leader.

He worked hard, as expected. Not only was the dormitory seized, but most of the company housing belonging to the engineers and executives fell victim as well. By day's end, Kita had decided on the place to which they (including the engineers and executives) would now relocate. Everyone was to live in the materials warehouse, located on the bank upstream. Kita boasted that the structure was solid because of the stable humidity level, and that one could walk to the old part of town once the river froze over. He assembled ten wagons. Eviction was set for the following morning. In the evening, a postal worker came to secretly refund their savings.

During that night, however, Kyūzō's mother went out to the back shed to find some empty packing crates. There she was hit by a stray bullet, shattering her back.

They called for a doctor, but after administering an injection he hurried away without issuing any clear instructions. Everyone was in a state of high agitation. Not knowing what to do, Kyūzō merely remained at his mother's bedside staring blankly ahead.

The sound of the first wagon could be heard at the crack of dawn. Kyūzō went off to seek advice from Kita. Standing squarely in the middle of a pile of boxes, Kita spoke agitatedly while nevertheless keeping his gaze lowered. "You can't rely on others at times like this. Everyone's a victim here. We're in a terrible situation. You have my sympathies. Of course I'll do everything I can to help. But the doctor said that your mother cannot be moved now, and even the Russkies would not go so far as to throw out someone who's sick and dying. So it's best to wait and see. Let's think more about this once things settle down. We know each other's whereabouts." He then added, as if suddenly remembering, "If you'd like, I can hold on to any money or valuables you might have. It may be dangerous for you to keep such things. Apparently quite a few people in the office have had their watches taken. I can hold on to those things for a while."

Kyūzō had no choice but to thank Kita and accept his offer. Regardless of whether the idea was a good one or not, it was encouraging to simply maintain ties with people from the company.

Although Kyūzō had nothing that could be called valuable, he nevertheless asked Kita to safeguard the pocket watch that his father had left behind, a silver cigarette case, his mother's ring, some clothes, and a gasoline can filled with cooking oil. As for money, Kyūzō had fortunately been able to withdraw their two hundred yen in savings. Keeping fifty yen for himself, he asked Kita to hold on to the rest.

After 4:00, the dormitory had become completely silent. "It's shameful, it's shameful," his mother droned on repeatedly. Leaving the room, Kyūzō began walking furtively around the empty dormitory.

Although he knew that no one was there, he nevertheless felt a strange sense of uneasiness upon reaching the second floor. Wood chips, a piece of rope, old, torn newspapers, broken bowls, and various other fragments of daily life whose original forms could not immediately be recalled lay scattered about, covering the floor entirely. Bare brick lay exposed beneath the torn plaster. The dank odor of mold, which seemed to have been hiding somewhere, presently enveloped the space like a shadow of vanished people.

An oddly sweet sense of liberation now seized hold of Kyūzō. Upon proceeding to middle school, he had been set to receive advanced schooling if his grades permitted. Angangxi was about two and a half hours north by train. If one changed to the main line there, Harbin could be reached in less than half a day. In Harbin there was a Japanese vocational school for engineering. During the semester this year, Kyūzō had filled in the name of this school on his survey form. "Get even with them!" his mother would often say. For her, Kyūzō was the warrior in whom all hope lay in overcoming the family's obscure origins. Naturally, everything appeared to him as an impregnable fortress. Unconsciously, he may have hated this task that had been thrust upon him. Now he found himself trampling upon the devastated remains of that fortress which had so tragically collapsed.

Kyūzō suddenly found himself standing in front of room twelve at the far end of the hall. This was one of four family apartments with three adjoining rooms. The door had been left open and part of the shattered furniture protruded outside. The room appeared painfully empty, as if a body part had been forcibly torn off.

The chief clerk lived here. He had a daughter named Sachiko, who was the same age as Kyūzō. Sachiko was considered quite beautiful even among the adults, but she was also rather impudent. One time Kyūzō had asked to borrow her kaleidoscope, and she had dismissed him out of hand. "You have trachoma," she said. This door had seemed so thick and impregnable! Now, however, it, too, had disappeared. Everything had become utterly equal.

He suddenly felt himself stricken by anxiety in being left behind. Stepping into the room, he saw a mouse looking back at him from the shadows of an overturned cupboard. Slowly it made its way along a post before fleeing inside a hole in the sliding screen. Inside some scrap paper, Kyūzō found a letter for Sachiko's father sent by someone with the same last name. It had been posted from a certain district in Shizuoka. He folded the letter, placed it in his inner pocket, and hurried out.

"Where have you been?" his mother demanded. Her face appeared larger with swelling.

"There are mice everywhere," he replied. His voice was flabby and weak.

"It's shameful, it's shameful," his mother repeated.

Kyūzō left the door open. The wind had died down, making it extremely humid. A horrible smell permeated the room. Perhaps his mother's wound had begun rotting.

The long dusk began. Somewhere an automatic rifle rattled like an engine.

There soon could be heard the plaintive notes of a war song. Someone sang in a high, clear voice, and this was followed by a chorus. It was just like a concert, Kyūzō mused. Upon realizing that the voices belonged to Russian soldiers who were coming to occupy the town, however, he began to panic. His mind raced about like a mouse searching for a hole, and yet his body remained paralyzed.

A military vehicle, crablike in appearance, was the first to arrive. Out stepped Alexandrov and three noncommissioned officers. Then a steel amphibious vehicle about the size of a small freight car appeared, fully loaded with communications equipment. Dark-eyed Mongolian soldiers rode up bareback, guiding their mounts smoothly like trick riders. There were four of these soldiers with a total of eleven horses. The animals had doubtlessly been expropriated from the Japanese forces, but were already following the Mongolians like shadows. Finally a group of Russian soldiers arrived, their footsteps echoing heavily. They immediately set to work hoisting a red flag over the gatepost, erecting an antenna tower in the garden, and attaching a large red star to the exposed red brick above the entrance.

Kyūzō and his mother were dealt with in a way that was simpler than they had feared. A young medic was called in. He readily examined Kyūzō's mother's wound, checked her pulse, and looked into her pupils. He then asked Kyūzō something.

"I can't understand Russian," he replied in poor English.

The doctor appeared to understand that this was English. Alexandrov offered to interpret. Fortunately, his English ability was at the same level as Kyūzō's. This would later prove useful in improving Kyūzō's situation somewhat.

"Can she urinate?"

In fact, she hadn't urinated since last night. Kyūzō tried asking his mother. "He asked if you need to urinate."

She shook her head slowly, her eyes half-closed. Kyūzō realized then that her face had completely changed. She seemed to want to say something but was unable to speak, with only a gurgling sound rising from her throat. Shining a flashlight on her, the medic pressed his finger to her face. Upon removing it, a gaping indentation remained.

The Russians conferred briefly with one another and left, leaving Kyūzō alone with his mother.

The footsteps that had shaken the entire building like a storm eventually faded, and all the various objects from the rooms that had been thrown out the window were now gathered and a bonfire started in the garden. Someone began playing an accordion. Another began singing in accompaniment.

Alexandrov returned together with a soldier carrying black bread and a large aluminum plate of soup. The soldier was a Mongolian named Punsha with a face that strikingly resembled that of a Japanese. He looked at Kyūzō with curiosity, laughing contentedly. Alexandrov stared hard at Kyūzō until he had finished eating.

Alexandrov passed by Punsha entering the room as he left. Pointing at Kyūzō's watch, Punsha gestured with his hands, repeating, "*Dat', dat'* [give it to me, give it to me!]." When Kyūzō shook his head no, Punsha suddenly drew the automatic rifle from his shoulder strap. Kyūzō offered up his mechanical pencil instead. With a flick of his hand, Punsha took the object between his two fingers, dropping it in his pocket. Laughing awkwardly, he took the empty plate and left the room while once again glancing enviably at Kyūzō's wrist.

Kyūzō hurriedly removed the watch and hid it in his pocket.

His mother tightened her lips, producing a sound like a whistle from deep in her throat. At first Kyūzō thought she was joking, but he was wrong. She lost consciousness and began experiencing difficulty breathing. In two hours she took her last breath.

It was the hottest part of the day, so the body could not be left out long. Alexandrov sent Punsha to help. Placing both the body and bedding on a makeshift stretcher, the two of them carried Kyūzō's mother to a sand dune by the river. Under the midnight sun, only the horizon remained constantly bright. They were digging up the roots of a shrub when a dog suddenly let out a terrifying growl. Two patrol officers approached with raised guns. After Punsha explained the situation, the officers lit cigarettes and watched Kyūzō work. When Kyūzō finally turned around as if finished, Punsha clicked his tongue in disapproval, picked up the shovel, and began digging rapidly. The officers departed, laughing among themselves.

Removing Kyūzō's mother from the stretcher, they placed the body and bedding at the bottom of the hole. Taking a bottle from his pocket,

Punsha sprinkled several drops into the grave. It smelled of alcohol. He began filling the grave with dirt. Kyūzō had the uncanny feeling that it was he himself who was being buried. Tears fell from his eyes, and yet he did not feel all that sad.

Having finished burying her, the Mongolian soldier took out a salt jar and piled a tower of salt about the height of his finger at the head of the grave. On the way back, Kyūzō cried in an increasingly louder voice without understanding why he was doing so. Nevertheless, he did not forget to firmly hold on to his watch from outside his pocket.

By the time they returned to the dormitory, lamps were already burning in the double line of windows and laundry was hanging out to dry. Rooms had been assigned, and things seemed to have calmed down. Someone was still singing.

Punsha called on Kyūzō the next morning. Pointing toward the river, he seemed to suggest that they visit his mother's grave. In the light of day, Punsha appeared decent and rather engaging. On the way there, he picked some gladiolas that were blooming in a garden. By the time they reached the sand dune, however, the flowers had already wilted.

The salt tower had become moist with evening dew and was nearly gone. Observing this change, the Mongolian soldier nodded contentedly, saying something as he pointed to the sky. He seemed to mean that Kyūzō's mother had now gone to heaven.

They went directly on to the warehouse by the river. Already there a red flag was waving and a Soviet soldier stood guard. Canvas-topped trucks had arrived, from which stretchers of casualties had been unloaded. Perhaps the site was being transformed into a field hospital. All was quiet and there was no sign of anyone around. Hurrying back, they came across a group of Japanese at the bridge leading to the old part of town. All were covered in sweat as they marched past, pulling their carts and carrying rucksacks. In front they held aloft a small red flag, and everyone had placed red ribbons on their chests. Yet this group was not from the company. Even if asked, they would of course know nothing about those from the company. Kyūzō tried to ask about their destination, but they themselves seemed unsure of anything beyond traveling to Changchun or perhaps Harbin. Upon watching them pass, Kyūzō suddenly noticed that they were being followed by ten or so powerfully built Chinese men. Unable to shout out a warning, however, he merely saw the group off in silence. Heavy cannon shots suddenly rang out in rapid succession, shaking the ground.

Kyūzō rushed back to the dormitory, stuffing as many of his belongings as possible into a rucksack, and dashed outside. He searched throughout the town for any Japanese people. For half a day he ran about looking for them. But where were the 865 Japanese who had lived there? They were now completely gone. Kyūzō alone was left, like a pool of water that remains on the tideland. Overwhelmed by fear and exhaustion, he sought support against the roadside wall when several Chinese youths appeared and wordlessly pushed him aside, putting up a poster in the very place where he had been leaning.

"Dongbeiren de Dongbei," it read in Chinese—northeast China for the northeast Chinese.

Lacking the energy to go elsewhere, Kyūzō remained motionless next to the poster, staring fixedly at the dried, whitened road. Tanks and trucks filled with soldiers passed by during this time, one after the other. Kyūzō would often find himself dreaming about that scene long thereafter.

It was close to dusk when First Lieutenant Alexandrov happened to drive past. Kyūzō called out to him, explaining the situation and requesting help in locating the whereabouts of the people from the company. Rather than replying, Alexandrov reached out for the red ribbon on Kyūzō's chest, asking suspiciously what it meant. When Kyūzō answered that it was the red of Russia, Alexandrov snatched it away with a faint smile and motioned for him to climb into the car.

The next day he was told by the Russians that the war was over. They sang with great joy throughout the night. Of course there was some fighting as well. Yet nothing dangerous happened to Kyūzō. At that time, hundreds of thousands of Japanese living in remote areas shook hands with death as they swarmed together to begin their desperate march toward the southern cities. Here, however, in the calm eye of the typhoon, there was no such desperation. Yet two years and seven months after these events, Kyūzō was forced to make his way through the remains of that devastating storm as well as through a storm of even greater ferocity.

In any case, these were the circumstances that led to Kyūzō's present situation of staying with Alexandrov. It was only much later that he realized that Alexandrov had misunderstood his explanation on that day. Alexandrov seemed to have misheard that Kyūzō's mother had been wounded and her belongings stolen by the fascist Kita. Of course that would explain why Kyūzō didn't know the whereabouts of the people from the company. However, this misunderstanding did not necessarily work against him.

For example, despite the fact that Alexandrov was cold and selfish and did not directly look after Kyūzō himself, he nevertheless appeared to take great pleasure in this mistaken fairy tale. With considerable senti-ment, he told everyone around that Kyūzō had been a victim of fascism, and for some time Kyūzō became quite popular as a result. Furthermore, Alexandrov seemed to enjoy the fact that Kyūzō had become so popular. Thus even when Kyūzō later learned to speak some Russian, he never bothered to correct that misunderstanding.

In late March of the following year, the Soviets began their frantic troop withdrawal. The region now came to be occupied by the Eighth Route Army. Nonetheless, Alexandrov and a dozen or so others remained behind as radio engineers. Kyūzō hinted several times of his desire to return to Japan, but Alexandrov flatly refused to discuss this. "After all, it's best for you to stay with us," he seemed convinced beyond doubt. Outside there are fascists with bared teeth roaming about.

(1946)

April 5: The United States, England, Soviet Union, and China commence discussions regarding the fate of Japan.

April 7: The Foreign Affairs Office reports that a total number of
4,039,447 Japanese remain unrepatriated.

May 1: The Chinese Nationalist government transfers the capital
from Chongqing to Nanjing.

May 3: Convening of the International Military Tribunal for the
Far East.

May 7: The Chinese Communist Party establishes a people's
government in Changchun.

May 12: Residents of Setagaya Ward in Tokyo attempt to enter the
Imperial Palace as part of the "rice demand" demonstrations.

July 1: The United States conducts its first nuclear tests at Bikini Atoll.

July 16: Formation of the first Yoshida Cabinet.

August 19: The Chinese Communist Party issues a mass mobilization
order, initiating a full-fledged attack on the mainland. Formation
of the Japanese Congress of Industrial Organizations; labor
increasingly goes on the offensive.

November 3: Promulgation of the new Japanese Constitution.
Renunciation of war.

December 30: Announcement of the 6-3-3 education system.

(1947)

January 31: MacArthur orders the suspension of a general labor
union strike.

February 28: Mass riots in Taipei result in over 1,000 casualties.

April 1: Promulgation of law banning private monopolies.

June 1: Formation of Katayama Cabinet.

July 18: The Chinese Nationalist government declares mass
mobilization.

July 30: New York stocks plunge.

September 12: The Chinese Communist Party announces a mass
counteroffensive.

December 14: Soviet currency is reduced to 1/10 its value.

(1948)

January 30: Assassination of Gandhi.

February 10: Record plunge of the Chicago market.

March 10: Formation of Ashida Cabinet.

During these two years, Kyūzō also experienced several changes. Without realizing it, what was once alien to him now became familiar.

Reckless joy and loneliness, undisguised desire and sadness . . . A sense of unyielding freedom that radiated throughout his life . . . These feelings were unpleasant at first, but at some point became easy to accept.

There was a continuity of crassness, simplicity, and boredom. At night, however, the restlessness of being left behind appeared in his dreams. He dreamt that he had turned into an insect roaming across a map or that he had boarded a train with neither ticket nor destination.

VII

A loud sound rang out and his body was sent flying. Numb with cold, he was unable to move for a while. Soon there was the sharp odor of smoke, the hard echoing of footsteps going to and fro, the groaning of iron, and the choking sound of steam . . . Finally Kyūzō remembered that he was concealed in a freight car, recalling also the circumstances that had led to this.

But what was that jolt just now? What of those hard footsteps? ("It seemed that people were walking on concrete. That might be a train platform.") And how much time had passed? Slowly he stretched his legs and approached the peephole.

First he saw a sign marked "Baharin." Then he glimpsed the dark red roof of the station. Kyūzō felt dejected. The time was 8:32—only an hour and a half had passed. Thirty minutes remained, and possibly a quite dangerous thirty minutes at that.

To his left he was able to see the ticket gate. Like dried-out caterpillars, two armed Eighth Route Army soldiers stood next to a station attendant, comparing the individual faces of passengers to their certificates. Fully sixty percent of the passengers were ordinary Chinese citizens. Waiting in a separate line for a routine baggage check, they carried their belongings in blue cotton wrapping cloths that were larger than they were. The other half of passengers consisted of administrators and civilian personnel, wearing stand-up collars with badges and armbands, while the rest were Eighth Route Army soldiers.

There also appeared to be some activity near the freight car. In the open door of the stationmaster's office directly behind the "Baharin" sign appeared Alexandrov, Bear, and Shiver. The stationmaster and a young Eighth Route Army officer stood immediately behind them, speaking animatedly. Alexandrov nodded, pulling down the brim of his hat with his left hand while pointing toward the train with his right.

Kyūzō jerked back, sensing that he was the one being pointed at. Had he been spotted? That didn't seem possible. Those three had probably come to the station on their own business. Hadn't they discussed something like that last night? Yet by now they would already have discovered that Kyūzō was missing. Assuming he had escaped, the first place they would search would be this train. Lying flat down in his hiding place, Kyūzō felt himself trembling as he awaited the attack.

Quite a bit of time passed. It was nothing more than fear, he thought to himself, when suddenly rough footsteps approached and the door was pulled open. Light spilled in, overturning the darkness.

"Kyuuzou," Alexandrov called.

Kyūzō remained motionless.

"Kyuuzou," Alexandrov called again far more gently, apparently locating him now. Yet still Kyūzō did not move.

Alexandrov climbed into the freight car. Kyūzō raised his head, staring at him in terror.

"Come," said the first lieutenant in a low voice, extending his arm.

Refusing his help, Kyūzō stood up by himself and then stumbled. With burly fingers, the first lieutenant caught hold of Kyūzō's flailing elbows. Wordlessly, the two men exited the freight car. Bear offered a hand in helping Kyūzō get down. With a faint smile, Shiver patted his trembling arms. Several eyes stared at him in the distance.

Surrounded by the men, Kyūzō began walking toward the stationmaster's office. "Don't you like being with us?" Alexandrov asked. Kyūzō silently shook his head. They wouldn't understand even with an explanation.

A stove burned noisily. His limbs felt hot and itchy. The stationmaster took out a scrap of paper, requesting from Kyūzō a signature and thumbprint. Alexandrov then signed underneath. Once the stationmaster had affixed a large stamp to the paper, the procedure was concluded. Yet it was unclear what kind of procedure this was.

Giving the stationmaster several bills, Alexandrov took the piece of paper and handed it to Kyūzō. "This is a special travel certificate," explained the Eighth Route Army officer beside him in surprisingly fluent Japanese.

"This train will go very close to Tieling. The city of Shenyang is occupied by Nationalist puppet forces, so please detour far around it to the east. This certificate will allow you to travel anywhere in the liberated areas. The train is heading to Andong. Please be careful not to show this certificate to anyone from the puppet forces. That might well prove dangerous. As for anything else, you'll need to actually see things for yourself."

This was the first Japanese that Kyūzō had heard in two years. "Are you Japanese?" he blurted out.

"Korean," the officer replied curtly.

Alexandrov gestured for Kyūzō to put away the certificate.

"Say thank you," prompted the Eighth Route Army officer.

"Spasibo"—thank you—Kyūzō answered in a small voice.

"It's nothing. Things will be fine wherever you go," laughed Bear as he slapped Kyūzō's shoulders. Kyūzō drew back in fear.

("I wonder if they found out about the map. And also about Shiver's knife and the Dania spoon.")

Once outside the office, Alexandrov stuffed into Kyūzō's pocket a wad of red military bills that was approximately one centimeter thick. Kyūzō stammered something, gesturing vaguely, but could only swallow hard. As the group walked toward the rear passenger car, Shiver gently held out a bag of sunflower seeds.

"This fellow can't get over the idea of revenge. It's because you're Japanese," Alexandrov wistfully remarked.

"Well, a lot goes on," replied Bear lightly, shaking his head. "In any case, I hope you arrive safely."

Shiver followed several steps behind, chewing on his sunflower seeds and spitting them out, oblivious to the people around him.

"Three minutes until departure," announced a station attendant, hurrying past. The train exhaled heavily, shaking all over.

"All right, then," exclaimed Alexandrov, pushing Kyūzō toward the passenger car.

Kyūzō hesitated for a moment and then began running. Turning halfway around in his stride, he uttered in a small voice that they could just barely make out. "Spasibo!"

Both cars were already full. There was still some room on the rearmost deck, as people disliked the constant wind blowing there. Turning his head, Kyūzō glimpsed over his shoulder the retreating figures of Alexandrov and the others as they made their way past the ticket gate. He found a place beside the lavatory and sat down on the floor. A guard stood on the exposed deck, his back turned to the passengers. Between his legs the rusted rail continued on indefinitely. On the right there was visible half a storage tank from a milling plant, while on the left a sea of hills stretched out, gentle and frozen white, for as far as the eye could see. High among the waves soared a large acacia tree, below which the walls of farmhouses appeared like black boxes.

The whistle blew. The connecting gear interlocked noisily as the wheels slowly began turning.

The station attendants waved frantically alongside those people who had come to bid the passengers good-bye. Seeing this, Kyūzō recalled that the train was the first long-distance carrier traveling southbound on this line. Surely being watched over by others was in and of itself a guarantee of safety. Eventually the platform receded in the distance like a soiled scrap of paper. In no time at all, the town of Baharin was sinking within the swell of the ground. Reduced to a black stain, all that remained of it were a gas tank and the pulp factory chimney.

As if obliged to do so, Kyūzō continued for a long time to gaze at this landscape that was fleeing from him. No doubt half his thoughts were dominated by the conventional emotions about the past that had been instilled in him. Yet the other half derived from the physical pain he felt in being wrenched from the twenty years that served as the basis of those emotions. However, even that appeared insignificant when considering the anxieties and expectations he bore toward the future, which was now approaching at a speed of fifty kilometers per hour.

Opposite Kyūzō, an old man in a padded jacket whose eyelids were caked with mucus lit a cigarette as the passengers around him hurriedly took out their own tobacco to request a light. There were a total of eight people in the deck, including Kyūzō. A sickly old woman escorted by a young man sat beside him in front of the door. By the aisle a hunchbacked middle-aged man who looked like a merchant sat on a trunk, and there was also a huge man over six feet tall with such a protruding chin that his forehead appeared to have been scraped off. Occupying the lavatory, which was broken, with no running water, was a man in his thirties wearing a stand-up collar who had a blank face with thick lips and a flattened nose. Upon seeing the badge on his chest and the strange hat on his head, which seemed to be a remodeled military cap, Kyūzō suspected that he must be a civilian employee or something similar.

The cold was piercing. Even the guard was trembling, moving away from the cutout aisle exit as he muttered to himself while squatting in front of the old man with the eye mucus. He was a young soldier about the same age as Kyūzō. When the old man offered him a cigarette, he held up his hand in refusal. His lips had turned a deep blue.

Even if all went well, the train would take fifteen hours to reach its destination. He should settle in for the long journey. Unfolding his blanket, Kyūzō separated it from the wrapping cloth inside. With that, the Dania spoon that he had stuffed into the side of the bag fell out, and he quickly pushed it back in. ("Someone might have noticed this.") Spreading out some of the blanket beneath him, he draped the remaining part over his head, placing the bag on his knees. The knife handle pressed against his chest, forcing him to move it slightly aside.

Grabbing a handful of sunflower seeds, Kyūzō offered some to the guard, who happily accepted. Kyūzō also began chewing on them. The seeds tasted like grass. While not at all delicious, they were the perfect thing to help relieve the boredom. The sick woman began sucking on a steamed bun, which was black and very hard looking. With a scrunched-up face, the hunchback noisily bit into some kind of fried food. Taking a sip of water, Kyūzō closed his eyes. He felt as if he were wearing a hat made of heavy stone that covered him all the way down to his nose. But he was unable to sleep.

Under the blanket, Kyūzō secretly counted the bills that he had received from Alexandrov. It was exactly ten thousand yen.

The aisle door opened and someone came into the lavatory. Although Kyūzō was not directly in the way, he was forced to stand up in order to move the hunchback's bag, which was blocking the lavatory door. Someone slightly tugged on his blanket, causing it to slip off. Quickly he hid the roll of banknotes. ("Damn! Someone might have seen that, too.")

The guard stood up, proposing that either Kyūzō use the baggage for a seat or that he and the hunchback trade places. Otherwise Kyūzō would have to stand up every time someone entered or exited the lavatory. Of course the hunchback immediately opposed this idea. He had taken this place for himself, he explained, and his weak constitution made it uncomfortable for him to sit somewhere windy. Also his baggage contained fragile items, making it unsuitable for someone to sit on. The discussion began to get heated when the man who had staked out space in the lavatory intervened to offer Kyūzō a place. He himself was sitting above the sink, so proposed that Kyūzō sit beneath it. The hunchback looked dejectedly at the man and Kyūzō. Clearly this was the premium seat in all the deck. The guard nodded in satisfaction, as if he himself were going to sit there.

From the start, however, Kyūzō had the unpleasant feeling that he couldn't let his guard down with the man. He noted with apprehension that the man's eyes strangely darted around as if searching for something. Having adjusted his seat, the man put on his glasses and began reading a book. Seeing this, Kyūzō suddenly felt relieved. Those everyday black frame glasses he wore gave the man the appearance of a schoolteacher. Moreover, any Chinese person who could read a book at moments like this had to be someone very important. During these past two years, Kyūzō had not read a single book. With the high cost of paper, he had sold nearly all his books when he moved. The only two that remained were a crude world map for students and *Tales of Inventions around the World*. Before Kyūzō had been able to reread this latter for a third time, however, it had been used as fuel for the stove. So it was that he felt a kind of hunger for books and reading.

Casually, Kyūzō tried to glimpse the spine of the book the man was reading when the latter held it out for him. The title, *Journey of Vengeance along the Tōkaidō Road*, was written in Japanese. Startled, Kyūzō looked up to find that the man had removed his glasses and was faintly smiling at him. He had an artificial left eye.

"So you're Japanese. I thought you might be," he whispered in a low, dry voice while shooting a glance outside. He spoke Japanese easily. When Kyūzō looked at him again, the features of a Japanese person rose to the surface on the man's face.

"Are you Japanese, too?" Kyūzō couldn't help but whisper back.

"No, I'm Chinese." The man patted the red badge on his lapel. "I'm a communications agent, so can speak several languages. I can speak Japanese, Korean, Mandarin, and Fujianese more or less interchangeably. And I can get by in Mongolian and Russian. But it's best to avoid speaking Japanese too loudly. There's a lot of anti-Japanese, anti-imperialist sentiment now."

"Are you like the secret police?"

"Who, me? You must be joking. I'm more like a newspaper reporter."

"But your Japanese is excellent."

"It's because my mother was Japanese."

"Then you're half Japanese," Kyūzō remarked, rubbing his hands together under the blanket.

"I guess that's true. But my name is Wang Muzhen. What's your name?"

"Kuki Kyūzō. The characters are "long time" and "tree" for Kuki and "long time" and "three" for Kyūzō."

"That's an odd name," Wang replied, closing the book noisily. "Shui-jiao ba"—let's go to sleep, he said in Chinese, turning on his side.

Kyūzō felt himself giving in to a sweet sense of exhaustion, one that gradually dissolved the anxiety in his body. Where could this fellow Wang possibly be heading? Since he of course must be a journalist for the Eighth Route Army, he'll hopefully travel all the way to Andong. Still, it's not impossible that he'll go as far as North Korea. There should still be Russki forces there. I'll ask Wang as soon as he wakes up. But seeing that *Journey of Vengeance along the Tōkaidō Road* book was really surprising. I wonder what time it is now . . .

It was exactly 11:33. Before he could confirm that, however, Kyūzō was already fast asleep.

VIII

Belching white steam as they heaved along, the twelve connected freight and passenger cars ran slowly on the rusted rails at a speed of fifty kilometers per hour. Vast grasslands, covered entirely in snow and ice, extended as far as the eye could see. Even after ten minutes—or even one hour, or indeed ten hours—the landscape showed no sign of change at all.

This was the eastern edge of the wetlands that cut across the plateau that stretched from Hungary to Central Asia. Here the black soil belt as transected by the Taklimakan and Gobi deserts appeared once more.

Weeds with stems over a meter in thickness grew densely. They supported a thin layer of snow and ice that accumulated atop them, but there were still areas that had folded in, unable to withstand the pressing winds.

These features appeared as caves from up close; slightly farther away they became a pockmarked face; and even farther they were like whitecaps in the sea. Wild beasts would pass below these areas and run through them. From midday the clouds faded and the sun began to shine. The ground glittered and yet the sky would grow dark.

They passed by a small village or hamlet every hour or hour and a half. But this train was traveling nonstop to Baicheng, where it would connect to a line heading toward Changchun. Every so often the train's whistle would frighten a flock of crows. The tracks provided a good hunting ground for these birds. Animals that were unable to walk on the snowy plains—humans, horses, and dogs—would walk on the rails. When attacked by those beasts that could roam the area freely—hunger, cold, wolves, and field mice—the crows would have their meal. Nevertheless, there seemed to be slightly even more crows than usual. At times the black vortex made up of thousands of these birds covered nearly half the sky, forcing the conductor to slow down and sound the horn.

The train continued on its way.

The sun was beginning to set as they approached the foot of the divide, which could neither be seen with the eye nor felt by the body—only water was perceptible. Far to the west the forest of the Great Khingan Range became fringed with red, rising up like a greenish shelf.

Far in the distance there could gradually be heard the sound of a whip. The ground was freezing, the snow was freezing, and even the ice had begun to freeze. It was the cold that awakened Kyūzō. Opening his eyes, he saw that Wang Muzhen rolled over at the same time. Kyūzō took a slice of dry bread and slowly bit into it, then began sucking a piece of sugar candy he had in his bag before also chewing on a bit of cheese and rind. Like an adult, he did not forget to finally take a swig of vodka. He waited for some time for Wang to wake up, but at some point fell back to sleep.

When night came and the temperature dropped even lower, the train's steam pressure also dropped, causing the vehicle to lose speed. The conductor's assistant was forced to add coal at twice the usual speed.

7:47—the conductor stared into the darkness on his right. Based on the report from headquarters, he knew that they were now passing through the most dangerous area. This was the number twelve railway bridge zone. The Khingan Range forest drew close, like an extended arm, while the upper course of the Sungari River branched out in several directions where it cut across the tracks before disappearing.

It was then that a dark, crawling shadow appeared exactly between the tracks and the forest. Of course the conductor did not see it. Even if he had, he would have imagined that it was a wolf roaming about. It was common in this area for wolves to emerge from the forest. Often there was more prey to be found near the tracks than within the forest.

The next instant, however, the conductor saw it—a red light flickered two or three times in the darkness, and then an orange beacon blew a pillar of sparks high into the air. Fearing that he would be blinded, he lowered the visor of his cap and pulled the brake. Raising his eyes again as he pulled, he now saw in the restored darkness the clear beam of a flashlight repeating a fixed signal. Three flashes and then, after a pause, two flashes, and then once again three flashes followed by two flashes.

The conductor applied the emergency brake and then in quick succession rang the alarm. The train shrieked, grinding to a halt. The alarm continued ringing for some time as the signals in the darkness continued even longer.

Abruptly awakened, the fallen passengers rose to their feet and looked at one another with pale faces as they silently strained their ears listening. Scraping the ice from the windows, several clearly saw the flashlight signals. Kyūzō, lying facedown, had struck his forehead hard against the foot of the sink. Had he not been wearing a hat, he would certainly have been injured. Wang was partly on his feet, his gaze fixed on something, examining the situation. His calm demeanor was such that it didn't seem as if he had just suddenly woken up.

The freight commander and several soldiers who had been riding in the front of the train immediately jumped down and ran to the locomotive. At the same time, the conductor and his assistant started running in this direction. The two groups met at the open freight car, where the trucks had been loaded.

"What happened?" the commander called out.

"Did you see it?" the assistant asked in a trembling voice. The conductor merely gasped roughly for breath.

"I saw the signal," the commander nodded.

"We must head back immediately," the assistant coughed violently. "The signal was three, two, three, two. It's dangerous."

"There's no need to panic. We have troops on this train. Also, the signal station is about one kilometer away. Let's wait until the messenger comes."

"We have no idea if he's coming or not. We don't know what the situation is there."

"Even so, the two of you blew the steam whistle for too long."

The assistant became silent. The commander turned around and issued orders to his subordinates.

"Have squads one, two, and three assume battle positions immediately. Squads four and five should get to work unloading the cargo. Also, I want you to take two men from squad three and scout the area."

The subordinates ran off.

"We must go back immediately," the assistant repeated.

Silently the commander turned on his heels, returned to the passenger car, and began addressing the general passengers.

"Unforeseen circumstances have taken place. The train must immediately turn back. The troops have changed their destination and will now head toward Changchun. For those of you who wish to turn back, however, please remain where you are. For those wishing to go to Changchun, please come with us. We will walk for four hours and then board another train. This is a message from headquarters."

No one could decide immediately. The passengers had waited two years to make this journey. For a while there was utter confusion. Some people crouched down, burying their heads in their hands. Finally, however, one person made up his mind and headed out. Someone followed, and then another, until finally most of the passengers (with the exception of the weak and infirm) changed their plans and would now travel on to Changchun. Once there, they would then try to figure out how to continue their journey.

Kyūzō also intended to get off the train. Now he had a certificate as well as money. It was all the same to him whether they traveled on the main line or a branch line. He hurriedly spread out his blanket, tied it with rope, and rearranged his things, gazing expectantly at Wang.

Wang nodded, holding Kyūzō back as if to say, "Just wait a bit." He remained still, sitting cross-legged above the sink, coldly watching the passengers as they scrambled past one another in their rush to exit the train. Kyūzō regarded Wang as one of the leaders, and so didn't view his calmness as particularly unusual.

The troops were already in position. However, the unloading of the cargo was proving extremely difficult. Trucks were the very life force for these troops, but the lack of any scaffolding posed problems in removing the vehicles from the train. The only thing to do was to have the men provide the necessary support. Twenty of them bent over below the freight car, steadily bearing the weight of the trucks as they were pushed out.

"We must leave now," the assistant called out once again. The conductor seemed to have returned to the cab of the train and was no longer in sight.

The commander did not remain silent. "It is because of the laziness of you station workers that no scaffolding was prepared for a case like this!"

"That is not the locomotive crew's responsibility."

"Then keep quiet."

"We've received orders from headquarters. This freight car is carrying important materials that absolutely must not fall into enemy hands. This is a request from Soviet Relations. That's precisely why advance troops were sent to protect this train. In any case, seeing a three, two, three, two signal means that we must return immediately."

"*We're* the ones who have received orders from headquarters. If one receives a three, two, three, two signal, then the cargo must immediately be unloaded and the troops deployed. But none of this makes sense to me. Why hasn't the messenger come? And you talk too much. You're an assistant. It's my understanding that only the conductor should receive signal orders."

"Then speak with the conductor. I might be the assistant in the locomotive, but I outrank him as vice-chairman back at the union. In any case, I'll call him for you, so please speak with him quickly!"

As if completely beside himself, the assistant bounded out and began running toward the locomotive.

The passengers began helping unload the trucks. Half the first truck had already been pulled out. The remaining passengers took hold of the second truck.

Kyūzō was about to run out after the last passenger when Wang reached out, grabbing his shoulder.

"They said that there's no need to panic. Let me handle this."

His tone was a bit strange, and Kyūzō was shocked, suspecting that his initial hunch may have been correct. Wang stared outside, keeping a strong grip on Kyūzō's shoulder.

Returning to the locomotive cab, the assistant found the conductor in front of the furnace, his head buried in his hands. Quaking visibly, the assistant addressed him.

"Get ready! Any moment now."

"Are we really going to do this?" the conductor groaned.

"Of course," replied the assistant, removing the furnace cover.

The conductor stood up, trembling. "Looks like I'm coming down with a cold," he muttered, wiping away the sweat.

Suddenly the outside lit up brightly as if it were midday. A flare had been fired. At the same time, the furious sound of gunfire rang out from all sides. A grenade had exploded.

The locomotive spewed out steam. With no signal, the wheels suddenly began turning in reverse.

Kyūzō tried to shake free and run when Wang lightly jumped in front of him, thrusting into his belly a pistol, which had somehow appeared in his right hand. Yet he spoke to Kyūzō in a voice as calm as before: "I won't harm you. Just stay where you are."

Most of the truck was tilting down when, slowly but irresistibly, it rotated to the right, twisting the men's shoulders, and overturned. Cries rang out as several men were pinned underneath. The second truck sent one soldier and three passengers flying as it continued rolling for one hundred meters before it fell upside down headfirst.

A solider turned around and took aim at the locomotive. The freight commander stopped him with a stern, dubious expression.

The train, carrying only Kyūzō and Wang as well as women, the aged, and infirm, gradually gathered speed as it reversed. But no one was able to concern themselves with this for long. Another flare was fired while the sound of gunfire that burst in from the darkness grew even more intense. The passengers groveled on the floor, trembling. They pressed their faces down into the ice.

Of course these soldiers also fought back. Caught unaware, however, they were at a disadvantage. If they were at all fortunate, it was only because the shots fired at them were largely inaccurate. But the grenades seemed to have caused considerable damage.

Kyūzō gave up struggling and did as he was told. Wang laughed. "Don't worry. Things will be fine." Yet his laughter was hard and stiff with tension. He swallowed constantly while walking restlessly around the train car, which was now nearly empty. It seemed that quite a long time had passed, but also that hardly any time had passed at all. However, exactly twelve minutes and thirty seconds had elapsed.

A third flare was fired. The sound of gunfire grew even more intense. For some reason, however, it seemed that these were now random shots. Suspicious, the commander bravely rose to his feet to check on the situation when an incredible sound reached his ears. Carried by the wind, it was the sound of an approaching train. The train was coming back, but why?

When the train came to a sudden stop and began moving south, Kyūzō was rendered speechless. Wang, in contrast, could not contain his excitement. Waving his gun about, he began speaking incessantly. "Serves you right! Do it, do it! All set! Shit! A huge fight! Get them! It's going well, isn't it, boy? Run, damn it!"

In the locomotive cab, the assistant thrust a pistol at the conductor. Crying aloud, the conductor performed his work. The train quickly gained speed.

Leading Kyūzō back to the sink, Wang told him that they would lie next to one another low on the floor. He grabbed Kyūzō's arm painfully, his eyes bulging and saliva beginning to drip from the edge of his lips. The lighting inside the train was turned off.

"The train is coming back!" someone yelled.

The gunfire grew more intense and yet also more inaccurate. At some point the grenades also ceased.

The train approached. Yet it showed no sign whatsoever of slowing.

At once the commander grasped what was happening. They were all in it together. The plan was to have the train fall into enemy hands. Immediately he issued a new order.

He explained that the truck that had fallen over onto its side at the edge of the tracks must now be moved directly onto them. Keeping only a small part of the firing squad, he had everyone get to work. The commander asked about the number of casualties. Eight dead and twenty-one wounded, came the reply.

The train echoed painfully. When the wheels touched the tracks, the sparks that flew off glittered like the lamps of a faraway town.

"All set? Hold on tight. Use your legs for support like this," Wang yelled.

The two grasped each other tightly, eyes closed, their legs pressed against the wall in the direction in which they were moving.

Chapter 2

The Flag

IX

The train approached with its headlights turned off, but the light from the small peepholes on each side of the furnace could still faintly be seen in the darkness. The roadbed shook and the rails echoed.

Although the freight commander had ordered the soldiers to block the tracks with the truck, he was far from certain whether they should destroy the railroad or allow the train to pass into enemy hands. With no time to hesitate and riven by an unspeakable agony, he simply went ahead and continued signaling the train with his flashlight. The train, however, showed no response.

Shooting still continued off in the distance, but the shots were now random, and the soldiers ignored them in order to focus on hoisting the truck up onto the tracks. Suddenly the bottom of the truck caught on the edge of the embankment. The vehicle stopped moving, its rear wheels suspended in the air. Four or five soldiers crawled underneath the vehicle to begin breaking up the frozen ground.

Sparks flew from the locomotive as it gained even greater speed.

Hurriedly putting away his flashlight, the commander yelled out in what seemed to be both an order and shriek. He jumped in among the soldiers, who were tightly lined up shoulder to shoulder, and joined them in their snapping cries of encouragement. The light that he had forgotten to turn off shone faintly through the cloth of his pocket.

The truck suddenly moved. Slipping sideways, its front left wheel crossed over the rails.

"Run for it!" the commander yelled.

At that moment, the front of the locomotive hit the truck with a terrible sound, appearing to hang over it. The train cut into the vehicle, bending it in two. Two soldiers who could not escape in time were thrown to the ground.

The locomotive slowly reared up as it continued running for another twenty meters, screeching as it dragged the truck behind it. Twisting to the right and coming to a halt, the train suddenly tumbled over onto its left, tearing up the frozen ground. A horrific sound echoed forth as steam spouted out.

The hobbled freight car behind it fell on the rails at a perpendicular angle, its front twisted to the right. The next car struck it as it veered toward the left. The train roared out as its cars crashed into each other, protruding from the tracks in a zigzag, and stopped. Suddenly everything fell silent. Then there was only the interminable rattling of wheels turning in midair.

Various groans began to be heard. From inside the passenger cars, voices weakly called for help.

The impact had caused Kyūzō to lose consciousness. He was largely unhurt, however, being in the last car and having braced himself for the crash. His only injury was a small cut on his finger caused by some shards of glass. A black stain formed at the tip of his glove. Grimacing, Wang stood up and tried to grab his fallen pistol only to quickly pull his hand back. He felt a burning pain on his left wrist. Using his foot to draw the gun closer, he picked up the weapon with his right hand. His body staggered slightly.

It suddenly grew bright. The fourth freight car had begun burning. The flame was at first a brilliant orange before changing to green. With a sound of ripping air, the entire car became engulfed in a vortex of flame.

"Hey, run for it, kid!" Wang called out. Yet Kyūzō did not move. "Hey, get a hold of yourself!" Wang repeated as if pressing down on him, but Kyūzō remained still. Shifting the pistol to his injured left hand, he began to slap Kyūzō hard on each cheek.

The soldiers had completely broken formation. Wandering from their posts, they stood in random positions, transfixed by the flames. Some distance away, the passengers clustered together frozen-faced around their belongings. Several of the wounded squatted or lay stretched out nearby. Some injured people also appeared to be lying flat by the side of the embankment. Perhaps they were not injured, however, but already dead.

Sensing danger, the commander turned around to issue an order when he suddenly collapsed, his upper jaw shattered by a bullet. This was a signal for the shooting to recommence all at once. Unlike the previous instance, however, the shots were now terribly precise. Men were quickly wounded, and while the soldiers on this side immediately sought cover and returned fire, they appeared to be overwhelmed. Assuming command, the aide-de-camp issued an order for the remaining trucks to be readied. Two vehicles seemed to be in working condition. Assigning the wounded and general passengers to each truck alongside five soldiers, he ordered them to cut directly east across the snowfields toward the station at Guoerluosiqianqi.

"Shit, get a hold of yourself! We're getting out of here now!" Wang shouted at Kyūzō, whose eyes were barely open. "We're leaving, so hurry!" Shaking him by the collar, Wang suddenly changed his tone and hurriedly asked him, "You were carrying a Russki certificate, right?" Kyūzō stared back at him in silence. "I know because I saw it!" Wang said, brushing away any objections as he forcibly thrust his pistol inside Kyūzō's pocket. Staying close to the floor, the two linked their bodies together as they crawled out from the deck, dragging their belongings behind them.

The passengers scrambled to hold on to the truck's side panel, fighting with one another to secure a place. The grenade struck this panel at its very center. The truck burst into flame and people fell to the ground screaming. The fire then spread to the other vehicle. The shooting grew even more intense. Although unseen, the enemy's approach could now be felt close by. The aide-de-camp realized that their only chance lay in finding an opening out to the plains. Until then, they had no choice but to wait out this time of terror. There was nothing to do but trust the soldiers. Turning around, the aide-de-camp saw something faintly shining in the pocket of the dead commander. He reached inside and turned off the light. The spurting blood on the lower half of the commander's face had now frozen, giving him the appearance of a child whose features had become messy from eating. The fire from the trucks had subsided, the freight cars were now burnt out, and darkness descended once again. The aide-de-camp quickly rose to his feet.

Kyūzō and Wang crawled beneath the train, lying flat on the ground as they intently surveyed the situation. The troops retreated and began to move out to the plains. Panicking, Kyūzō found himself about to start running.

"Fool!" Wang grabbed on to his bag, pulling him back. "Do you want to die?"

Rifle fire flew just past them. Kyūzō tried to say something, but the chattering of his teeth made it difficult to speak. He was not simply afraid, however. In his own way, he had assessed the situation. Those who occupied the south appeared to be in a superior position. Although Wang of course couldn't be trusted, he did seem to have some secret connection with those in the south. While things had not gone well, Wang had clearly grasped this chance and possibility. For Kyūzō, anyone who might help open up a path to the south was an ally.

Sparks flew from the rails as they were struck by bullets. Gradually, however, the gunfire tapered off as the fighting shifted to the east.

"What should we do?" Kyūzō asked. Discovering that the area around his mouth had grown numb, he rubbed his lips with his palms so much that they grew itchy. Also, his eyes had become so chilled that he could not open them all the way.

"We wait," Wang replied. His voice had frozen over so much that his words sounded like, "We way."

"For what?"

"Comrades."

A plane approached from the northwest. All at once the firing stopped. The plane passed by and then returned, swooped down with a sharp, metallic sound, and then flew off with a heavy roar.

"A Soviet plane," Wang said hoarsely.

The battle ceased for some time. The groans of the wounded sounded just like the call of beasts. Although cold dulls the pain, those who cannot move from loss of blood soon freeze if they don't scream and warm the body. A cry like a large-throated bird rang out two or three times from the passenger car above. Perhaps it was a baby. The wind began to pick up.

Suddenly, the shooting recommenced. The battlefield was far on the other side, and it seemed as if the two forces had now drawn close. Battle cries rose up as grenades exploded. The fighting continued for twenty minutes before the shooting abated, and it seemed as if things were coming to an end.

"I wonder who won," Kyūzō asked in a murmur.

Staring into the darkness, Wang gave no reply.

The shooting continued for some time, but there were now large intervals between the shots, making it impossible to grasp what was going on.

"This is too much. Let's go over there." Wang felt around and poked Kyūzō in the back, and the two crawled to the western side of the embankment. "This cold is like December. It has to be forty-five degrees below."

Kyūzō didn't think it was that cold. At most, it was probably around thirty degrees below. Maybe twenty-five. Urged on, he climbed down together with Wang and found a comfortable place safe from the wind. The two sat down alongside one another facing the unseen forest, instinctively pressing their bodies together. They seemed to hear the sound of wolves calling out, but perhaps their ears were playing tricks on them. The wind, pounding in their ears, carried with it all manner of groans. Yet the cries from the train were certainly those of a baby.

"Strange . . ." Wang turned around and partly got up before sitting back down again in resignation.

"Hmm, maybe you should give me back my pistol now."

Kyūzō moved sluggishly but finally did as instructed. He didn't have any ulterior motive. It was simply that his body had grown so cold that it was too much trouble to move his limbs.

Someone gave a brief yell slightly beyond the embankment. The shooting stopped.

X

"Don't go to sleep." Perhaps two hours had passed since Wang had begun poking Kyūzō in the ribs.

"Damn it!" Wang screamed as he tried to stand up before staggering to his knees. Crawling over to Kyūzō, he thrust his face at him and gasped weakly, "Hit me, hit me. Hey, I said hit me!"

Kyūzō raised his hand as requested, but the pain in his joints made it difficult to generate any strength. Rather than strike him, Kyūzō stumbled over and pushed Wang down. Grappling, the two rolled around for some time on the frozen ground. They grew winded and nauseous, but it now became easier to move. Standing up next to each other, they began stamping their feet.

"I've got some vodka," said Kyūzō.

"Let's have a sip. I'd be grateful," Wang replied excitedly.

While Kyūzō unfolded the blanket and fumbled around for the alcohol, Wang continued to make strange cries. He bit on the bottle to uncork it, making a snapping sound as if breaking a tooth. Without pausing for breath, he seemed to choke down three swigs. Kyūzō took only a mouthful before sitting down. He felt as if he had imbibed a stick of fire.

"Vodka is the best thing for the cold. Take good care of this bottle."

Dissolving, the stick of fire spread throughout his body in five minutes. Wang let out a groan. The pain in his left wrist had returned. Kyūzō suddenly remembered the question that he had wanted to ask since the afternoon.

"Mr. Wang, where are you going?"

"It's not a question of where. I receive new assignments wherever I go. A newspaper reporter is not well paid."

He still wants to insist that he's a correspondent. ("He's underestimating me.") Of course there's no way he can be trusted.

"It's quieted down. I wonder if everyone's dead."

"I'm sure the engineer is dead."

"That baby is probably dead, too."

"There was absolutely no reason to go back that far. He was too scared."

Wang then began cursing in a language unfamiliar to Kyūzō.

"Why isn't anyone coming?"

"It's absurd!"

"Mr. Wang, which side are you on?"

"Which side? Oh, I see . . . But that's no simple question, something that could be easily explained. Damn it, the air pierces all the way to one's teeth. One's mouth gets frostbitten by speaking too much. In any case, there's no need for you to worry about such things. Shit, once we join them, there will be fire and hot soup."

"But what if they don't come?"

"They'll come."

"But still . . ."

"Believe me, they'll come. The deal is too big."

For some reason, Wang suddenly began walking toward the locomotive. Kyūzō hurried after him. The joints in his knees had stiffened and his body felt three times heavier. Wang fell over with a scream. There was a ditch. "Be careful," he said, making a sound as if striking a thick wall. This was the roof of the livestock freight car, which had tipped over and derailed. There was the smell of something burning.

Wang was trying to reach the third freight car. This was the covered car that was directly in front of the car in which Kyūzō first tried to hide. It was leaning over to the right, its front plunged into the ground below the embankment, with its bottom half alongside the slope projecting out into the black sky like a shadowy tower.

"It's completely wrecked."

Wang tried to open the door, but it had become bent and would not move. A sickening odor rose up. He passed below and emerged on the other side. Although the door had broken off, the unusual stench prevented one from looking inside.

"What is that smell?"

"Well, it's just as I thought." Yet Wang appeared to be devastated. "Had everything gone well, it would have been a huge job worth at least five hundred thousand."

"What was inside?"

"Polytar. It's a special paint coating made from copper line."

That's right, Alexandrov and the others had mentioned something about that. Yet Kyūzō remained silent. It no longer concerned him. He stamped his feet while striking his earlobes.

"We can't just stay here," Wang said, blowing his nose with his fingers.

"Shit, my nose feels like it's being ripped off!"

"What should we do, then?"

"I'm saying that we can't just stay here. A Russian plane just flew by. In four or five hours a train full of soldiers will be coming."

Kyūzō turned around to look at the town of Baharin from which he had finally escaped. A slight rift appeared in the white clouds. The air fluttered in the distant wind. He suddenly felt afraid.

"Isn't there a village nearby?"

"No, there's not. And we wouldn't be welcome even if there were."

"Why not?"

"No welcome is given to someone who can't be determined as friend or enemy."

"I've got a certificate."

"Certificate? Plenty of people have them. This area marks the very border between friend and enemy. What good is a certificate if you haven't yet decided who is an ally?"

"We could offer money."

"You've got that much? At any rate, best not to play tag in a land-mine field."

Shivering, Wang spat and began walking back to their previous place.

"What are you doing?"

"Leaving."

"Mr. Wang, aren't you going south?"

"Yes. But I want you to stop calling me 'Mr. Wang.' I'll soon tell you a new name. But only if you decide to come with me. What do you want to do? Shall we go on together?"

Kyūzō hesitated slightly. As if overtaking that hesitation, however, he quickly answered. "Yes."

"Then wait there. I need to take care of something in the train." He started off and then turned around. "Meanwhile, why don't you scrounge around?"

"What?"

"Various things fall out of the pockets of the dead."

Kyūzō didn't reply. This of course indicated his refusal.

"In any case, someone will clean them out." Snorting, the man who was no longer Wang climbed into the passenger car. "Tell me immediately if anything strange happens."

Crossing his arms, Kyūzō dug his hands into his armpits and rocked up and down on tiptoe. He wanted hot water, if only a sip. The man groped around inside the passenger car. Crouching down in the middle of the car, he removed his right glove and used his frozen hand to take from his inner coat pocket a match, which he struck against the floor. He used his left hand to cup the match so as to prevent the light from scattering as well as to avoid blinding himself. Blood flowed from his wrist from beneath the glove. But he could not think about that now. Between the seats lay a small old man whom he had kept his eye on. The match went out. The man thrust his hand under the old man's bellyband and grasped his thick billfold—indeed, it was so thick that he was unable to hold it with one hand—before trampling on the old man's belly and ripping the cord. Kyūzō watched the train window become slightly brighter, feeling the inside of his mouth grow numb as if he had tasted electricity. His reaction was partly out of fear and partly because he was now reminded of the window of the room where the stove burned red. There was a sound as of paper being crumpled in the distance. Or perhaps it was of many legs treading on thin ice as it began to crack. Taking a step forward, Kyūzō was about to convey this message when the man suddenly jumped down from the deck.

"You there?"

"I'm here," Kyūzō replied in a murmur, and with those words unwittingly began to feel a bond with this man who was no longer a stranger. "It seems that someone's coming."

The nameless man now pricked up his ears. There was certainly some noise. But it was unclear whether or not it was footsteps.

"In any case, it doesn't seem to be people we'd be glad to see."

"Is it all right not to wait?"

"Not now, in these circumstances." He began walking away and then added brusquely, "Let's go."

Kyūzō started after him.

"How about the baby?" he asked and then immediately regretted it.

The man, however, said nothing.

XI

For a long time the two remained silent as they continued walking south on the western side of the tracks. Frozen lips made it difficult to speak, while frozen ears made it irritating to listen. Their entire bodies were focused on their legs—and rather miserable legs at that—so as to avoid straying from the embankment and stumbling. There were stones and hollows, the weather was freezing, and it was after all pitch-dark. The only thing in their favor was the tailwind.

They crossed two small rivers and one large one.

While crossing the large river, Mr. Anonymous turned around and spoke. "This might be the Taoer River."

On their right the wind began howling especially loudly. It seemed as if the very mouth of the wind were right there. After walking for a while, there appeared a large black mass. This was the edge of an overflowing forest.

The man stopped, suddenly changed direction, and began walking toward the woods.

"Let's have our meal there."

Kyūzō hesitated.

"Won't there be wolves?"

"We'll build a fire. Besides, dead bodies are scattered about over there."

"But they're frozen and so won't stink."

"Idiot! I mean that the wolves will go there to take care of business."

The ice gave off a terrible sound as it cracked underfoot. It seemed less like ice than ceramic. The overlapping layers of ice, snow, ice, snow clung tightly to the roots of the withered grass. The grass gradually lengthened until it felt like one were crossing a rough, solid swamp. When it sprang back, it felt painful, like needles. At times there were thickets that grew higher than face level.

The situation was even worse inside the forest. Stiff ice covered the fallen larch leaves, but when one became stuck in areas where the ice was brittle, one would sink all the way down to one's groin, making it nearly impossible to extricate oneself without help. At worst, there was even a risk of breaking or spraining a limb. Moreover, one could only grope one's way forward at such moments. The man experienced this situation twice and Kyūzō three times, sapping them of the energy to continue moving. Besides, there were signs of living creatures about.

Nevertheless, they penetrated quite deeply into the forest. From the perspective of the forest as a whole, of course, they were still only at its entrance, but they had come far enough so that the lighting of a small fire would not be visible from the outside. There was an archlike cave between two large, intertwined trees, beneath which the ground appeared to be dry. When they struck a match to investigate, a round bird the size of a human child suddenly appeared before them, flying off with a loud squawk like the sound of horse hooves.

Yet the place was quite suitable. They smashed the ice and collected withered grass and twigs, which immediately began burning when ignited. The blaze was perhaps slightly too strong. However, there is no resisting the lure of fire. Although the sparks singed their clothes and eyelashes, they opened their coats and embraced the flame. When the front of their bodies became hot, their backs became cold. Upon warming their backs, they once again heated their front. Repeatedly turning around in circles, they finally removed their shoes and warmed their feet. Every inch of their bodies became itchy, and then the itchiness turned to pain, until finally their entire bodies unwound, melted, and became engorged with blood. Groaning, they scratched themselves all over.

Screaming, the man slumped over clutching his left hand. There was a hole in his wrist, as if he had gouged it out with his fingers. The inside of his glove was filled with blood, which stuck to his hand and flowed all the way down to his elbow. He covered the wound with ashes, binding it tightly with a scrap of cloth from a hand towel.

The man put snow into his small cooking pot and placed it on the fire.

"Are we sleeping here?" Kyūzō asked. For some reason he appeared to be in good spirits.

"Don't be ridiculous! We'll only eat our meal here. We sleep during the day."

With this blunt reply, the man removed something from a bit of wrapping in his bag and began chewing. It was beans.

Kyūzō unrolled his blanket (taking care to conceal his other belongings, such as the Dania spoon), took out some food, and placed it in the hat that he held on his knees. Tonight he would have dry bread and cheese as well as splurge on a slice of bacon.

But the man merely continued chewing beans. Convinced that he would begin his meal after first boiling water, Kyūzō chewed on his sunflower seeds and waited. The man stared into the fire. Yet was he was really looking at it? Once this doubt emerged, the man's gaze took on a very suspicious air. It almost felt that he was looking at me. It was clear what his unmoving artificial eye was gazing at, but that made it hard to know where his seeing eye was looking.

The water began boiling. They each took turns drinking. The water smelled of earth, but it was sweet and delicious. Yet the man continued chewing on his beans, showing no sign of preparing a meal. Kyūzō grew slightly concerned.

"Aren't you eating?"

"I'm eating now, aren't I?" The man looked up, his lips curled in a smile. So his gaze had been directed at me! He had been peering inside Kyūzō's hat. "But you've come prepared, haven't you? You've got quite a feast there. I had no idea that all this would happen."

Unthinkingly, Kyūzō replied at once. "Please have some."

"I really shouldn't, but . . ." The man immediately sidled up next to Kyūzō, skipping over the preliminaries.

Kyūzō quickly prepared some additional food for the man.

"You're very kind," the man remarked while reaching out to grasp Kyūzō's hat, carefully dividing the food between them. "Is this all right? Will the food last?"

"I should have enough for seven days."

"For both of us?"

Kyūzō felt his blood run cold. "No. If it's for both of us . . ." he trailed off timidly. In his heart, however, he realized that there was nothing to be done, half resigning himself to the situation. He didn't feel capable of walking through this dark wasteland alone. Indeed, he couldn't even warm himself by the fire alone, as he was doing now.

The meal ended simply, as if they had gulped the food down.

"Now, let's boil some more water and use that to fill our bellies."

They gathered more twigs and threw them on the fire. Grease oozed up between the wood as the flame spread and the smoke rose. Lifting his injured left hand high above his knees, the man appeared relieved. "I like to think about things, lots of things," he murmured.

Enjoying the sense of fullness that comes after digestion, the two waited for the water to boil. Once again Kyūzō observed the man's clothes and facial features. He supposed that he wanted to put himself at ease. Other than a vague childlike quality in the middle of the man's face, however, there was really nothing that reassured him. The light of the flame below threw into sharp relief an inch-long scar that ran along the line of his cheekbone underneath his artificial eye. Because of the man's peculiar gaze, Kyūzō had not noticed this. It was a mark that told of the severity of the man's past. Also, the base of his coat sleeves was pulled up toward the neck, barely covering his broad shoulders. And the worn-down area just below the line at the coat's base was proof that he had bought it second-hand or received it from someone else. Dog fur could also be glimpsed below the collar—even Kyūzō's collar was lined with rabbit fur—and the amateur craftsmanship could clearly be seen in the shoddy tanning of the hide. It could not really be doubted that the clothes were acquired hastily, and that the man had previously worn something quite different. But Kyūzō did not wish to think about this any further.

"I wonder where we are now."

"We're probably about twelve miles outside of Taonan."

"Will we go into town there?"

"No, we won't be able to. We're still at the border between friend and enemy. When all is said and done, I think, the most dangerous thing is a border. They're more dangerous than being in the midst of enemies. At least in my experience, they certainly are."

"Then how about the next town?"

"The next town is Shuanggang. That's also on the border. The towns after that, Kaitong, Bianzhao, Tanyu, Taipingchuan, as well as the towns thereafter, are all on the border. In times such as these, the border definitely expands."

"Then where should we go?"

"We'll make our way through areas without towns or villages."

"All the way to Siping?"

"No, I think it's best if we go to Shenyang."

"Shenyang?"

"We should be there in two weeks."

However, the Eighth Route Army officer had warned him against going to Shenyang. Various doubts arose. Yet he lacked the courage to confirm these. He felt anxious in feeling anxiety. Disappointment was terrifying. A phantom path was better than no path at all. In any case, it was important to get closer to Japan, even by one step.

Hearing a sound, the man pointed beyond the fire. A beast that looked like a filthy dog slowly passed by with slanted, faltering steps, its neck hanging so low that it nearly touched the ground.

"Is that a wolf?"

"Yes."

"I guess I should've picked up a pistol too."

The man offered no reply. The water boiled.

Putting down his cooking pot, the man waited for the water to cool to a drinking temperature. "Are you happy to be returning to the Japanese mainland," he asked idly, as if half speaking to himself.

"Yes, very happy."

"I imagine so. I like to think about things, and I've found myself wondering where I come from. It's strange. Perhaps because of that, I guess I've got something like a conviction. Japanese people also tend to think about things. The Japanese are all right. But they lost. I think that in the next three years the Americans and Soviets will go to war. I'm quite certain. The intelligence is solid . . . How old is your father?"

"He died a long time ago."

"I see. Seriously, what nationality do you think I am?"

"You're Chinese, right?"

"Do I not look Korean? How about Taiwanese?"

"I can't really tell the difference."

"All right . . . So who will take care of you when you return? Is your mother in the Japanese mainland?"

"No, she died too. I'm still not sure where I'll go."

Repositioning himself, the man took a long, burning branch from the fire, tilting his head as he watched the smoke rise from the smoldering wood. The sound of the wind enveloped the outside of the forest like a wall.

"If I wanted to, do you think I could look Japanese? What do you think?"

"Of course you could."

"Right? My mother is Japanese and her father was Korean, but I'm not sure about prior to that. In any case—ha-ha—this question of where I come from is quite something. I think about various things, such as not blowing my nose with my fingers when I become Japanese or that I must use tweezers to trim my whiskers when I become Korean. Either way, though, it's not so important. One good thing about Japanese people is that they read. I like to read too. Still, I have a Fukuoka accent. Is it hard on the ears?"

"I wouldn't know about that."

"Well then, shall I tell you my new name? I'm going to trust you. My next new name is perhaps Kō Sekitō—kō meaning "high," seki for "stone," and tō as in "tall building." Kō Sekitō. It's rather distinctive, isn't it? This name is somewhat well known in the south."

"So it's Mr. Kō, then?"

"Yes. My acquaintances all call me Kō xiansheng—Mr. Kō."

"Shall we put on more wood?"

"No, it's time for us to get going."

Reaching into the bottom of his bag, the man who had newly become Kō carefully removed a crumpled cigarette. Tearing it in half, he placed one part in his bag and stuffed the remainder in a small brass pipe that he took from the earflap fold of his cap.

"This is a real Ruby Queen cigarette. I'm down to my last two."

He inhaled slowly, getting all of it. Cradling his face in his arms, he remained motionless for some time.

"The soldiers haven't seen this, right?"

"Haven't seen what?"

"This fire."

"It's fine even if they have. They're afraid, too. Isn't there some proverb about shadows?"

It suddenly grew bright. The two looked up at the sky at the same time. Through the intertwined branches, the moon, shining painfully white, appeared slightly distorted. Above, clouds like old spider webs scudded across the sky. Their surroundings began to fill out, and the trees appeared like willed animals. Kyūzō was very glad not to be here alone.

"The moon's beautiful, isn't it?"

"Did you call the moon beautiful? Not for me. Only women are beautiful. But even women become unpleasant if they're too beautiful."

They gathered some snow and put it on the fire. Black steam spouted up, within which sparks like red glass appeared to be swimming. A greasy stink enveloped the air. It suddenly became cold, as if one were being skinned. Kyūzō recalled the moment when he opened the door when escaping from Alexandrov's room. Hope was written on the front of that door, but perhaps despair had been written on the back. This was perhaps the nature of doors. A door always appears as hope when standing before it, but then turns to despair when one turns around. Kyūzō thus resolved to look only at the front of doors without turning around. He wanted to tell Kō about Alexandrov's room. Yet he didn't know how to speak of it.

9:45. Leaving the forest, they returned to the edge of the tracks and began walking, driven on by the north wind. Rocks lay scattered all about. While resting, their feet had become painfully swollen. Yet the moon was out, which made things somewhat easier.

With the forest gradually receding, they soon arrived at a waterless river. The riverbank was dense with willow shrubs, in which they stumbled over the bones of a large animal. If the previous river was the Taoer, Kō remarked, then this might be the Najin.

The area beyond the river was completely treeless, with only gentle swellings of the ground that continued on indefinitely. It was like an ocean that had been hardened and rendered motionless by lead. Yet Kyūzō knew about the ocean only through photographs and films. After four kilometers there stood a small wooden sign with a sharpened point, beyond which the tracks began to turn widely to the left. The sign was simply inscribed with the numbers "9.4." Perhaps this meant that Taonan Station could be reached in 9.4 kilometers. The two argued there for a while. Kyūzō wanted to at least follow the tracks. But Kō was unyielding in his insistence that they take a straight course that led away from the tracks. They decided to use the North Star as a marker. At first, it was quite difficult to find. There were far too many stars in the sky.

In walking by the railway, one could somehow still sense the presence of people, even if this were only the tens or hundreds of coolies who worked here building it years or decades ago. In wandering further into the wasteland, however, one's very breath changed weight, making one dizzy with an unbearable loneliness. Shortening the space between them, the two hurried along as if fleeing despite the fact that they had just started off. Yet the landscape was so vast! There were only pebbles and slightly larger stones, narrow, irregular ditches gouged out by heavy rains or floods, handfuls of withered grass dotted all about, and an endless repetition of low hills that continued on into the horizon.

11:00. When they reached the top of a relatively larger hill, there appeared near the peak of the next hill two adjacent towers in the shape of overturned buckets. They seemed to be brick kilns. A sorghum field lay between the hills. Kyūzō felt a sense of relief. However, it would be quite troublesome to walk along the perimeter of the ridge. Also, the peace of mind that came about too quickly was all the less welcome in that it seemed to hint at some future anxiety. A narrow path created by the tracks of a wagon cut across the center of the field from east to west. If one listened, the cries of people could be heard on all paths. Leaving that behind required tremendous courage. If Kō had shown even the slightest hesitation here, Kyūzō would surely have stopped in his tracks and refused to go further. Perhaps sensing his feelings, Kō said nothing until they reached the brick kilns.

The kilns, decayed and crumbling, looked like many years had passed since they had been last used. They were like ruins from ancient times.

They gave off an eerie feeling, as if something would leap out from inside them. Kō stopped and abruptly announced, "Let's rest." Had he known that this would be the last place to rest for some time?

They dug up some stumps of sorghum, but after digging up three of these the heels of their shoes seemed about to fall off. For the remainder, they made do with a bit of withered grass. The fire was quite poor. Not only could they not warm themselves, they were barely able to melt the snow that they placed in the cooking pot. They gathered the sparse snow and drank it without boiling it. It stank horribly of mud, making them both nauseous. They drank vodka to remove the bad taste.

Rough breathing could be heard just behind them. Four stray dogs appeared, becoming entangled with one another as they circled the brick kiln towers. Although pretending to play innocently, they seemed to be trying to decide whether the two humans might make a suitable meal. Or perhaps their unpleasant frolicking meant that they had already decided to eat them. Waving their hands about, Kō and Kyūzō tried to chase the dogs off, but the animals showed no reaction. As if completely ignoring them, the dogs approached ever closer. They were no doubt used to people. Kō suddenly pulled out his pistol and fired. The most ferocious-looking dog—the one with the ripped tail—fell forward with a yelp, turning his body in circles with his muzzle flat on the ground. As if nothing had happened, the other three dogs leisurely ran off, abandoning the victim.

XII

Descending the hill, they found themselves back in the wasteland. They walked throughout the night, their backs bent stiffly as they stared at their feet. Their faces grew wrinkled in trying to cover too much ground. There was an endless repetition of stones, ditches, withered grasses, and swelling hills that continued far off into the horizon. And beyond the last hill, a door that could only be seen in the mind's eye, on which was written the word "hope."

("A town inhabited by men, women, and children, with a warm fire burning, a bed in which to mindlessly fall asleep, a garden outside the house, a road outside the garden, and nothing else. A safe and peaceful place where this deathly wasteland would become a mere joke, and one would laugh at something amusing, and quietly close one's eyes leaning back against a chair if one were bored, knowing that all one's actions had meaning.")

Kyūzō realized, of course, that if Kō heard such things he would burst out laughing. He and Kō were people who belonged to entirely different worlds. Precisely because of that, he was unable to shake off two questions that had been haunting him.

What had driven Kō to undertake this two-week march? And why had Kō chosen him as a travel companion?

He had probably just randomly decided on this period of two weeks. Doubtless he was planning to soon hire a wagon in some large town. It would then be cheaper for two people to pay for the wagon rather than one. And even prior to that, it was more reassuring to have someone else along on the journey. Even if such reasons were foolish, one had to believe them in order to stop thinking about these questions any further. Kō probably mentioned two weeks in order to drive away my fear and make me ready, Kyūzō added to himself. Yes, that is just what adults do ...

The morning sun was red, flabby, and absurdly large. For some reason, Kyūzō suddenly felt sleepy when he looked at their long shadows lined up alongside one another. His body suddenly felt light, and before he knew it he was sitting down. He felt no pain whatsoever as he collapsed to the ground.

"It's time we found a place to sleep," Kō remarked.

Yet the sights around them were so cruel! In this vastness, humans appeared exceedingly small, and for at least a four kilometer radius there was nowhere for these small humans to hide. To sleep there or here amounted to exactly the same thing. If one refused to sleep here, one would be forced to travel beyond the horizon in search of somewhere else. In any case, they decided to rest here for an hour each. They lined up two stones as a landmark so as to avoid mistaking the direction. Gathering grass, they made a small fire, and Kō went to sleep first. In this instance, Kyūzō's blanket was like treasure. With the sparse fuel and strong wind, the fire quickly died if one neglected it. In a daze, Kyūzō collected more grass in anticipation of the next hour. The grass had frozen before withering, its color fading as a result, and was so fragile that it crumbled in his hand. He worried whether Kō would go to the same trouble of tending the fire for him.

Now then, my turn to sleep. Lying on the edge of the spread-out blanket, Kyūzō rolled over together with the blanket so that it wrapped around his entire body. His head was covered, but he felt helpless when his feet stuck out. Feeling Kō tuck his feet back in the blanket, Kyūzō soon fell fast asleep. He awoke shocked by the punishing cold. It was like sleeping on ice. His body temperature seemed to be the same as that of the ground, and other than the tip of his nose it felt like he had frozen to death. The pain centered solely on his nose. He was then struck by the idea that Kō had abandoned him. Desperately moving his numbed body, Kyūzō finally crawled out of the blanket to discover Kō asleep, pitched forward with his knees splayed and head plunged into the extinguished fire.

Kyūzō called out to him, shaking him, but he showed no response. Kō finally opened his eyes when Kyūzō hit him hard, but his teeth were chattering and his seeing eye was swollen a deep red. There was something wrong with him. He started to say something, shuddered, and then twice vomited a yellowish substance. Nevertheless, he curled his lips to the right, revealing a frozen smile spread across half his face. In that smile Kyūzō sensed affection.

A large flock of crows flew by from south to north, squawking loudly. After one group flew by, another followed. It took four or five minutes for all the crows to fly past.

Gesturing to the birds and then pointing south, Kō spoke in a hoarse voice that was barely audible. "There's a river or forest."

Gently stopping him when he tried to immediately stand up, Kyūzō gave Kō some vodka and built a fire to boil water for him. People become strong when alongside those who are weaker than themselves. Conversely, they become weak when alongside those who are stronger than themselves. Yet Kō showed no weakness whatsoever. He insisted on leaving soon after drinking the hot water. Some hardship was needed so as to rest properly, he seemed to say. His gait was surprisingly steady.

But it appeared that Kō had miscalculated the omen of the crows. No matter how far they walked, there was neither river nor forest. They continued walking all day, but the landscape showed no change at all, as if they had constantly remained in the same place. However, the several hours of daytime were relatively more temperate. It was perhaps twenty degrees below zero—possibly even above fifteen. They looked for grassy places and, just as before, rested an hour each and ate their meal. Yet they regretted this later. Why didn't they sleep then for at least two hours each? Night returned, and during the time of darkness before the moon rose—or rather, prior to that, when with bent backs and dragging feet they followed the sunset at a near trot ("the crows should have returned, but didn't!")— they bit their lips until the blood flowed, feeling terrified by a sense of despair, no longer able to believe that they could hold out any further, and continually wondered why they hadn't slept for at least two hours each.

Unable to find a resting place no matter how long they searched, they were forced once again to spend the entire night walking. Everything, from this to that, was exactly the same as last night. Stones, ditches, and, raising one's eyes, an ocean that had been hardened and rendered motionless by lead. Their fatigue had increased several times over. Many times they wished to throw off and abandon their belongings. They wanted to lie down right on the spot and go to sleep. Prodding and dragging each other along with faltering steps, as if drunk, they moved through the vast expanse like tiny insects.

"Give me some vodka," Kō demanded, grabbing on to Kyūzō's elbow for support. This was already the fifth time he had made such a request since sundown.

Kyūzō shrugged him off without reply. Kō then forcibly took hold of

Kyūzō's belongings, attempting to snatch them away. Kyūzō didn't wish to defy him further. Nevertheless, Kō refused to return the vodka after drinking. As if quite naturally, he corked the bottle and placed it in his pocket. At once Kyūzō grabbed hold of Kō's left hand, grappling with him head-on. With a scream, Kō shook himself free, backed away covering his hand, and then stumbled to the ground.

"Give it back!"

These were the only words exchanged between them then, either before or thereafter. Silently, Kō responded by drawing his pistol. The incident was thus settled. Neither of them seemed to feel that this event was particularly significant. Kyūzō, somewhat absentmindedly, even interpreted it to mean that all was going well. As if nothing had happened, they once again set off walking. The northern wind continued blowing as always.

Dawn broke. Soon they discovered a broad, gray expanse of low ground beyond a hill. This was a frozen wetland with a dense growth of tall, withered grasses that were as thick as bamboo poles.

For them, the area was like a mountain of fuel. Shouting, they ran off at a stagger. Despite appearances, the stalks were quite fragile, breaking easily when touched by one's body. Rolling around, the two flattened the grass and then gathered it together using every part of their bodies. Setting aside some of the grass for their beds, they piled up the remainder and started a fire.

Thick, milky white smoke rose up, and flames soon burst forth loudly as if sprinkled with gunpowder, appearing to force back the sunlight. For some reason, however, the two didn't feel especially warm. The parts of their body exposed to the fire were burning hot, and yet in their core they felt even more chilled. Perhaps the cold came from their sleeplessness, something that couldn't be warmed by fire. Kō, in particular, looked miserable. Holding his left hand, he couldn't seem to stop moaning and shivering. He complained that, from the tip of his pinky to the area below his ears, the left side of his upper body felt broken with pain.

The fire, although strong, did not last long, and one was forced to add new grass nearly every five minutes. Imploringly, they gathered grass and threw it on the fire again and again. Half-awake and half-asleep, they repeated these actions until they found themselves at some point buried in grass, asleep, their arched backs turned toward the fire.

They slept perhaps two or three hours. Kō woke up. In the cold fire lay Kyūzō, fast asleep and covered in ash. Kō was shocked when he looked up. While they were sleeping, everything around them had burnt down. The fire had fanned out downwind, and an expanse of several hundred meters was still smoldering. Come to think of it, Kō realized, the taste of smoke had permeated all the way to his chest.

Wishing to gain a clearer sense of the situation, he exerted great effort to finally reach the top of the hill. In the open vista, there appeared a large marsh that seemed to be fully one kilometer around extending in a long, narrow strip in a north-south direction. The near bank was only fifty meters away. The fire had spread alongside the marsh's western bank, leaving the eastern side virtually undamaged, perhaps because of the sparseness of grass there.

Intuitively, with perhaps the instincts of a wounded animal, Kō felt that they must go there. Shaking Kyūzō awake, he dragged the bag and crept across the ruins of the fire, which emitted a slight purple smoke. The low ice surface had become a steep cliff. Between the ice and cliff lay an expanse of dry red clay, approximately two meters in length, covered in grass roots and forming a small sunny spot. This area received sunlight from the south-east, was sheltered from the wind, and appeared quite comfortable. As if tempted, Kō slid down when, suddenly blowing his nose loudly with his fingers, he lost all the strength in his body.

("We should have found this spot before building the fire. One makes a mistake by rushing. Before doing anything, one must make sure of things first. We should boil water, but at times like this some sugar can give one energy.")

Kō felt as if he were speaking to Kyūzō about these things, and yet fell into a frantic, senseless nightmare.

Shocked by the change around them, Kyūzō watched still somewhat groggily, believing that Kō had lost his footing on the cliff. Kō leaned against the cliff, snoring. He was not dead yet, Kyūzō thought, but he surely would die. On the far bank of the marsh, a low thicket of shrubs spread out over the gentle slope. Two or three times, Kyūzō walked there and back carrying twigs. Allowing Kō to sleep, Kyūzō built a fire next to him and removed his shoes, warming his feet. He broke off some ice and boiled water. Holding him so that he would wake up and drink, Kō suddenly began laughing and, pointing to the marsh, shouted meaningless words: "Andara, tsoan, chii, rururu."

With that, he dropped back off to sleep. His entire face was swollen black and blue, a large tear covered his seeing eye, and his lips were white and dry, around which had formed a black ring of frostbite. Touching his forehead, Kyūzō discovered that it was surprisingly hot. He was terrified, convinced that Kō would die.

XIII

The fields in the distance were still burning. Kyūzō suddenly felt hopeful. Perhaps someone might see the smoke and come. A farmer, hunter, shepherd, woodcutter, or perhaps a traveler passing by or soldiers out on patrol.

Kyūzō remembered that he had a map. He unfolded it, but at first had no idea where they might be. For it was impossible to believe that, after traveling for two nights, they could still be in such a place. Walking directly south (contrary to expectations, their course had veered slightly west), the abandoned, townless wasteland that extended for another hundred and seventy or eighty kilometers measured one hundred kilometers in width—the area appeared on the map as a small, unremarkable blank space—while the symbol for the marshland that he finally located appeared as if they had only just entered that space. Even then, the closest town (a place beyond the marsh called Daiqintala) was roughly fifty or sixty kilometers away. Who would possibly concern themselves with such a small fire in the plains? Kyūzō had heard of the Khingan Range fires that burned for ten or even twenty days. What of this tiny fire in the plains! And yet this small fire had just appeared utterly massive and terrifying to him.

He burst out crying. He hated Kō so much that he wanted to kill him. Even if he didn't kill him, however, the man was dying. He then began to feel immense anger at himself. The tears froze and began to itch, making him stop. He had already forgotten why he was crying anyway.

In Kyūzō's mind, Kō would die that night. Without question, the large flock of crows had swooped down from the far bank of the marsh that evening because they wanted to eat him. He would take his last breath when the moon rose, Kyūzō suspected, taking care to avoid letting the fire burn out. He quietly took back the bottle of vodka.

The moon rose while he slept. Kō, however, was still alive. Kyūzō stirred the fire and ate. Wishing not to depend solely on the provisions he had brought, he decided to search for food tomorrow, and thus ended up eating a bit more. Dissolving the dry bread in the hot water, he fed Kō. Kō, muttering gibberish, immediately spat out the liquid. "Idiot!" Kyūzō shouted, dropping Kō's cradled head to the ground. He hit him one more time before covering him with the blanket.

The night was filled with sounds. There were sounds that existed in reality and those that did not. The fluttering of the wind, the howling of beasts, and the screeching of birds all truly existed. As if plagued by nightmares, the beasts made incessant howling sounds that, Kyūzō suspected, must have been terrifying even to themselves. Yet it was the voices that had no real existence that were the most hostile. The wing flapping of countless phantoms. How could one possibly escape the phantoms created by one's own desire to escape? The more tightly Kyūzō grasped the handle of the knife under his shirt, the more forceful those phantom lives became. Approaching footsteps, a voice calling out his name, approaching footsteps, screams of terror, approaching footsteps, sobbing, approaching footsteps, the creaking of a wagon . . . After hesitating a long time, he gently removed Kō's pistol. This was a natural course of action under such circumstances. It was both his unbearable fatigue and the hatred he felt

BEASTS HEAD FOR HOME ○8 73

for those who had abandoned him that gave him just enough courage to endure. The night was a terrifying one.

Near dawn, while Kyūzō was rebuilding the extinguished fire, Kō began singing in a spooky nasal tone. "Young lady": he sang only the single lyric and hummed the rest in a melody that was irritatingly cheerful. Rather than hum the full song, however, he would like a broken record soon return to the "young lady" at the beginning. Young lady, young lady... After the sixth time Kyūzō could no longer bear it. Extending his leg, he kicked Kō in the shin. "Ah," cried Kō in surprise, ending his song. They say that some people sing right before dying. He'll finally die at dawn, Kyūzō thought.

Dawn came, however, and Kō still wasn't dead. Kyūzō now believed that he might not die. Using vodka to wash out the wound on Kō's wrist, he then rewrapped it in a hand towel. The wound didn't look like it had gotten worse.

He climbed up to the top of the cliff. The fire on the field had stopped. It had blackened the right side of the marsh, and another marsh could now be seen near the horizon, where the fire had finished burning. Kyūzō walked for a while along the bank. Making a rustling sound, the dried ashes buried his shoes to the ankle. The wind had fallen off, and it seemed like the temperature would grow higher than yesterday. Once the wind changes, it will soon be spring. A large mouse had burnt to death, its teeth bared and white belly swollen to the point of bursting.

A thin, square cloud passed by. It was quite unusual. Perhaps somewhere there was someone else who also regarded it as unusual. Suddenly Kyūzō thought about putting up a flag. Crossing to the far side of the bank, he began looking for moderately sized branches. The knife came in handy. He cut down five branches about the length of his arm.

He opened the wrapping cloth and made a pouch by tying together the sleeves of a shirt. Transferring the contents of the wrapping cloth to the shirt, he ripped the cloth in two. Using one piece as a flag, he tore the other into several smaller pieces, forming strips of rope, which he used to join the branches together. The flag fluttered lightly when he mounted it on top of the cliff. It was like an invisible hand reaching out, calling to the distant world. The flag was clearly visible from the bottom of the cliff. It appeared as high as the cliff itself, which was especially wonderful. After gazing up for so long, Kyūzō's neck began to ache. Walking to the opposite bank to gather firewood, he could still see the flag when he turned around. It was too white to be red and yet too reddish to be white. In the light, it could appear as either color, and seemed likely to attract notice. The flag was more oblong in shape than most flags, making it seem as if it were looking for something, while its constant fluttering gave off the impression that it was trembling in despair. It was as if the object standing there were no longer a flag but rather Kyūzō himself.

In the afternoon he arranged their provisions. He tried to divide the food so that it would last for ten days, but the portions were too small. If he were to split the food between them, Kyūzō estimated that they could each have seven pieces of dry bread at a single meal (with each piece no larger than the tip of one's thumb). They clearly needed fifteen pieces. On that basis, there would be enough only for five days. He calculated that it would take three or four days to travel to and from the nearest town. Subtracting the amount of bread he would need for the trip there as well as the amount he'd leave for Kō while he was gone, Kyūzō realized that he would need to depart the day after tomorrow at the latest. He then divided the other foodstuffs in the same way.

He suddenly realized, however, that these thoughts were all quite foolish. Couldn't he be using this time to head south, even a bit? Without walking, it was absolutely impossible to arrive anywhere.

("That's right. I should prepare my things right now.")

Of course Kyūzō knew that he shouldn't abandon Kō. But if he waited for Kō to die, then they would both perish. And even if Kō were to recover, that might take too long and they would both still perish.

("But someone might see the flag and come rescue us.")

That would be fine if Kō could receive help.

("But it might be possible for both of us to receive help here.")

But still . . .

Regardless of the disturbance in his heart, however, Kyūzō continued doing what he had to. Having assiduously gathered the requisite amount of kindling, he then went off in search of ice. The ice by the bank had become weathered and full of dust, and when melted would turn an inky color while producing a centimeter of sediment made up of sand and debris. Once one's thirst was quenched, one realized that the water was foul and undrinkable. Preparing some sharp stones, Kyūzō walked all the way to the center of the marsh. The surface ice was also gritty, but in scraping that off he saw that the ice inside was somewhat cleaner. It was difficult to break off. There was no way he could use his knife. He was forced to smash the ice and gather up the broken shards. Upon boiling, however, the same color and odor appeared even if there was less sediment. He shuddered in disgust as he imagined what the marsh was like in summer.

The wind faded and it became colder. A thin, milky white film began to spread over the ice. Another day had ended. The flag, which had not yet been seen by anyone, was now drooping and wrapped around the pole.

Kyūzō stared absently at the fire, listening to the sounds of the darkening wasteland. In his mind there appeared a white map, fully spread out, on which emerged a single point. It was so tiny! It's too small, he thought, bringing his eyes closer. And yet the point escaped the closer he approached, never becoming any larger. Pursuit, escape. Pursuit, escape . . . Then he himself became the point, disappearing in the boundless white. In order to divert himself, he thought about borrowing the book that Kō had been reading on the train, *Journey of Vengeance along the Tōkaidō Road*. He began to reach inside Kō's bag but suddenly stopped, feeling guilty. He then took out the Dania spoon. The woman engraved on it was well developed, with double curves from her waist to her buttocks. Imitating Alexandrov, Kyūzō rubbed the ball of his thumb across her breasts, belly, buttocks, and thighs. Hard and cold, the spoon simply felt like metal. It was much more amusing to just look at it.

"Oh, ah," groaned Kō.

It was unbearable to think about spending another night like this. Tomorrow he must put an end to it somehow. If nobody sees the flag by noon . . . Kyūzō suddenly realized that Kō had opened his eyes. He gazed around with a disoriented look before staring at the flag. Had he regained consciousness? Kyūzō felt so happy that he wanted to shout out. He was peering at Kō's face when Kō, with almost no change of expression, whispered to him in a breath.

"Idiot! A flag?"

"But it's been two days already."

"Take it down."

Feeling betrayed, Kyūzō remained silent. Kō began moving his body, groaning, and then muttered something between clenched teeth. Kyūzō heard the word: water. There was some water that was just cooling, and Kyūzō poured a bit into the corner of his mouth. The stubble on Kō's face had grown surprisingly long. They say that beards grow quickly on the faces of the dying. He choked, tears rising to his eyes, and appeared to be suffering. His eyes were bloodshot and his temperature still high.

"How are you feeling? Are you in pain?"

"I'm cold."

"Do you want to try to eat something?"

Moving his Adam's apple up and down, he consented with his eyes. Kyūzō fed him pieces of cheese with dry bread dipped and softened in hot water. It took some time, but Kō ate eight of them. Did it really seem that he was going to die?

"It's been two days already."

"Take down the flag!"

"Why? I don't want to starve to death."

"Idiot!"

"It really seems like you're afraid of coming across people."

"Then give me back my pistol."

"I'll return it as soon as you've recovered."

Gingerly raising his right hand, Kō painfully grasped his left arm. "Is it morning or evening now?"

"Evening."

"It's shameful. I really owe you. But the flag's a problem."

"So just tell me the reason."

"You're very stubborn. All right, I'll tell you. I'll tell you once I get better."

Kyūzō kept silent. I bet he's some kind of criminal who doesn't want to be seen. Kō chuckled.

"You have a face like a native. There's a ring around your mouth."

"So do you."

Kō smiled again before the blood drained from his face. He cried out, slurring his words, "I can't bear it. Could you look at my hand?"

It was extremely difficult to remove his glove. Kō bared his teeth, screaming and kicking the ground with his feet. The tip of his pinky was dark red and swollen to twice its normal size. The nail was ingrown and white like a shell.

Kō looked at it and said immediately, "Cut it off!"

Kyūzō said nothing, but Kō urged him on. "Do it quickly before it gets dark. There's a knife in my left pocket. Hold the finger tightly at the base and sever it from the second knuckle. Please hurry . . ."

Closing his eyes and averting his face with a look of utter exhaustion, Kō held his left arm away from his body and turned it over on the ground. For a long time, however, Kyūzō could not decide what to do. Kō remained still and seemed to have again lost consciousness. I can't cut his finger if he's unconscious. First of all, how much can I trust what he says right before he loses consciousness? Next, I couldn't bear it if he were to wake up and, forgetting what had happened, screamed that I had cut off his finger. However, Kō had not lost consciousness. Opening his eyes wide, he shouted in a frightful voice, "Quickly!"

Kyūzō hurriedly followed Kō's instructions to wrap his pinky in a piece of the hand towel.

"Tighter! Wrap it more tightly!"

Soon the entire finger was cold and black. The knife, which was slightly larger than a pencil sharpener, was quite unsuitable for use on the human body. Gathering his courage, Kyūzō thrust the blade into that part of the finger located slightly above the knot. Dark blood flowed slowly from the broken skin. But he could do nothing more than this. If the finger could not be severed by moving the blade sideways, then the only thing left was to tear it off. With no other option, Kyūzō plunged the knife into another part of the finger. After several thrusts, the veins, nerves, and tendons all stuck out like entrails, and the finger now looked like a piece of sinewy meat that has been vomited out without being fully chewed. Kyūzō's hands were slippery, making it difficult to grip the knife firmly. Yet there was no way he could stop at this point. Finding a large branch among the kindling, he placed it on the ground, put Kō's finger on top, and twisted down with the blade. Even that didn't work. The hard, flexible part of the finger kept disappearing under the bone. Abandoning Kō's knife in favor of his own Mongolian blade, Kyūzō used the same technique while stepping on the finger with the heel of his shoe. He could hear the bone being crushed. As he forced his foot down once again, the front of the knife severed the finger and then cut in half the branch underneath before plunging into the ground. Kyūzō felt sick.

Kō, however, remained motionless and silent. He had again lost consciousness at some point. Worried that he was too quiet, Kyūzō placed the glass of his watch under Kō's nose to check that he was still breathing. 5:02—might as well wind the watch. Kyūzō stirred the fire and boiled water. While waiting, he sacrificed some of the remaining vodka to wash the severed end of Kō's finger, wrapping it thickly in a new piece of hand towel.

Kyūzō felt chilled. His body would not stop shaking. He added as much kindling as possible to the fire, increasing its heat. Looking at Kō's sleeping face, exposed and exaggerated by the quivering flame, Kyūzō felt less pity than disgust. Why must I be so tightly bound to this bastard who refuses to die and who can't reply? What significance could this man have for me? Something small and white suddenly began wriggling on the back of Kō's neck. This white thing was slowly moving along his collar toward his ear. It was a louse. The louse had crawled out in search of warmth. ("So shouldn't he be cold already?") It was not cold yet. The insect immediately turned around and headed for its original territory. They say that it's a bad omen for mice to move about. Lice that move about might also be a bad omen. Kō's pulse was already over one hundred and thirty beats per minute, and was so faint that it seemed about to vanish.

Washing his hands, Kyūzō wiped the blood from the knife. He then threw the severed finger far off the cliff.

XIV

The next morning was also mild, with no wind. Thin clouds appeared in the southern sky.

Kō was still alive. His fever was high and he had not yet regained consciousness, but he had continually stirred since early morning. He had spoken deliriously, ground his teeth, and struggled to turn over, but Kyūzō wasn't sure if such changes were signs that his condition was worsening or improving.

Kyūzō sprinkled some vodka on the wound and changed the hand towel. Kō seemed to be in no pain whatsoever. When Kyūzō fed him some dry bread dipped in the juices from the sausage, Kō seemed to turn into a different creature and tried to greedily swallow the food down. Perhaps it was good that Kyūzō had cut off his finger. Kō was a man who had overcome the challenges posed by his own head, his unshaven face, and the omen of the louse. He might just end up surviving.

The wind picked up as the sun rose. It was a strange wind, blowing irregularly and constantly shifting direction. Like a caged beast, Kyūzō prowled around the fire.

In any case, I'll set out tomorrow afternoon. It should be enough to leave Kō enough food for three days. Once I arrive at some village, I'll pay someone to come and rescue him. Of course I'll prepare not only food for him but also kindling and ice for water. It's absolutely meaningless to wait here with him and starve.

And yet . . . another voice whispered. That all depends on Kō's regaining consciousness. If he can't eat and make a fire for himself, then my leaving would be the same as letting him die.

"Mr. Kō!" Kyūzō shouted in his ears. Still no response. It was so disappointing. All his squirming about was nothing more than an internal impulse.

He spent the entire morning gathering kindling. Separating out the large branches from the small, he piled them in front of the cliff hollow. He then collected some withered grass. The place now looked ridiculously comfortable, and this thought made him extremely irritated.

Around noon, clouds covered the entire sky and there was some flickering snow. It stopped in an hour. In any case, Kyūzō thought, it's good that I gathered kindling. The wind faded when the snow stopped, leaving the rust-colored sky a blurry red. He spent the afternoon collecting ice.

Gathering together the ice shards that he had broken off with a stone, Kyūzō carried them in his coat, wearing it backwards and rolling up the bottom. Impressed by what he considered to be a brilliant idea, it was nevertheless unfortunate that no one was around to see it. His technique for breaking the ice had improved as well. It was hard work, however, for the shards had to be as large as possible in order to be stored.

Returning from his second trip carrying the ice, Kyūzō was surprised to see that the flag was fluttering slightly to the north despite what he took to be a lack of wind. Come to think of it, the southern sky appeared a bit cloudy.

On his third trip back, however, there was something even more surprising. In the shadow of the gathered kindling something was moving. At first Kyūzō thought that Kō had been attacked by a wolf or wild dog, or perhaps even a bear (he didn't know if there actually were bears in the area or not). He dropped the ice and drew his pistol while running toward it. However, he soon realized that it was neither wolf, wild dog, nor bear. Rather it was Kō himself. Had he regained his sanity? What was he doing?

Having come all the way to this spot, Kō should have heard Kyūzō's footsteps. But something was strange. Kyūzō called out to him in a loud voice. There was no reply. Joy turned to suspicion. And then it turned to rage.

Tearing open Kyūzō's shirt that was filled with provisions, Kō lay on top of it, devouring the food. He was holding the sausage in his otherwise painful left hand and stuffing it into his mouth, while with his right hand he was ransacking the dry bread.

"Stop!" Kyūzō yelled as loudly as he could, instinctively raising the gun.

But Kō didn't even turn around. He was desperately stuffing food into his mouth, barely chewing as he swallowed it down. He heaved in convulsions, from his shoulders to the underside of his stomach. Food dribbled out of his mouth as he was unable to swallow it all. It almost looked as though he were taking revenge on something.

"Idiot!" Kyūzō yelled, rushing over and knocking him down from behind. Even then Kō didn't stop eating, clinging to the ground as he screamed, "Eh, eh." Kyūzō screamed right back at him. Grabbing Kō by the nape of his neck, he pulled him up and flipped him over onto his back.

About seventy percent of the food had been devoured. It was unbelievable! No matter how much one filled one's belly, there was plenty of food for three meals. What the hell was wrong with him?

"You can't do this, you idiot!"

Kyūzō's anger turned to despair.

"You can't do this!"

He tasted something bittersweet in the back of his throat. His head felt cold inside.

Kō remained flipped over on his back, not even trying to move. His tongue protruded from his open mouth as he drooled incessantly, the white of his eye exposed, and only his artificial eye stared straight ahead with a terrifying look.

"Really, you can't do this!"

With another yell, Kyūzō grabbed hold of Kō's hair, banging his head against the ground repeatedly. Kō let out a brief groan each time. He seemed to have no idea what he had done. Suddenly his body began shaking, and he vomited up the food he had just eaten. Largely undigested chunks of dry bread, cheese, and sausage spurted out covered in phlegm and white foam.

("Maybe he's lost his mind.")

Kyūzō felt that the feeling in his entire body had shriveled, giving off a dry, rustling sound as it concentrated in the depths of his nostrils and middle of his face. The tears flowed to the back of his throat. As he stood near Kō, who was still shaking, having thrust his face in the middle of the vomited food, Kyūzō began to sob quietly. A thought quickly flitted through his mind: Alexandrov had been kind.

"Young lady." Kō sang in a soft voice, frothing at the mouth.

Beating his fists on his knees, Kyūzō turned toward the hazy white wasteland and began crying loudly.

His tears soon gone, Kyūzō sobbed convulsively while staring at the fire that was now almost out. It seemed that his emotions had disappeared. The food was effectively gone. Everything was finished. He understood this rationally, and yet for some reason this fact did not feel terribly urgent. Something would come up, he believed. However, there were no doubt people in this situation who starved to death believing to the last that something would come up. They said that no deserting soldier ever returned alive after trying to pass over the Khingan Range. Kyūzō had heard many times of military badges emerging from the bellies of wolves. This is how some people died! I wonder if I'll also die like this, refusing to believe it until the end.

("But it's possible—no, certain—that Alexandrov has heard about the train accident. And he must certainly have sent word to a rescue team to investigate my case. What would he do without a corpse and any knowledge of my whereabouts? For example, he might feel responsible if he suspected that the certificate he had given me had caused trouble, resulting in my being abducted by the Chinese Nationalist troops. In which case, he might send a pursuit team—assuming that such a force exists, and that they were more powerful than the Nationalist troops—to investigate and rescue me. In any case, the escape route for the Nationalist troops was south. The pursuit team would thus come south at some point.")

Kyūzō would surely die repeating such a fantasy, unwilling to give up hope until the end.

But it's been a strange twist of fate, he thought. I was abandoned by Kita and his group because I had to take care of my mother. Now I'm about to be abandoned by fate because I'm taking care of a stranger. Even if I'm somehow saved, I won't take care of anyone ever again.

XV

Afterwards, Kō vomited up the contents of his stomach twice more before immediately falling asleep and snoring terribly. Kyūzō spent the entire night sitting still, mechanically burning kindling. He thought he hadn't slept at all, but upon realizing that the squawking of the crows had awakened him with a start, he supposed that he might have dozed a bit. There was dark swelling under his eyes from too much crying, and the smudge of the tears made his face appear shrunken. Kō was sleeping in the same place as last night, lying facedown with his chin thrust out. He must have suffered horribly, as his hat had come off and his coat was twisted below his chest. Dried vomit encrusted his entire face, glistening in his beard like frost. The same vomit was also clogging his throat, Kyūzō suspected, judging by the whistling of his breathing. For all that, his breathing was surprisingly regular.

Kyūzō boiled and drank some water. He suddenly felt hunger. He gathered up Kō's leftover food. There was only enough to fill two hands. He felt an involuntary twitch in his jaw as his back teeth began grinding. As if the small scraps of sausage possessed legs and were about to escape, Kyūzō eagerly stuffed them in his mouth. They were utterly flavorless. It was like tasting lye. If hunger and appetite were two different things and he had no appetite, then he thought that he shouldn't eat. Hunger, however, would not allow him to stop eating. It was a terrifying thing, far more compulsive than appetite.

Once he began eating, there was no end. He became unbearably anxious to not move his mouth even a bit. This anxiety might be less from hunger itself than from the fear of hunger. It was only after he had consumed nearly half the food that he realized he must stop. He began to think that hunger was like a tangible thing. He was even on the point of believing the ridiculous notion that hunger had taken possession of Kō yesterday and was trying to take hold of him today. He looked for food within hunger in the same way that one seeks light within darkness. His head was filled with the colors and shapes of all kinds of food.

The first thing that naturally occurred to Kyūzō was the fish in the marsh. He could break through the ice and catch them. Suddenly everything was solved. It was so simple that his thoughts became hazy. He walked off to the place where he had broken the ice and began to dig deeper. Ten centimeters had already been shaved off, so the water should be reached by digging another twenty or thirty centimeters. However, the ice was unexpectedly hard compared with the weathered surface above it. He did not mind the labor involved in digging. But he was afraid of how much his hunger would grow through these exertions.

Lying on his belly, his face covered with ice, he dug down strenuously, careful to avoid wasting even the slightest energy. The hole was becoming too narrow. Widening it by digging sideways, he proceeded deeper. After repeated attempts, the resistance he encountered suddenly changed. What he felt was not ice, but neither was it the surface of the water. Putting his hand in and scraping about, he discovered chunks of ice mixed together with slimy blue humus.

Dejected, Kyūzō lacked even the energy to stand up for a while. He remained still for so long that the cold of the ice directly penetrated his skin through his clothes. His exposed wrist was stinging and swollen red. Wiping the ice from his face, he got up slowly, and yet he felt extremely sharp and clearheaded in thinking about the challenge of the marsh.

Quickly taking in the surrounding terrain, Kyūzō saw that the bottom of that part of the marsh would obviously be shallow. The water seemed to be sufficiently deep closer to the cliff.

He marked out a spot just thirty meters from the fire. However, he had no energy left to continue wielding the rock to dig through the ice. Taking out the pistol, he suddenly pointed downward and pulled the trigger. With a brief, dry sound, the ice scattered about. A hole about the size of one's pinky appeared. It was deeper than the length of one's finger, but it was not as deep as he had hoped.

Opening the magazine, Kyūzō took out the bullets. He didn't know what kind of pistol it was, but it was an automatic handgun that fired seven shots in rapid succession. ("Five bullets remained if one subtracted the bullet used to shoot the dog at the brick kiln and the one used now.") Removing three bullets, two remained. Holding the cartridge with frozen fingers, he used his teeth to detach the front shell of the three bullets. Blood oozed in his mouth as one tooth became loose. He then stuffed the gunpowder in the ice hole. Returning to the fire, he brought back a bundle of thin branches and withered grass. It was quite strange how his next course of action was decided virtually without thinking.

Covering the hole with the grass, he piled on the branches and lit them on fire. Once he was sure that the fire had caught, he quickly ran back. The fire was burning properly. He waited, holding his breath. A long time passed. The flame's radiance faded and smoke rose up, and then the smoke gradually thinned and disappeared. But there was no explosion.

Cautiously he approached. Clearing away the ashes, he found the wet grass, underneath which had formed a small pool of water. Yes, the heated ice had turned to water.

Enraged, he fired the remaining two bullets. One struck close by and made another hole. His aim was good with the other one, and a spray of water spouted up in the air.

Upon turning around, Kyūzō saw that Kō had propped himself up on his elbow, looking at him. Had he awakened from the shock of the gunshots? For a moment, Kyūzō's eyes shone with pleasure. He stood on his tiptoes and inhaled. Immediately, however, he realized it was hopeless. Kō was a madman. He had devoured all their food. He was beyond control. Closing his eyes, Kyūzō slowly walked back as if the joints in his body were dislocated. Ignoring Kō's questioning gaze, he sat down with his back to him.

"What happened?"

Kyūzō spat between his legs by way of response.

"I feel like my body is about to break." Kō's voice was dry and lifeless, and the words caught in his throat. "What was that sound just now?"

Surprised, Kyūzō looked up. Had Kō regained his sanity? Suddenly all his reproaches came bursting out.

"The sound just now? All right, I'll tell you. Why are you saying that now? Why now? It's already too late. I had calculated the provisions, but then you ate five days' worth of food at once. Something is wrong with you! Understand? Five day's worth of food at once!"

Kyūzō was so eager to say everything at once that he began to ramble—repeating himself, making leaps, and reversing things in his vehemence.

"All right, I understand." Kō interrupted weakly, scraping off the crud around his mouth. "I've caused you trouble. It's been a feverish nightmare. Could you give me some water?"

Expecting Kō to be shocked by his words, Kyūzō felt instead that he was being evasive. Kyūzō brusquely pushed the icy cooking pot toward him. Drinking all the water in one gulp, Kō lay back down in exhaustion.

"My body is about to break. And my finger. What's this? Right, you cut it off for me. Strange how the finger still hurts even though it's gone. What did you do with the finger after cutting it off?"

"I threw it away over there."

"Huh. I feel like I'm about to break. Did I sleep a lot?"

"For six days."

"That's awful. It's incredible. Are you still angry at me? What for?"

"It's fine if you don't understand."

Kō narrowed his gaze. Licking his lips, he tried to peer into Kyūzō's face. His expression was one of suspicion, as if he had just been betrayed.

"Fine. Those who know nothing of the world can be very sure of themselves."

"The people who are most sure of themselves are rather those who say such things while waiting to die."

"What! Who's waiting to die?"

"Didn't I say that there's no food left? We're both going to starve here!"

"You shouldn't exaggerate so much. But was that sound just now from the pistol?"

"Yes."

"What happened?"

"I tried to break through the ice and catch fish."

"Did it break?"

"No, it didn't."

"That's right. You shouldn't be so wasteful. Those bullets are our life-line. Are you going to keep your promise and give me back my gun?"

"Here. I used up all the bullets."

Kyūzō carelessly tossed the weapon at Kō's feet. Without moving, Kō closed his eyes and, with pursed lips, let out a long breath.

That breath became a sharp needle of regret that pierced Kyūzō's chest. Damn it, it's as if I've been rushing toward my own destruction with my way of doing things. If I just had a pistol, things might still have worked out somehow. Deep in the marshland there must be rabbits. There should be wolves and wild dogs as well. There might even be deer. If need be, even crows would help.

He secretly stole a glance at Kō. Kō's face, wan and filthy, was tightly closed, and he lay unmoving as if he were dead. But it's not just my responsibility! First of all, this man caused everything. And it was only because I took care of him that he even regained his sanity. But he was so optimistic about our food situation just now. It's possible that he had a solution in mind. But everything has now turned to despair for him. Maybe the pistol really was crucial? It's as if the two of us are killing each other.

With an audible gulp, Kyūzō swallowed the saliva that filled his mouth. The sound was unexpectedly loud, making him feel beset by a dizzying fear. Again, something was there, approaching much closer now. It was hunger.

The sun reached its height in the hazy southern sky, shining a dull red. Kyūzō knew that this was a sign that the southern wind would blow much harder. In that dull radiance that stirred life he sensed the kind of despair that could rip one apart.

He began running. Climbing up the cliff, he ran around the remnants of the plains fire where he had previously walked. He searched for the burnt mouse that was turned faceup, exposing its white, swollen belly. It had disappeared from where it should have been. He ran his hands through the ashen grass, knowing that the search was futile and yet unwilling to give up.

Suddenly he heard a hoarse voice, like the sound of a dog barking. It came from the bottom of the cliff. Kō was calling to him.

"Hey, take down the flag!"

Peering down, Kyūzō saw that Kō was leaning against the cliff unsteadily, that he had somehow stood up and was tentatively twisting his head back and forth. He was overwhelmed by Kō's incredible strength of will. When Kō realized that Kyūzō was watching him, he called out in a decisive and almost cheerful tone.

"Take down the flag! Time to leave."

Sticking out his lower lip, Kō held his breath as he let go of the cliff. With furrowed brow, he made a show of walking a step. Immediately, however, he sat back down.

"Well, let's leave tomorrow. But in any case, take down the flag. I don't want to pretend that you're taking advantage of my weakened condition."

"But you promised to explain why."

"All right, fine. I'll explain."

Kyūzō didn't believe this verbal promise. Despite his reservations, he disconnected the pole, breaking it down into its individual branches, and folded up the rope and flag before sticking them in his pocket. Selecting two of the sturdier looking branches, he threw one down to Kō.

"That one should make a good walking stick."

"I see. Yes, a good walking stick."

Chapter 3

The Trap

XVI

As Kyūzō climbed up the slope, the trailing sound of Kō's footsteps suddenly stopped. It was the fourth day since leaving the marsh. Five or six steps behind, Kō appeared as a dark mass as he lay groveling on the ground. Ignoring him, Kyūzō began walking on, but his stride gradually slowed, and he finally stopped in resignation. He tried calling out to Kō, but his voice was now gone. It was easier to walk than to raise his voice. Slowly he made his way back.

"What's wrong?" he asked in a frozen voice. He placed a hand on Kō's shoulder as he tried to help him up, but Kō's body suddenly went limp as he collapsed on his belly. The right half of his face, reflected in the slanting moonlight, appeared puffy and swollen. With each breath, the edge of his lips trembled slightly and the sides of his flattened nostrils expanded and contracted. His overflowing saliva formed white icicles that hung from his unshaven beard. He even seemed to be faintly snoring.

"Wake up!" Kyūzō yelled, using the back of his hand to hit Kō repeatedly behind the ears. His voice stung as it stuck to the back of his parched throat.

Muttering incoherently, Kō twisted his body to escape the blows from Kyūzō's hand. Tucking his wounded left hand underneath his own body, he gave a hoarse cry and returned to his senses. Clutching Kyūzō's arm, he jerked himself back up. As he knelt with his head lolling back and forth, he yelled out in a shrill voice, "Hit me again!"

Kyūzō continued beating him with both hands. His senses became dulled—it was just like beating cotton. However, his fingertips hurt so much that they felt like they were broken, the pain reverberating from his shoulders all the way to his ears. And yet it was only this pain that allowed him to confirm what he was doing.

"Enough. Let's go."

With a grunt, Kō used his unsteady hands to block Kyūzō's blows and then looked fearfully around at the swelling hills of the wasteland, which with its back turned to them gave off a white radiance. "Shit! Let's go." Finding his grip on the walking stick, he staggered off with a bent posture, not yet standing fully erect. Around his waist was coiled a rope, which dangled long behind him and at the end of which was affixed his bag. With each step, the bag bounced back and forth as it slid along the ground behind him.

In the darkened minds of the exhausted men, the sound of the bag formed a line like the tracks made by some crawling insect. In fact, Kyūzō repeatedly conjured up the image of an insect slowly crawling from one end to the other of a broad white cloth, and he tried to identify that insect with himself. In this way, he began to feel that his insecure fate had now been given a secure foundation. Perhaps if one calculated the width of a single step as fifty centimeters, then the next step would be one hundred, then one hundred and fifty, two hundred, and three hundred. Eventually growing confused as the number approached ten thousand, he felt secure in approaching that much closer to hope.

It was only this morning that Kō felt that he could no longer carry his bag. As soon as it began to grow light, they came across a long and narrow thicket of bushes in the hollow of a hill. There they built a fire. Rather than try to rest, however, Kō sat there cringing, only his bloodshot eye moving as he anxiously looked around.

"Let me see the map."

After peering at it for a while, he climbed to the top of a slightly elevated hill in front of them before turning around and beckoning to Kyūzō. Pointing south, he asked in a suspicious tone, "Do you see anything?"

The fatiguing simplicity of the unchanging, desolate plains merely called forth once again a sense of numbing frustration and draining fear. When Kyūzō shook his head no, Kō, goggle-eyed and obviously dismayed, began looking around on the ground as if searching for something.

"These ... these are not fields."

He looked forlorn, as if on the verge of begging Kyūzō to tell him that these were indeed fields. Of course they were not fields.

"What's wrong?"

Kō said nothing as he returned to the fire with a blank expression, lost in thought. Kyūzō added more branches when the fire began burning strongly. Smoke billowed up as the sparks furiously scattered about. As there was no wind, the smoke swirled straight up to a considerable height and, trembling, fluttered slightly to the northwest before disappearing. Kyūzō suddenly grabbed Kō's arm.

"The wind is coming from the south!" he said.

Absorbed in chewing on a grass root that he had plucked at his feet, Kō looked up at the sky and then yelled at Kyūzō.

"Idiot! Don't let the smoke build up like that. Someone might see it." Flicking at a branch with the tip of his walking stick, he waved his hat about, fanning the flame. As the flame spread, the column of smoke faded.

"Someone might see it."

Kyūzō curled his lips in response to this foolishness. Staring at the map Kō had returned, he suddenly understood the reason why Kō had just gotten so upset. Following the arranged course, they should now be at a point forty kilometers west of Tanyu. There should be fields in this area, while in the south there should appear a series of hills that form the border with Inner Mongolia. Had they gotten lost?

"Where are we now?"

Kō made no attempt to reply, however, merely shooting a cruel look at Kyūzō. Boiling water with the snow he had gathered, Kyūzō then placed a fifty-sen piece in his hat and offered it to Kō. This was how they typically decided who would sleep first. Waving his hand, Kō replied in annoyance.

"Put out the fire. We're pressing on today without sleep."

Kyūzō was about to protest but, shocked by the cornered look in Kō's eyes, decided to remain silent. Kō then staggered when trying to lift his bag. Hunger appeared first in one's flesh before it was registered by the senses. Last night they had consumed the last of the beans that Kō kept in one of his socks. Other than water, they had put nothing in their bellies for twenty hours now. Also, the cold had returned for the past two or three days. Having expended a great many calories, their hunger would be that much greater.

"Damn it! My hand's gone numb. Just wait a minute."

There was fear in his voice. Stamping out the remains of the fire, Kyūzō didn't wish to respond.

"Just wait. I'll make it worth your while. I'll give you a hundred yen an hour."

Kyūzō removed from his pocket the rope that he had made at the marsh by shredding the wrapping cloth in order to bind together the sticks for the flagpole. He threw this over to Kō.

"You can use this to hang the bag from your body."

Attempting to grab one end of the rope that had fallen at his feet, Kō pitched forward on his right side, his nose plunging into his bent arm.

"Well then, make a fire. Two hour shifts!" he said in an echoless voice.

Crouching down by Kō's ear, Kyūzō pressed for an answer.

"So I guess we're lost, right?

Kō, however, merely shivered slightly, closing his eyes and saying nothing. He had already begun snoring softly.

Yet Kyūzō now deeply regretted having given the rope to Kō. The bundle of his belongings wrapped in the blanket was nearly empty, but it now felt like iron in sharply digging into the top of his shoulders. Since their confrontation, what had sustained the two was not rational will but merely fear, phantoms, and a beastlike visceral impulse. The other one was sustained by that impulse, and it was only the stimuli derived from the fact that each continued his unyielding struggle that functioned as their final reserve of strength that even now spurred on their attachment to their own fading lives.

The hilly paths were especially painful. Even the barest slope stung deeply. The same distance felt several times longer, and Kyūzō tried to find any reason to make excuses, wishing to rest even for a moment. He felt something like a mystical awe for Kō's strength of will in continuing to walk on. And no doubt Kō himself felt the same way about Kyūzō.

In this way, the two sustained one another. Hence if the stimuli from the other were to stop, thereby causing the support they received to waver, it would be quite doubtful whether either could have distinguished in any sensory way between stopping and continuing to press on. When the slope of the hills became steeper or a huge rock face suddenly appeared, Kyūzō at times believed he was walking when in fact he was on all fours. Or perhaps he thought he was going forward when, with stooped back, he rested his hands on bent knees and shook his body from side to side.

It was the most dangerous for Kyūzō to consider such thoughts as "I should experiment and try walking with my eyes closed" or "I'll try to experience what it would have been like to drive a car." The gap between fantasy and reality virtually disappeared, and his senses became gloomily clouded, like the small, dirty peephole of an ice room enclosed by thick lead walls. The cruel world of lies at once flickered and vanished. The large steaming basket under the eaves of an eating house on a street corner, hens that run about and push their way through the narrow alleys, the cat that is so fat that it cannot move, fading advertisements on a telephone pole, a room with a bed, hot water, and soap in a washbasin, the silky white surface of a boiled egg . . . The uncertain, wobbling ground, filled with dark noises and screams, would intermittently rise up and try to swallow his feet, leaving Kyūzō unable to press forward. Absentmindedness occurred frequently, if only instantaneously, but those instants might form a continuity and hold him back.

In fact, didn't Kō just now fall asleep while walking?

Rather than rouse Kyūzō's courage, however, his companion's stumbling seemed to unnerve him. Although he vaguely sensed that the distance between himself and Kō was gradually increasing, there was nothing he could do about it. Previously that was all right since he was the one walking ahead, but now the situation was reversed. Now it was Kyūzō's turn to be left behind. Somehow this thing called stumbling seemed to be contagious.

Kyūzō recalled the dispute he had had last night with Kō. The night was pitch-dark, enveloped in clouds. He had opposed the idea of continuing on, since at such times it is easy to get lost and merely circle around the same area. Also, he thought that at several moments he had heard the sound of wolves howling in the distance. Yet Kō made no attempt to listen. If they ended up getting lost, it would doubtless be his fault. In so saying, however, they of course did not have a precisely determined course and were at any rate trying to head south, so they would probably not stray so far that it would be impossible to correct. With their limited strength, however, there was a danger that even the slightest detour might prove irrevocably fatal.

Unbearable fear gradually paled, turning to despair. It then paled further, turning to anger. That anger took on form and became increasingly focused on a strand of rope. This was the rope that Kō was using to drag his bag. Kyūzō began to become obsessed by the strange idea that his entire fate was now hanging by that rope.

Startled by the sound of the bag sliding on the ground, Kyūzō returned to his senses. He was on his knees, lost in thought. Leaning on the walking stick, he finally got back up.

("Yes, I need to get that rope back.")

Just in case, he used his elbow to confirm that the knife was still tucked under his belt. However, it required a great deal of effort to begin walking again. A new blister had peeled on the outside of his right little toe, and it stung painfully.

He finally arrived at a ridge. The distance between the two of them was now over fifty meters, and Kō was already approaching the swell of the next hill. Kyūzō despaired at the shortness of the descent on the current hill. The bones in his shoulders felt as if they were about to crack. He felt his stomach convulse with severe nausea, as if he were seasick. While descending the hill, he found himself instinctively yelling, "Wait!" His voice was blocked by frozen lips, however, and the sound produced was merely a weak shout: "Ay." Even that sound was swallowed up by the thick, frozen walls of the wasteland. If someone were ten steps away, the only sound he might hear would surely be no louder than that of paper being torn. At its end, the yell had turned to crying.

The next slope was the longest and felt even steeper. Kō did not bother turning around. Kyūzō felt that he could go no further. Grabbing some dry snow entangled in withered grass, he placed it in his mouth. Although it didn't feel the least bit cold, the unmelted snow scraped his upper jaw as if he were chewing rock dust. Thinking that he might feel more energized if he chewed on some grass roots, he kicked at the ground with his heel only to find it unyielding, wounded only slightly with a small, white cut. Instead, he felt a pain so sharp that he wondered if his tendons had snapped, rendering him immobile for a while.

Suddenly at his feet there lay the remains of a mouse. Its white belly was exposed, burnt, and swollen a pale pinkish color. It was a large field mouse. "What? It was right here?" he thought giddily, leaning over it, when the mouse disappeared. Kyūzō shuddered, stupefied. In the next instant, it occurred to him to build a fire. Above all, he needed heat, besides which it would surely force Kō to come back. It would indeed be a case of killing two birds with one stone. Yet there was nothing in the area that could be used as fuel. Handfuls of withered grass encrusted with weathered snow could be found scattered about here and there on the hollows and stone remnants, but it was virtually impossible to gather enough to make a fire.

In any case, though, Kyūzō wanted a fire. Although realizing it was meaningless, he used the tip of his walking stick to scrape off the snow from some grass, lighting a match directly upon it. Only bits and pieces of a few blades caught flame, and the fire went out without generating any smoke. The match ended up burning the longest. Holding on to the splint until it burned the tip of his glove, he then went on to the next patch of withered grass.

Kō suddenly stopped. Kyūzō lit another match. Kō shouted something in a hoarse voice. Ignoring him, Kyūzō continued lighting one match after another. Hearing Kō return, he finally lit many matches together in a bunch.

Kō grabbed Kyūzō by the shoulder, pulling him up.

"Idiot! What are you doing? Stop it!"

Shaking his hand free, he yelled back at Kō.

"Give me back the rope!"

"Rope?"

Kyūzō began lighting another match.

"Hey, I said stop," Kō insisted, trying to brush Kyūzō's hand away with the tip of his walking stick. "Stop it. You're wasting them."

Turning around, Kyūzō suddenly let out a growl and lunged at Kō. He missed him and fell over, digging up the ground with his elbow. Rising to his feet, he immediately struck another match.

"Idiot! People can see from far away!"

"It's fine if they can. Give me back the rope!"

When Kō approached, Kyūzō merely turned his back to avoid him, seeming quite unwilling to stop lighting matches. He had finally finished off the first bunch. Removing the second bunch from his inside pocket, he tried to light them as well. Following closely behind, Kō raised his walking stick, striking Kyūzō on the right shoulder. The stick flew off, broken. Weeping, Kyūzō suddenly grabbed the knife handle under his jacket. Kō began to draw his pistol but, recalling that there were no more bullets, quickly put it back.

For a long time, the two remained glaring at each other. Finally, in a doleful, dreary voice, Kō slowly spoke.

"Let's go. We're almost there."

"Almost there!" Kyūzō's jaw quivered hysterically. "It's your fault, you bastard! I'm the one who saved your wretched life!"

As Kō silently walked off, however, Kyūzō followed five or six steps behind.

XVII

With each ascent of the swelling ridges slightly before dawn, Kyūzō thought that he saw something off in the southern horizon. With the sinking of the moon, ringed on the bottom with its cloudy white crescent, that something gradually took shape and appeared as a forest or knoll, or at moments even a large town. But he knew only that it was a dark mass, and that with its constantly changing form it might simply be a cloud. Yet are there shapes in the night that do not move? Even a changing form might be an illusion in the eyes of the person looking.

Gradually the sky became brighter. Crossing over a slightly elevated hill, the dark mass suddenly appeared directly before Kyūzō. His visual confusion was to some degree correct. Clouds dirty as sediment settled in part of the southern horizon. In front of those clouds, the multilayered series of hills that they had seen on the map blocked off what lay ahead.

Yet that group of hills was completely bare. Although the hills didn't appear to be particularly high, in the dry season they become barren as bone, and the grass was eaten away by mice before it could take root, leaving a ragged surface that was washed away and eroded by rain. When those peculiar slopes were illuminated in relief by the morning sun at their side, they shone in such colors as red, yellow, green, purple, and black. They were like some great mountain range, possessing an overpowering quality about them. Kō also didn't know what the hills were called and they were not listed on the map, but Kyūzō would not have thought it strange if they were designated as some mountain chain.

"Are we crossing those mountains?"

With exhausted, half-open eyes, his feet dragging, Kyūzō asked this question in a voice that was no less dragging.

"Beyond them lies Horqin Left Middle Banner."

"Is that where we're going?"

"I don't know."

Yet Kō's stride appeared more forceful now, and this in turn affected Kyūzō, who recovered some energy. The clouds gradually rose higher in the sky, and Kyūzō felt a slight southern wind on his eyes and cheeks. Sensing a kind of roundness when he inhaled, he suspected that the temperature was climbing.

Traversing two more hills, they came upon a broad expanse of lowland that lay between them and the series of hills. There a road heading in an east-west direction cut across their route. Shaking irregularly, the road headed east along the edge of the hills before turning right, where it stretched off a long distance before disappearing into the shadows of a ravine.

"It's a road!"

Kyūzō's voice was shrill with excitement. It had been exactly ten days since they had last seen signs of human existence. Yet Kō made no reply.

Lying one level lower than the surrounding ground, the road might have been mistaken for a dry riverbed were it not for the traces of wagon tracks. While it was not a riverbed, the road obviously became something of a stream during the rainy season. It had been built up as much as possible before freezing over. An unusual abundance of withered grass appeared on each side, and in the shadow of the embankments grew trees that were somewhat undernourished. They were less trees than a pile of twigs measuring no more than thirty or forty centimeters in height. They looked like elm stumps that failed to grow. The buds that annually appeared on them were probably picked off by rabbits or mice or perhaps even hungry travelers, leaving them no time to develop. Nevertheless, it was interesting that the trees by the roadside were more protected than others. One reason for this, no doubt, was that rain gathered and flowed there, allowing the trees to better conserve water. Another reason was that the signs of human presence perhaps functioned to discourage the approach of small animals.

Alighting on the road, Kyūzō breathlessly turned around and laughed. Kō slid down from the embankment next. Immediately crossing the road as if to avoid Kyūzō's gaze, he prepared to climb up the opposite side.

"Aren't we going to rest, Mr. Kō?"

"We should get to the Kai River while it's still light."

"But why? It's fine here."

"Stop joking. Resting by the road after all this?"

"I'm not going. I'm resting here."

"It's only another six miles or so. Having come so far, it's pointless to rest now."

"Then we don't need to push ourselves so much."

Putting his belongings down on the embankment, Kyūzō began gathering branches by the roadside.

"Hey!" Holding his breath, Kō hailed him in a blurry voice. "I'm saying this for your own good, so let's go."

"Please help me with this."

"I'm saying this for your own good. I've got a plan."

"If we're going to rest anyway, then it makes the most sense to rest here. I hope that a wagon passes by."

"Stop talking nonsense!"

"I'm hungry!"

"That's why I'm telling you to listen to me. Don't you want to get back to Japan? Then listen to me. It's dangerous here. That's why I made such a fuss about the flag. Let's go. We should get there while it's still light and find out about the Middle Banner. Come on."

"But I don't have any reason to be afraid." Piling up a bundle of branches on the road, Kyūzō quickly began gathering some withered grass. "It's been very dangerous until now. There's no need to worry at this point."

"That's why I said that I'd explain things!"

"That's what you said. But you haven't done so yet."

"I'm . . ." Quickly licking his bottom lip with the short, dark tip of his tongue, Kō then wiped his mouth with the back of his hand. "I'm being pursued."

"I knew that. Even I could tell that much." Crumpling up the withered grass, Kyūzō stuffed it among the branches before striking a match. The first match went out before lighting the splint. The wind was up. Shivering, he struck the second match.

"Damn it, you bastard! If you hadn't played around with those bullets . . ."

"I know."

The fire caught and white smoke billowed up. The smoke flowed west alongside the road, scattered rapidly at that part of the embankment where Kō was standing, rippled over the wasteland, and then swirled off toward the north. Coughing violently, Kō slowly moved away from the smoke before walking over to Kyūzō's side of the embankment. Yet he did not go near the fire. The firm resolve with which he sought to overcome temptation caused him to raise even his artificial eye, and in the shadow of the eyelid his pupil appeared small and dark as a hole.

"Is this horse dung?" Kyūzō used the tip of his walking stick to poke a gray, pebble-sized lump lying in the hollow between the furrows of the tracks. The lump easily peeled away from the ground, facing upwards. Stripped of the frost, it was the vivid color of horse dung. Drawing it closer, Kyūzō stepped on the dung with the heel of his shoe, splitting it apart. Raw grass fibers stuck out from the powdery opening. "It's still fresh."

"Dung always looks fresh once it freezes."

"But the ice around it is still quite thin. And something would have come and eaten it if it had been here long."

"Like what?"

"Maybe crows, dogs, or mice."

"You should stop these empty hopes." Stooping painfully but with no change of expression, Kō tapped the tip of his broken walking stick against the main part of his boot. "Nothing is going to come no matter how much you wait. No damn way anything would come! I'll say it clearly, this area is the most dangerous. You can't tell where or what kind of bastards might be lying in wait. No fool would pass through this place nowadays."

"Then you've got nothing to worry about."

"Stop talking so impudently. In any case, it's for your own good."

"In any case, I'm staying here," Kyūzō replied dismissively, setting off to gather more kindling. "I've had enough of your advice."

Slowly curling up his lips as the cartilage in his throat twitched vigorously, Kō heavily dragged his right foot and turned the other way. Only his face remained still as he stared at Kyūzō's ear.

"Well then, I'm leaving."

Returning to the fire with the kindling he had gathered, Kyūzō removed his shoes with an air of impatience. Half his right sock had become stiff with half-dried blood. Warming the sock over the fire, he replied in a flat, listless voice.

"Fine."

"All right. Don't regret this."

Kyūzō pulled the blanket over himself and closed his eyes. Shivering, he felt that he was already half-asleep. Kō set off walking. For Kyūzō, the increasingly distant footsteps Kō made as he dragged his shoes, climbing along the slope in a roundabout way toward the left, sounded like a death sentence. Yet Kyūzō's fervent desire for rest extinguished all anxiety. "After all, I've made the best decision," he repeatedly told himself, nodding.

He tried to sleep cradling his knees to his chin, but for some reason it was quite impossible. The sound of the slowly moving air brushing up against the ground made him feel that the world was absurdly large, and the small bud of anxiety that was otherwise hidden by the relief he felt in unburdening himself now began to grow together with that expanding world. Suddenly he felt that he was already dead. The wagon had come just a moment too late.

"Oh, that poor Japanese man," remarked one wagoner.

"He seems to be the same age as my daughter," the other chimed in.

"Let's remove his clothes so that it will be easier for the crows to eat him," the first wagoner said, rolling Kyūzō over and stripping off his coat and inner jacket.

As the second wagoner began removing his pants, his magnificent knife with the engraving suddenly fell out. The first guy quickly picked it up. The second one complained. The first one then unsheathed the knife and suddenly ... At that moment, the heavy heel of someone's shoe trampled forcefully on Kyūzō's exposed flank.

What a stupid dream! Kyūzō tried to collect himself, blinking repeatedly as he sat straight up. It was at that instant that he realized something crucial. His cooking pot! Kō had taken it with him. Without that he could not boil water. Reflexively he rose to his feet and pricked up his ears. Yet the only thing he could hear was the sound of the wind. He thought that he should follow after Kō. At that very idea, however, his body refused to listen. All the pain of a hunger march was ingrained in Kō's presence, such that the very thought of returning to him produced in Kyūzō an instinctive sense of anxiety. Of course there was no clear guarantee that his present situation was any better. But the fact that he had finally arrived at a road, that he was actually on the road right now, surely meant that he might still hope for something.

He remembered that he had put the empty vodka bottle in the pouch that he had made from his shirt. Yes, that should do just fine. That's a good sign! But it took a lot of time and energy to stuff it with snow. When the bottle was finally filled, Kyūzō buried it in the ash. So far so good.

He unfolded the map, intending to assure himself further. He was now precisely where the projecting southern part of Heilongjiang Province bordered the crooked, hooklike eastern part of Inner Mongolia. It was possible that this road formed the boundary between those two regions. The road headed directly east from Baoshunhao before splitting off midway: one branch led to Tanyu, the other to Horqin Left Middle Banner. If Kyūzō's reading of the map was correct, he would need to travel east for ten kilometers to arrive at that junction before going another forty kilometers southeast in order to make it to the Middle Banner. Altogether it was a distance of fifty kilometers. Walking, it would be a journey of two days at best. Two days at best? "Come on, human beings can survive on water for twenty days!" Repeating Kō's pet phrase, Kyūzō quickly dismissed the cruelty of that blunt number.

Besides, walking was the worst-case scenario. Baoshunhao lay at the entrance to a series of hamlets in the plateau region, while the Middle Banner was the central village in the black soil region. Was it really nothing more than an unrealistic desire to hope that a wagon might pass through the one main corridor that connected these two regions? Of course Kyūzō didn't know the frequency of such trips. He didn't know whether wagons would come by twice a day or once every three days. In either case, however, there was no proof that a wagon would not be coming in the next hour.

Yet that thought was immediately replaced by another concern. If he were to go to the Middle Banner, he would find there a triangle of land wedged between the railroad where the soil was good and villages were everywhere. There would no longer be any desolate wasteland. With money, he could buy food and get water. There would be no need to have such frightening experiences. However, might not other terrors await him there? Could anyone promise that human beings were less cruel than nature? Another issue was whether the Middle Banner was now occupied by the Nationalist troops or by the Eighth Route Army. Kyūzō knew how to deal with the latter. He also had his certificate. He desperately wished that it was the Eighth Route Army occupying the area.

Come to think of it, Kō also seemed to harbor some kind of hope for the Middle Banner. Judging by his actions thus far, however, it was clear that he didn't hope that the area was occupied by the Eighth Route Army. Besides, in considering this question alongside the train attack incident, it seemed just as dangerous to have too much hope. Yet the Eighth Route Army had planned to run the train directly to Tieling, so at least the area along that line should be under their control. From the Middle Banner, the distance to, say, Sanlin Station was at most only fifty kilometers. It thus seemed quite possible that the Eighth Army was indeed occupying the area.

("As Kō said, this thing called a border region is really vast.")

The fire made a small, very dry, slightly echoing sound. With a strong hiss, a bundle of ash suddenly spouted in the air. The fire continued hissing and ash continued spouting, and it didn't stop until it had thrust its way through the blackened part. The bottom of the bottle had burst.

His heart racing, he felt as if he were about to choke. Just like the feeling one gets after running hard. Furious, he grabbed the neck of the bottle and flung it. Suddenly his throat felt intensely parched. Unable to stand it, he bared his teeth and let out a cry.

He was wide awake. Had he slept until now? Perhaps he was thinking while he was sleeping. Or sleeping while he was thinking. Imperceptibly the sun had risen quite high, glittering in the leaden sky like a polished sheet of copper, and everything shone the color of old porcelain. The wind was mixed with the clear smell of spring.

With the southern side of the embankment at his back, shadows had already begun to engulf him from the waist down. If he moved to the northern side, he would receive sunlight but the wind would be rather bad. It was not only the wind that was a concern, for he might be choked by the smoke if he were not careful. Ultimately, however, the sunlight offered the greatest advantage. He plucked up his courage and changed position, discovering that neither the wind nor smoke was as bad as he had imagined.

But he wanted water. With water, he'd be able to survive for twenty days. Regardless of how much it smelled of spring, the temperature was such that it was still quite impossible to gnaw on unmelted snow. His body began quivering in irritation. He felt like he was still fighting for breath. He wondered if this pain would gradually increase, and he would finally reach his limit and die writhing in agony. It was unbearable to even think about that limit. He had heard of travelers in the desert who got lost and were forced to chew their own wrists in order to sip their blood. This area here was like a desert. I wonder if I, too, might soon be forced to chew my own wrists and sip my blood. No, I'll definitely freeze in my sleep before that. Thanks to the cold, I'll surely be spared such pain.

Perhaps it was his imagination, but he somehow felt his eyelids grow heavier. Opening his eyes wide in shock, he pressed his clenched fists against his forehead and began forcefully turning them.

("I wonder if there's not a good way . . .")

He suddenly thought of a wonderful idea. He could use half the wrapping cloth that he had made into a flag. Folding the cloth in two, he placed some crushed snow inside and tied the four corners to the walking stick, which he then held over the fire. The snow melted, soaking into the cloth. Squeezing the cloth, he then sipped the water from the bottom. The taste was bad, but it was drinkable. He had truly hit upon an excellent idea! ("I suppose I'll get by somehow.")

After filling his belly, Kyūzō felt nauseous and vomited a bit. This happened often, however, and so was nothing to worry about. He also felt slightly more calm. While staring at the burning branches as the oil bubbled forth, he realized that those small bumps on the surface, as yet unripe and covered by a thick sheath, were buds. They appeared to be an excellent source of nutrition. Why hadn't he realized this earlier?

Removing those branches that were sufficiently burned, he cooled them off in the snow, held a piece at each end, and chewed as he rotated it like corn on the cob. The taste was slightly bitter but there was also some sweetness. The taste wasn't much, but the smell was awful. His mouth was filled with a greasy stickiness and an intensely fishy smell rose through his palate, spreading viscously all the way to the back of his eyes. Nevertheless, Kyūzō chewed on three pieces, each approximately thirty centimeters long. Eventually he felt as if a soft rubber stopper had been crammed down his throat. His scalp twitched and he felt queasy. Believing the buds to be nutritious, he tried to hold them in, but finally could no longer endure it and vomited everything up. Writhing in agony on the hard ground, he still thought that he shouldn't abandon the idea, that he had simply eaten too many buds too quickly, and that he must try again later, as things would certainly be better if he mixed in some grass roots.

XVIII

Kyūzō awakened to the sound of groaning. At first he saw the soles of the shoes of someone sitting cross-legged. The heels were worn down at an angle, extending all the way to the highest strip of leather. The toes wiggled nervously, covered by the shadow of the person's upper body as it swayed rhythmically and vigorously back and forth.

Kō had returned unnoticed. He was groaning—his body shook and his facial features were distorted—as he held his left wrist aloft with his right hand. It took some time for Kyūzō to remember that they had separated. Squinting, Kyūzō cautiously examined him. The sun still hadn't moved all that far. It must be between 1:00 and 2:00. The fire was burning well. A small pile of newly gathered branches had been placed in a spot where they would be immediately noticed. Kō must feel ashamed, Kyūzō surmised.

The two looked at each other. Instead of speaking, Kō suddenly screamed so painfully that Kyūzō rose up in shock. Kyūzō was dubious, as it seemed to be a trick, but reflexively began speaking first.

"What's wrong?"

"Take out a cigarette and pipe from my bag," Kō replied, theatrically gasping for breath. "Damn it, I fell and hit my injured hand. Remove half the tobacco from the cigarette. On the inside of this front collar—there—you'll find a bottle. Ouch, damn it! Take just a tiny bit of powder from the bottle. No, about half that. Mix that in with the tobacco and then stuff it back inside the cigarette."

"Is this opium?"

"You know what opium is? It's heroin. Once you stuff it inside the cigarette, place it in the pipe." Small flecks of saliva sprayed out from between his bared, clenched yellow teeth.

Lying on his back with the pipe pointed up at the sky, Kō lit the pipe with trembling hands, quietly inhaled deeply, and then held his breath for a while. As if solemnly performing a ritual, he repeated this action three times. His expression then began to change. His upper eyelids drooped heavily, his face became reddish, and his lips slackened. Licking the dark, fleshy sack of his lips with the tip of his tongue, he smiled meaningfully as his head slumped to his chest.

"How is it?"

"This always works best." He tried to lift his head, but the base of his neck was too wobbly. "You can try some if you want," he offered, swaying back and forth unsteadily. "But I'm not an addict. You shouldn't get addicted—just do a bit. I nearly got addicted when I was young. It's a powerful drug, and I had a hard time quitting. But addicts are all worthless. They don't have any definite goals. In my opinion, it's not that people fall apart because they do drugs, but rather they become addicted because they've fallen apart. A real man doesn't get beaten by drugs . . . Regulating opium is stupid."

"Why did you come back?"

"Why? There's not much of a reason why. After walking a long way, there was a very steep, rocky hill, and I slipped and hit my finger. Damn it! It's strange to feel pain in my fingertip when it's no longer there. There's only a tingling feeling. Let's boil some water. I'm very thirsty. It must have been hard for you without a cooking pot."

"I melted some ice by wrapping it in cloth."

"I see, I see. You've held up well. I suspected as much. Didn't you get lonely being alone?"

"I've decided to travel along the road . . . Shall we go to sleep?"

With a vague laugh, Kō blew his nose with his fingers, which he then wiped on his knee.

"There seem to be rabbits in these mountains. If only we had bullets . . ."

His gaze fixed on the hollows of the tracks, Kyūzō made no reply. His skin, darkly sunburned and downy, was permeated by a light coat of dust, which made it that much thicker. The rigidity of his expression seemed to extend all the way to his heart. He was himself shocked by the psychological change he now felt in remaining silent upon hearing Kō's words.

Kō scratched his back against the embankment. Kyūzō gathered snow and placed it inside the cooking pot. Muttering to no one in particular, Kō began speaking.

"People say that it was opium that ruined the Chinese people, but that's a lie. It's because they're so ruined that they began smoking opium in the first place. It's the fault of their leaders. Still, the Chinese are not ruined yet, as if that were possible! They're like pigs, constantly producing new young. Such a pathetic bunch of people." Suddenly his tone changed. "Do you know anything about Hitler's early life?" he asked.

"No, I don't."

"Hitler was just a corporal. The story that I heard took place before he became a corporal."

"I don't know about it."

"Really? Neither do I."

The sky suddenly began to grow red. There was still some time before sunset, but everything now looked like a summer evening. Invisible particles of dust rained down on them. In an instant, the radiant swells of the hills rusted and clouded to a yellowish gray. Kyūzō noticed that a thin, milky white film had formed on the water in the cooking pot. When touched by the wind, this film rippled slightly as it was blown over and again to one side.

"It's spring," Kō said flatly, rubbing his chin with the back of his glove.

Hearing this comment, Kyūzō felt his lips grow numb as something in his face became unraveled. He swallowed quickly. Everything was so unfair, he felt, as tears began to well up. "Shit!" Kyūzō exclaimed, clutching his knees and squeezing them tightly.

Having nearly fallen over, Kō gave a cry and lifted himself up. It seemed that he had momentarily fallen asleep.

"I just had a strange dream. Where was I? Around Fukagawa, I guess. I often dream about Japan. It's because my mother's Japanese. I went to elementary school until my third year. I can't recall her face very clearly. When she appears in my dreams, she always has her back to me. Her hair was dark and thick, and her toes were curled tightly inward, always stretching her sandal straps. She ran around all the time and often ended up breaking her sandals. 'Brat!' she used to call out in a small voice, suddenly picking me up by my ears. Hah! I wonder if she's still alive somewhere."

"Won't you try and get some sleep?"

"Wait a minute. In the dream, I was in a small gutter under the eaves of a house somewhere. No one could see it from the outside, but some canned food was lying at the bottom. When I grabbed it, I realized that it wasn't a can but an insect. The insect had a thick shell, like a rhinoceros beetle, but when I peeled off the skin there was canned food on the inside. It was surprising to see what kind of canned food it was. It was fresh . . ."

"That's enough. It's foolish!"

"Ah, I talk too much when the heroin starts taking effect."

"Please get some sleep. Time is precious."

Kyūzō rose to gather some kindling. By the time he returned, Ko had already fallen asleep.

Throwing all the kindling on the fire, Kyūzō also lay down next to it. There was no need to take turns standing watch since he planned to leave once the fire was out.

XIX

Kyūzō couldn't quite remember the dream's content, but it was horrible and oppressive. He was being chased by something, and was trying to escape down a steep and narrow slope that continued on indefinitely. He couldn't see the person, but a gangly man whose entire body was covered in scabs—between which grew several wet, black hairs—bounded after him in constant pursuit while playing a violin with a broken, screeching sound. The sound was horrible. Unable to withstand the tension, he intentionally slipped and tried to plunge into a cold, pitch-dark cave—at which time he awoke.

The wind blew harder and harder, and the sky, completely tinged in a dark orange, shone eerily. Kyūzō's eyes hurt. The inner lining of his throat and nose burned with sand and dust. Something heavy lay on his chest. It leaned over his face with both hands on his chest, pressing something cold against the bottom of his nose. He then heard some rough panting by his ear.

Quickly raising his elbow to push the assailant's flank to the right, he tucked in his knees, turned his body to the left, and sprang up. Yet his attacker jumped back even faster. With a low hanging head, it looked searchingly at Kyūzō from five or six steps away.

It was clearly some kind of dog. In any case, it certainly wasn't a wolf. Yet Kyūzō couldn't tell whether it was an actual feral dog or a stray that had become separated from its owner. Its coarse fur as well as the bared teeth jutting out from its dark lips were like those of generations of feral dogs, but its small, thin body, protruding ribs, and timid look evoked a sense of servility and weakness more characteristic of pets.

With its unusually large and unshapely head turned to the side, the dog quickly averted its eyes from Kyūzō's gaze and kept its short, filthy tail curled between its legs. Only its ears were pointed attentively at Kyūzō. He tentatively reached out a hand and called to the dog, but the animal moved one step away with a low growl. However, it made no attempt to move farther. Sitting down, the dog began busily scratching its belly with its hind leg.

The fire began to go out. Kyūzō reached out with the walking stick to sweep up the scattered embers when the dog suddenly leaped up with an asthmatic bark, staggering clumsily.

It's sick, Kyūzō thought, and immediately felt his body stiffen with a raging appetite for the dog. If he were lucky, there was a possibility of catching the animal. As if sensing something, the dog snarled, baring its teeth. Perhaps the animal also felt some appetite for Kyūzō and Kō. But no doubt its sickness prevented it from daring to make a meal of them, and the animal simply hoped to hang around until they died. Kyūzō thought with revulsion that the dog, with its sensitive nose, might perhaps have smelled that he was already half-dead.

He poked Kō's shoulder with the back of the walking stick, waking him. Sluggishly, Kō rose to his feet and let out a long yawn, which sounded as if he were blowing on the mouth of a bottle. Backing away, the dog coughed hoarsely.

"What's that?"

"A dog. A dog that's sick."

The dog again shrank back a bit, but then, as if settling down, lay on its belly growling.

"That's no dog. It's a wolf."

Kyūzō was unconvinced. Wolves, he thought, were larger and skinnier. Kō himself didn't seem quite sure, adding vaguely, "It might not be a wolf, but it's not a dog either. Maybe it's that something or other animal that's a cross between them. I forget the name, but there's an animal like that. People say that they're even fiercer than wolves. They're called something like Korean mountain dogs."

"But it's sick."

"You might be right."

"Let's catch it."

"I wonder . . ." Kō's lips were curled cynically as if wanting to say something.

Kyūzō immediately understood that he was referring to the bullets from the pistol. In his mind, however, he repeated to himself: it's no use talking about the past, for on balance I'm the one who comes out ahead. Didn't I save your life? And you also tried to abandon me once. Ignoring the cynicism, he rose to his feet.

"That thing just crawled on top of me trying to smell my throat. It's got to be very weak because it didn't even bite me."

Kyūzō took out his knife, readying it in his right hand. When he straightened his back, the nerves and muscles of his body—particularly his lower half—attacked simultaneously by sleeplessness, hunger, and fatigue, lost control and became entangled together. Panting, he couldn't step forward as he wished. Kō also rose to his feet. Gripping his small knife, he slowly walked hunched over around the remains of the fire, intending to appear on the dog's far side.

"Keep the blade pointed up!"

The dog also rose to its feet. Growling, it began listlessly sniffing the ground.

As Kō approached, he started to whistle as if to calm the dog. The animal turned around and lazily walked away. When the two men stopped, the dog stopped; when they advanced, the dog retreated just as much. They were planning a pincer attack, but the dog seemed aware of this, and constantly maintained its position at the top of the isosceles triangle formed by Kō and Kyūzō at its base. The animal showed no confusion whatsoever about its positioning. Its gait was very unsteady, and the men felt that they could soon catch up with it. Yet even if the dog didn't run faster than the speed at which it was pursued, it didn't slow down either. Drawn by the dog, the men continued after it from both sides of the road. In their eyes, the animal appeared as a piece of meat that would soon be consumed.

Suddenly the dog jumped to the side and disappeared along the southern end of the embankment. Shouting, the men gave chase but had already lost sight of it. There were many small hills around them. They stood side by side on a slight elevation nearby, their teeth chattering as if by common consent. For some time they could neither move nor speak. Suddenly Kyūzō broke off a withered branch, gnawing on the raw bark. Seeing this, Kō immediately began imitating him.

Dragging his legs, which had lost all feeling and felt so heavy that they seemed to have sunk largely into his torso, Kyūzō finally returned to the fire. There was the dog, which had somehow slipped ahead of him. It lay atop the embankment sprawled on its belly with its mouth open, gazing at him with a look of indifference. Kyūzō ran after it but tripped and fell to the ground with a cry. As if in response, the dog began barking, its fur standing on end.

A desperate chase began once more. The dog cut across the road and fled north along the wasteland. The terrain was rugged and uneven compared with when Kyūzō had walked through it. With each step, his feet got caught up in stones, grassy stumps, hollows, and ditches. He staggered constantly, bruising his elbows and kneecaps. His center of gravity shifted continually on its own accord, at moments exceeding his own body, forcing him to crawl on all fours as he could no longer walk standing up.

The dog was also exhausted. Once the edge of Kyūzō's knife even grazed the fur on its legs. As the dog twisted away, he heard the sound of its clattering jaws next to his wrist. Yet that happened only once. As one might expect, the dog was quicker. But perhaps it was the animal that was toying with the men. Perhaps it wasn't being chased about but was merely pretending to be chased while secretly waiting for the two men to eventually tire and stop resisting.

Moving slowly, Kō was virtually no help. He merely panted for breath and lagged far behind. Yet he never became completely separated from Kyūzō. At a certain point, the dog would invariably turn and run around behind him. It was as if the animal were anticipating that Kō would be the first to collapse. Once it even attempted to slip by his legs. Trying to twist his body, Kō toppled over, apparently angered, and with a shout flung his knife at the dog with all his strength. The blade grazed the dog's back, but it did not turn around.

As dusk approached, the sky was covered in yellow sand dust. Untiringly, the three hungry rascals continued their game of tag, their shadows dancing faintly about the vast wasteland. Their efforts had now clearly exceeded their willpower. The only force that drove on these three puppets was the feel of the inner lining in their throats in the expectation of warm meat passing through it.

Yet Kyūzō now felt that even that force was beginning to ebb. It was no doubt because of the temperature, but he was dripping in sweat from his shoulders to his armpits. That had never happened before. Overwhelmed by an unchecked sense of lethargy and bewilderment, as if his body had flown off somewhere far away and left only his face, he even lost sight of the dog. At those moments he barely managed to get hold of himself and crawl after the animal. The dog waited for him then, maintaining its distance as it ran slowly ahead once it had confirmed that Kyūzō had begun walking again.

Nevertheless, the time was approaching for him to muster all his remaining strength and resolve things at once. Fearing the outcome, however, he was unable to make up his mind. Yet it was not as if Kyūzō had any particular plan of action. He would merely pretend to collapse, drawing the dog to him as closely as possible—perhaps three or four meters—and then suddenly spring up and throw himself upon the animal. He shuddered to think of the drain on his muscles and the pain in his heart that would be required then. In any case, he would have only one chance. There was no hope that the attempt could be repeated a second time. But he considered that such an action was better than having one's life erode away bit by bit. Above all, it was the raging hunger that waited, stretching painfully wide the entire inner lining of his throat so as to devour the dog's flesh.

Kyūzō sent a signal to Kō, who, already wanting to lie down, immediately rolled over on the ground without quite knowing what the signal meant. Kyūzō then drew one of his knees tightly to his chest, held in both arms, and bent over at an angle, ready to pounce at any time.

It was then that his worst fears were realized. While it would certainly have been horrible to lose and fall victim to the dog, as the animal wished, this result was even more devastating—it was a draw.

This time the dog did not stop. Nor did it turn around. Perhaps even the animal had reached the limits of its strength. Its tail curled inward and muzzle pressed to the ground, it ran off unsteadily with a floating gait heading straight east into the wasteland.

Kyūzō tried to get up but could not. Like a wet rag, he lay stuck in place. Although his battle with the dog had ended in a draw, he was losing the battle with life. The defeat was irrevocable. It was doubtful that he possessed the energy to go on living.

Kō inched toward him, pulling his head up.

"This wouldn't have happened if we could use the pistol. Listen, you bastard, it's your fault. Shit! Shit! Because of your stupidity, you bastard, we're going to hell!"

Kō removed his hands, allowing Kyūzō's head to fall onto the ice with a thud.

"Even going to hell isn't possible since we can't use the pistol. One shot for you, one for me, and things would quickly be over. At this rate, it won't be easy even to get to hell. One shot and everything would be done. And such a shitty dog. I'm sure you realize the consequences now. Idiot!"

In a wet nasal voice, Kyūzō began crying as he lay sprawled on the ground. The tears gathered on his filthy cheeks, the dust particles floating around inside them.

The two men were loath to even move. The sweat on their bodies gradually chilled, however, and the cold wind reached its bare hand inside their collars and sleeves, rubbing their skin that now felt peculiar with fatigue. Their sense of discomfort was so strong that they could no longer remain still. Sighing and shivering, they controlled their shaking long enough to crawl back to the road.

The fire, however, was now extinguished. Around the black ash, only thin strands of cobalt-blue smoke appeared weakly hectored about by the wind. At this point the men had no energy to gather more firewood. Tearing off his gloves, Kyūzō thrust his dark, frost-swollen hands into the remains of the fire. He sensed a sharp pain, but the dryness felt good. Using his free hand to pull the blanket to him, he closed his eyes. Kō collapsed on top of the ashes, his body shivering within the whirling dust.

"Don't go to sleep," Kō said breathlessly, reaching out a hand to Kyūzō.

Seeking warmth, Kyūzō dug himself more deeply into the embers, his left shoulder pressing firmly against Kō's elbow. Kō clutched the edge of Kyūzō's blanket and silently crawled inside. Instinctively, the two men sought out each other's body warmth, huddling closely together. The pungent smell of ash mixed with their own body odors soon filled the blanket, providing an indescribable sense of well-being.

"Don't go to sleep."

Despite this repetition, however, Kō's voice was already partly engulfed within the membrane of sleep, blurring the contours of its sound.

(Thin creases of light streamed down from throughout the pitch-dark sky, flowing into Kyūzō's eyes. Upon solidifying, the light turned into the white wall of a room. In the crack of the wall climbed an insect. The insect disappeared, and there rose up the smokestack of the paper manufacturing factory in Baharin. A man with a dog stood up in the shadow of the smokestack. It was Lieutenant Alexandrov. As Alexandrov turned around, his face changed into that of Kyūzō's dead mother, in whose eyes soup was simmering. Ladling some of the soup with his hands, he poured it into the hole of some black bread. The many men gathered around him then dipped their hands into the soup.)

Choking on the smoke, his fingers thrust into Kyūzō's armpit, Kō said again as if remembering: "On't go slee . . ."

The dream shattered, changing now to a new scene.

(The empty dormitory. As Kyūzō walked around it alone, he gradually turned into a child. Opening a door, he saw an elementary school classroom. The army medic Dania stood at the lectern holding an attendance book. Someone was hiding below the lectern. In the shadows of the door and window, the cunning gazes of several people were directed at him. Laughing, Dania motioned him over. She looked like Sachiko when she laughed. Someone whispered in his ear: say Sovet, not Russki! All the women must cut their hair! Dania opened the attendance book. A thin silk handkerchief fell to the floor. Looking at it, Kyūzō now saw sand dunes and a large salt tower. Below the tower it was he himself who lay dead. Outside in the school yard his classmates practiced their skating as they followed the whistles of their teacher.)

XX

4:30. For a long time, the men under the blanket barely even moved as they clung together in the ashes. At one point the area around them grew dim, but when the wind fell and dust cleared it again became bright. There still seemed to be some time before the actual dusk.

It was then that several wagons happened to pass nearby. Only their sounds appeared, however; the shapes remained unseen. For some reason— perhaps the air temperature or wind direction—sounds as far off as three or four miles would, at this time and place, appear as if they were suddenly in front of one's nose. It was probably a sonic mirage caused by the refracting airwaves.

The unseen wagons approached. They were the most primitive two-wheeled wagons, the wheels large and wooden. Their axles creaked, singing their sad, plaintive appeal, and the large, black oilcans hanging underneath offered perfect accompaniment each time they banged against something. The sound of whipping rang out. Riders were probably urging on their idle horses. The rumbling grew heavier.

A hand reached out from the edge of the blanket. The glove was made of black fur, so the hand was Kō's. The blanket rose up, slipping from his shoulders. Leaning on Kyūzō with all his weight, Kō tried to shake him awake. Distraught and covered in ash, he looked around quickly. Suddenly the sound of the wagons faded. He seemed stupefied for a while, but quickly sank back down absorbed within the ashes, and in the next instant was already fast asleep. His breathing sounded as if his throat had been torn out.

The next unseen wagon came by five minutes later. Kō reflexively stood up. As soon as he got to his feet, he heaved and vomited. Yet nothing came out from his empty stomach. As he tried to ascertain the nature of the sound, his red, bloodshot eye that shifted around frantically made for an uncanny contrast with his clear, white artificial eye that stared straight ahead indifferently. Shrieking with a teary voice, he began pounding Kyūzō's chest.

"Wake up! Hey, there's a wagon!"

In his blurry conscious, Kyūzō had also heard the sound. But he could not move his body. He lacked even the energy to straighten his bent finger.

"Can you hear that? It's a wagon!" His vocal chords numb, Kō murmured into Kyūzō's ear with all his strength.

Kyūzō returned his gaze with half-open eyes, nodding as he drew his chin back in such a way that it was unclear whether he could see or not. Assured that he was not hearing things, Kō fell silent with relief. His hands trembled as he gripped Kyūzō's shoulder. The trembling gradually intensified, and he suddenly began yelling at Kyūzō while roughly shaking him.

"Wake up! Hey, wake up! Hey."

The sound of the wagon began to slowly recede in the distance, swaying back and forth before once again vanishing somewhere. Kō hurriedly pressed his ear to the ground. At first he heard nothing. After a while, however, he was able to faintly distinguish from within the heavy groaning of the earth some thin, weak vibrations of a wagon mixed together with horse hooves. Compared with the phantom sounds he had just heard, these vibrations were so distant and faint that they were barely worth considering. Nevertheless, the sound was unmistakably real.

Kō slowly got up. Folding down the earflaps of his hat and rubbing them lightly, he gazed around him in a vacant stare. Recoiling, he caught a glimpse of Kyūzō from the corner of his eye. He gave a low grunt, as if forcibly coming to a decision.

First, he tore off his chest badge and buried it in the ash. Picking the badge back up as he reflected for a moment, he decided that it really had to be buried. Jabbing his fingertips against his knees in an effort to stimulate blood circulation, he proceeded to the next task. Pulling his bag over, he took out a document, folded it in half, and concealed it in the bottom of his shoe. Once that was done, he again tried to awaken Kyūzō. Yet Kyūzō wriggled away, clutching the blanket and showing no sign of releasing it. After some struggle that appeared fruitless, Kō gave up and began removing his coat.

He then unbuttoned his jacket. His teeth chattered and his filthy face was utterly drawn of blood, the color that of a rusted metal clasp. Only his lips were shockingly white. He threw off the knitted shirt that he wore underneath. A thick muslin vest appeared. Running vertically along the garment were several evenly spaced stitches, between which seemed to be a kind of padding that was round and swollen. It looked like a bullet-proof vest.

It appeared that this was what Kō wanted. Untying the strap, he threw off the vest. Now he put his clothes back on as if grappling with them, beginning with the shirt. He had grown terribly thin. Twisting his body as he groaned with cold, he began cursing.

"Hey, wake up!"

Kyūzō screamed, covering his face with his arms. Kō placed his hand behind Kyūzō's neck and pulled him up roughly.

"I said wake up!"

"Let me be! Stop it!" Kyūzō replied in a hoarse voice, falling back limply.

"Kuki, come on, boy. Please wake up."

While uttering these words, Kō began to roughly undress Kyūzō. Just as Kyūzō was about to raise his hands to resist, Kō crossed them together at the knee and continued his work.

"You can't sleep. Listen to me, all right? You'll die if you sleep. You won't be able to return to the Japanese mainland. Just put on this vest. It's for your own good. It's warm. You can still feel my body warmth in it. Come on, be tough!"

Wriggling away, Kyūzō spat in Kō's face. Kō, however, showed no reaction. Fully unbuttoning the outer part of Kyūzō's coat, he grabbed hold of the collar and yanked it down. With his arms restrained behind his back in the manner of a straitjacket, Kyūzō could no longer move.

"Stop it! What are you doing?"

"Like I said, I'm putting this vest on you."

Kō pulled Kyūzō's arms out through his sleeves. His face drawn, Kyūzō let out a horrible scream. Waiting for his arms to be released, he groped for the knife handle and brandished the blade at Kō, who shouted at him.

"Idiot! Hurry up and put the vest on!"

Twitching, Kyūzō stared at Kō with a frightened look, screaming at him intermittently. Kō struck his cheek with the back of his glove and repeated harshly, "Hurry and put it on!"

Kyūzō no longer resisted.

The vest was very heavy. It was a strain just to breathe, as his body was already numb with cold. The garment was slightly too large for him, but he was big for his age and could more or less get away with it if he put it on from the top.

Shoving Kyūzō as he staggered about, Kō continued to press him.

"Where did you put the certificate? The certificate . . . the Russki certificate?"

"Why? Give me back my knife!"

"Idiot! A wagon's coming."

"Wagon?"

"Haven't I been telling you for a while now? We can get food and there might be water. Hurry! Hide it in your shoe!"

"Where?"

"In your shoe."

"The wagon?"

"That's enough!" Without thinking, Kō struck him hard across the cheek.

Slowly removing his shoe, Kyūzō murmured in a low voice, "You'll regret that."

As he regained his physical sensibility, the stiff vest became a terrible hindrance.

"What is this thing you're making me wear?"

"I'm sure it feels warm."

"Don't give me the runaround!"

"I'm not. I'm making a request, so I'll tell you."

"Damn it!"

Kyūzō was utterly unable to tie the laces on his shoes. Kō tried to help but was unsuccessful. Leaning over the shoes, Kō finally managed to tie the laces together with his teeth.

"Give me back my knife."

"Sure." Spitting off into the distance, Kō lay down heavily on the ground. Suddenly his voice became leaden.

"Listen. Can you hear it like this?"

"Yes." Kyūzō lay down alongside him. Drawing the blanket up around him, he suddenly yelled frantically, "It's a wagon! It's the sound of a wagon!"

"Of course. It's still far away, though."

"No, it's near!"

"There's no need to rush. You know, I . . ." Kō continued in a gasp. "I'm not an ungrateful person. I'm entrusting you with all my fortune. I'm sure you'd be shocked to know how much it is. Maybe you won't believe me. There's probably enough to buy fifty foreign cars. Are you shocked?"

"It's opium, right?"

"I'll do what I can. I'll give you one hundred thousand, two hundred thousand—even five hundred thousand. With that much, you should be able to start your own small business. Please, I'm asking you. I'm a wanted man. I'll look after you until we board the ship. Hey, are you listening to me?"

"But . . ."

"Don't sleep. Just hold out a bit longer. It's easy to lose heart at the end. Try hard. Just a bit more effort."

"But why me?"

"As I said, I'm a wanted man. Don't fall asleep!"

"Damn it! I wonder if there's food in that wagon."

"Of course there is."

"But I don't understand why you first sought me out."

"It was out of sympathy. Seeing someone from a defeated nation wandering about all alone."

"Only that?"

"No."

"So then I was a scapegoat, right? Damn it, my head aches."

"I'm not someone who uses people for nothing. In any case, I'm asking you. It'll be good for you, too. Just take my word on this and listen to me. Soon you'll understand. I'm not like those other bastards. In several years from now you might hear rumors about me. I'm sure they'll shock you. Perhaps you'll recall what we talked about now."

"I don't know. I've suffered a lot because of you."

"You may not feel that way later. Soon you'll understand. What! That's right, you won't know until much later in the future."

"My head is aching!"

"Just hold out. It won't be long now."

XXI

There was only one wagon. It was a large type used for long-distance travel, and was roughly covered in the front by a sedge canopy. The setting sun shone brilliantly from behind, hurting the eyes to look at it. The horses were clearly old, with exposed ribs, but there were in any case two in harness. Swinging his legs one after the other, a young man wearing a rubber raincoat and wrapped in dog fur skillfully drew his three-meter whip in the air.

Seeing the two men suddenly appear from the shadows of the embankment, the young man first recoiled with a start. He had heard rumors of suspicious people in the area, but this was the first time he had actually encountered any. He deeply regretted the fact that he had not listened to his wife's warning that the day was an unlucky one. Yet he felt relief when he noticed that the men were miserably covered in ash and barely able to stand on their feet. They did not appear to be capable of doing any great harm. The young man felt confident in his ability to fight, if it came down to that.

Summoning his last ounce of strength, Kō continued standing straight.

It was his abiding belief that the measure of human dignity could be found in the fact that man stood upright. He was perhaps not entirely wrong in this. Although intending to stand erect, he in fact kept wobbling strangely. It was thus at the same time impossible to regard him as having dignity.

Kyūzō had already sat down. A sense of laxity that they were now saved enveloped his body in a kind of sweet lethargy, numbing him even to his hunger. Even the thought that they were playing with the rapidly growing possibility of death must have brought him pleasure.

"I'm afraid we're lost," Kō said to the young man, walking ahead to hold the horse by the muzzle when he saw that the youth had no intention of stopping. Using all his strength to avoid falling over with inertia, he spoke loudly in a voice that was like a draft of wind. "We've gotten lost."

"Lost? Lost coming from and going to where?" the young man asked mockingly. Yet perhaps his intent was not to mock. Rather, it may simply have sounded that way on account of his strong, virtually unintelligible accent—which was perhaps from the plateau region beyond the Stanovoy Range. "We got lost," Kō replied, avoiding the question. "Are you taking this wagon across the Kai River?"

"Yes."

"To Horqin Left Middle Banner?"

"That's right."

"Are there soldiers there?"

"Uncle, the man is asking if there will be soldiers," the young man inquired, turning around to address someone in the canopy before then asking Kō with an innocent look, "Would it be better if there were soldiers?"

"Which side are they from?"

"Well, which side would be better for you?"

Shivering, Kō leaned on the wagon shaft, barely holding himself up. Placing his hand in his pocket, he intimated the shape of a pistol and shouted forcefully, "Don't fuck with me!"

"I'm not. I'm serious. I ask because I left the Middle Banner one week ago. Some of the Nationalist troops were still there. But they were quickly pulling out. They said that all the troops would pull out soon. I'm serious. I wouldn't know these things."

"How much to give us a ride to town?"

"How much do you have?"

Crawling on all fours by Kō's feet, Kyūzō said under his breath, "Ten thousand yen."

"Three hundred yen," Kō answered, drowning out Kyūzō's reply.

"So you're Japanese?"

"Take us to town for three hundred."

"If you've only got three hundred, I bet it will be difficult to pay that much."

"We've got five hundred in total."

"But uncle, the regular price for two passengers is really five hundred." A low groan and gurgling-like cough escaped from the canopy.

"All right, five hundred. Take us to town."

"Really?" Laughing amicably, the young man got down off the wagon. Easily lifting Kyūzō, he offered his arm to Kō. "Hey, that's a nice blanket. Uncle, make some room for them."

Soon raising his whip high, the young man deftly made two parallel strokes in the air, driving on the horses as he struck one and then the other side of the road. "Uncle, share some food with them," he said after a while, turning around. "We'll arrive in town tomorrow morning."

By then, however, the two men had already slipped under the pile of empty gunnysacks and were sleeping like *things*.

XXII

The wagon stopped once after sundown. The old man warned the younger one when he grew concerned that Kyūzō was no longer breathing. After placing his ear next to Kyūzō's mouth and confirming that there was still some life in him, the young man built a fire and boiled water on the roadside before carrying the two men out. He shook and hit them, but still they did not wake up. It was only when he poured strong spirits into their mouths that they finally regained consciousness. He then grilled some fried bread that was now frozen cold, spread some miso paste on it, and fed them. He had them chew on some garlic and sip hot water laced with alcohol. Although half-asleep, the two men greedily devoured the food. Kyūzō was so hungry that he at one point mistakenly bit into his own finger. Shrieking, his gaze met the surrounding scenery for the first time. The old man, with hollow cheeks, large eyes, and a protruding lip, fidgeted as he lit the tip of his tobacco pipe with thick, sinewy fingers. The film of flame, red on the surface and green below, flickered like the hands of a dancer. Beyond there stood a high cliff made of red clay, and the pattern of lines visible on the soil layer appeared to be dimly floating. Apart from thickets of rough bushes dotted here and there, the filthy snow and weathered rock face endlessly overlapped, creating the deep mountain folds that surrounded them. The dark sky bent with the weight of the stars. Turning around, Kyūzō saw that the moon, like a nail mark, was shining strongly in its ascent. There rose up a large pine tree that he had not previously noticed. Just one tree as far as the eye could see. Suddenly he began sobbing.

If left alone, the two men would never have stopped eating. When Kō had finished his third and a half piece of fried bread and Kyūzō his fourth, the young man extinguished the fire and sealed the willow basket containing the food. He was a kindhearted fellow.

When night broke, however, the two men awoke in an abandoned, roofless house. The afternoon sunlight was already waning, and shadows climbed up nearly one meter on the wall. All the parts made of wood— the floor, posts, door, and window frames—had been removed. On the earthen floor, which was roughly fifteen to twenty square meters in size and surrounded by a sky of exposed brick, fragments of broken roof tile and concrete lay scattered about everywhere.

Kyūzō was the first to awake. He had no idea whatsoever as to where he was or what had happened. His entire body ached heavily, and he even had no idea about his sleeping posture. A tree stood outside the broken window. As he stared at the tree, feeling somehow drawn to it, it overlapped with the image of the pine tree from the mountain last night, and from there he recalled in succession the wagon, the young man, the wasteland, and the dog. But he knew nothing about what had happened after the wagon. Where could this place be? Why was he here?

Like yesterday, the sky was a dull red and the temperature noticeably higher. A dog was barking somewhere in the distance. Turning his head with great effort, Kyūzō saw that Kō was sleeping right next to him. On the edge of his slightly open lips, several small icicles hung down along his unshaven beard. One of the icicles had grown quite long, nearly five centimeters. Beside it the fur from his raised collar fluttered slightly, and this alone proved that he was still alive.

It took a long time to awaken Kō. During this time, Kyūzō realized that his blanket had been stolen. Wrapped inside the blanket were just a couple of pair of underwear. No matter what, the loss of the blanket was disappointing. Gazing around, he noted that Kō's bag also seemed to have disappeared.

Provoked by the theft of his bag, Kō suddenly got up. Shivering with his head in his hands, he grumbled and cursed for a long time. Based on what he was saying, there didn't seem to be anything of particular value in the bag. He was especially vexed about losing the book, *Journey of Vengeance along the Tōkaidō Road*, as well as a half dozen bars of soap. The book, *Journey of Vengeance*, had been a gift from an officer in the secret services division of the Kwantung Army named Lieutenant Yoshino, who on the title page had written the following words in his own hand:

Gift: to Mr. Kō Sekitō
If I'm a man, then you're also a man.
Army Lieutenant Yoshino Hiroto

"I suppose you've never heard of him. He was a great man, originally from Fukuoka. That's right! In our line of work, there wasn't anyone who didn't know Lieutenant Yoshino. After all is said and done, he was a great man. Good memories, damn it! It was his own handwriting, and so was of some value, after all is said and done . . ."

Kō's memories of the soap were similarly unrestrained. The soap wasn't like those substitutes made from fish oil. Rather, it was made from acacia in the good old days, was of a beautiful color, and lathered up entirely differently. Grumbling for a while alternately about the soap and *Journey of Vengeance along the Tōkaidō Road*, he then turned to the lost bag itself. Apparently it was made in Tianjin from a single piece of cowhide. Kō had received it from a certain government purveyor with military contacts, and it was far better than the stuff one could buy nowadays.

Suddenly he turned Kyūzō around, asking uneasily, "Everything all right?"

"My blanket's stolen."

"And the other thing?" he replied, striking himself firmly in the chest. He meant the vest.

It's fine, Kyūzō nodded. Relieved, Kō appeared now to begin thinking of things more normally, tilting his head as he thrust his fingers into his shoe and then placed his hand inside his pocket. For some reason, neither the money nor pistol had been stolen. Following his example, Kyūzō also checked his belongings. His money was safe, as were his knife, the Dania spoon, and even his wristwatch. The very fact that his clothes were not stripped from his body was incredible, but how strange it was also! Really, that young man must have been exceptionally decent.

"No, that's not it," Kō considered, narrowing his eyes. The spasms that crawled up from his feet gathered around his neck, intermittently erupting around his jaw. After the eruptions subsided, he let out a long sigh. "No. There must be some reason for this. Those men ran into some trouble, panicked, and then left us. They must have been so hurried that they didn't have time to check what was on us. What could it be? Yes, they must have come across thieves who were even more ruthless than themselves—tough bastards who would've seized the bag, blanket, and money for themselves."

"I bet they were soldiers."

"That's my guess too. Rather than run into that kind of trouble, they stole only the blanket and bag, as those wouldn't be noticed, and then tossed us here. Damn it, it's a high price for that travel fare."

"Shall we get going?" Kyūzō asked, stretching to peek out the southern window. There was a road that turned left after two or three hundred meters, beyond which appeared a long earthen wall. "The town is nearby."

"Hmm, wait a moment. Which side do you think those soldiers are on? Yes, the way I see it . . ."

"In any case, let's go. We need to find some food."

"That's why I'm thinking. The way I see it, they must be from the Nationalist Army because the Eighth Route soldiers behave properly. The way I see it, well . . . Yes, this question is important."

"Which side would be better?"

"That's obvious."

"I wonder."

"We're going to Shenyang," Kō replied curtly as he slowly got up. Staggering, he leaned against the wall. With a loud sound, a mouse suddenly jumped out by his feet and ran outside.

"You stay here."

"Why?"

"Because it's better to be alone when negotiating with soldiers. Don't worry. What do you think I've entrusted with you? Leave it to me."

"But what are you going to negotiate with the soldiers?"

"I won't know until I try."

Kyūzō didn't like the idea. If he followed Kō's suggestion, then the time before he could eat would be delayed that much longer. Nevertheless, he decided to stay behind because he was suddenly overwhelmed by an intense drowsiness and thought that there was no way he could walk all the way to town.

As he listened to Kō's pitiful footsteps receding in the distance, Kyūzō leaned against the wall and absentmindedly dozed off. While sleeping, he slowly moved toward the remaining small sunny spot by the northern wall, in front of which he came across something like rotting wood. He felt that he recognized the object, but it was strange and inexplicable. It was a mummy that had been devoured by mice.

There were a total of five mummies. All were completely naked. Three were large, one medium, and the last one extremely small. Long hair still remained on the head of the medium-sized mummy as well as on one of the larger ones. They were each in different positions, but all were lined up alongside one another. Their faces and internal organs had all been completely gnawed away in identical fashion.

By their heads, partly bathed in sunlight, characters could be read that appeared to be carved out by stone.

Alas
halfway there
all of us
died
here
with a feverish disease
summer, year 21
Mizuura Takeshi
and four others

At first, Kyūzō was annoyed that his rest had been interrupted. Given that these people had also been Japanese, however, he then felt a bit sorry for feeling this way. Who were they? Where had they come from? Seeing that there was a child among them, he suspected that they might have been a family or perhaps colleagues from a company or something. The small mummy must be the child of the female mummy. Which one had died first? Suddenly Kyūzō somehow felt afraid. Perhaps this group had walked through the wasteland like us. Could they possibly have believed that they still had to die after so much suffering. No, there was absolutely no way they could have believed such unfairness. Kyūzō drew back in horror. He felt that these mummies hated him.

There were other markings that appeared to be characters. However, he could barely make them out. Only in one place there seemed to be the form of the character for "water." Could that be the "water"—*mizu*—from the name Mizuura? Or did it refer to drinking water? Of course it had to be drinking water. Suffering from high fever, there wasn't one of them who could fetch water. All they could do was think about it, and so they had carved out that character. Its sound still seemed to be floating around. Year twenty-one was the year of the typhus epidemic. Speaking of typhus, there was lice. Kyūzō recalled the louse that had crawled out from Kō's collar by the marsh, and his entire body suddenly throbbed with itchiness. The mummies clearly wanted to entangle him in their fate. He quietly tiptoed away so as not to awaken them.

His throat stung. Swallowing his saliva when he finally reached the exit, his throat's inner lining made a sound as it peeled off.

XXIII

Kō was furious to find Kyūzō crouching outside the hut.

"Hey, come on! How about being a bit responsible?"

"There are corpses inside."

"There's nothing in the world more gentle than the dead. It's the living who are scary. From now on, be more careful!"

Yet Kō was in a good mood. His negotiations seemed to have gone well. Forcibly dragging the reluctant Kyūzō inside, he proudly spread out the food he had bought before jokingly spitting at the mummies.

"Just look at how gentle the dead are! They don't complain no matter what you do!"

There were steamed buns, salty meat in oil, and some spongy fried food. On top of which, it was a real luxury to have cider. It would have been ideal if there were a fire, but Kō strictly forbade that.

"How did it go?"

"We're very lucky! They were Nationalist soldiers after all. I was able to bribe them. Don't be shocked, but we can get a ride on a truck—a military truck. Now that they've agreed to take us, we're practically already there. We're very lucky! And they said that it's the last truck."

This was certainly welcome news. After such long suffering and despair, it was at first unbelievable that things were now going so well.

"That was typhus over there, right?"

"That's enough! You're going to ruin the food."

"Shit, I'm unbearably itchy."

"Me too. We'll get used to it soon. By the way, the soldiers had already heard about the train accident. Their unit is indirectly involved, and it seems to be a topic of gossip among the officers. Well, that was helpful. They trusted me because of that accident. I suppose I can tell you now, but in fact I was the one who provided them with the train information."

"I knew that already."

Kyūzō greedily devoured the food. Drinking some cider, he choked a bit. Kō began laughing loudly. Kyūzō thought that this was the first time he had ever heard Kō laugh like that. Yet this did nothing to help his gloominess.

Alas
halfway there . . .
all of us . . .

As he chewed the meat, it had a mummified taste. Yet the taste was at the same time wonderful and joyous. Happiness and guilt mixed together in such a way that, for him, emotions themselves became a heavy burden.

The plan as Kō explained it went mainly as follows: The person whom he dealt with was a paymaster-general named Bai. Yet there was nothing surprising to hear that Bai was a general. The Nationalist Army probably had the highest number of officers in the world, and at times that number was even greater than the number of soldiers. In any case, Bai was a man of considerable talent and possessed a truck for his own private use. As Kō described, he had fortunately been passing by when the Nationalist troops were beginning their rapid clearing out upon news that the Eighth Route Army was set to lay siege to Qianjiadian, which was located immediately to the south. Here, too, Kō employed his typical ruse of introducing himself as a newspaper reporter. He also managed to introduce Kyūzō by explaining that, while escaping, he had rescued a Japanese youth who had been enslaved by the Eighth Route Army. General Bai was a reasonable man, and so the two had soon struck up a friendship. At first the general was planning to travel to the Rear Banner, but would now "go all the way to Shenyang for a patriot like you"—and this, as Kō added, after a mere thirty-five minutes of conversation. Kō had nothing but praise for the general, whom he described as smart, cultured, and beyond reproach. A poem that the general had composed hung on the wall, he remarked, and the calligraphy was stunning. Since they had to pass through the Dalin railway bridge before dawn, their departure was set for early the next morning. Dalin was the railway station located just one stop east of Qianjiadian. The general had suggested that we rest in his quarters until then. However, he asked that we wait until dark before visiting him. There were a great many people seeking a ride on the truck, stated the general, and it would cause resentment if we were too obvious.

Kō's plan indeed made sense. Above all, Kyūzō found himself strangely moved by the word "patriot" that Kō had casually mentioned. What had now disappeared, of course, was the heavy echo that the word possessed during that period in which all one's conscious thoughts existed as a result of external coercion. Kyūzō even felt a strong repugnance for that word itself. Yet he seemed to feel a kind of wistful longing for that very world that was governed by such an insubstantial sign. This feeling was not unlike the relation between hate and love that he experienced with regard to that past world that had abandoned him and escaped. Moreover, the old, hackneyed quality of the word "patriot" somehow called to mind a Korean floor heater. There would certainly be such a heater in the general's residence. His idle thought about the moment of lying there crudely seized hold of all his senses, refusing to release them for even a second. Although he tried not to dwell on this thought for fear of betrayal, it doubly or triply exacerbated his current pain. In any case, it was the mummies more than any floor heater that were physically closest to him now. Instinctively he almost cried out, gasping for breath.

"By the way, how much did you say you have? Ten thousand yen?"

"But why?" At first Kyūzō could not believe his ears.

"And you've got a wristwatch."

"But I can't give you everything. I still have a long way to go."

"You'll manage somehow or another. The important thing is what we need to do now, breaking through the border. Even I gave that guy a gift of twenty-five grams of heroin. In terms of money, that would be no less than fifty thousand. Also, we'll prepare exactly thirty thousand in cash. At any rate, I promised a total amount of one hundred thousand . . . Just think if we had been robbed by that kid in the wagon. We really can't complain. We're asking the military to take care of us!"

"But you have that thing on the train, Mr. Kō."

"Well, if that load of polytar was safe, there would have been change left even after paying a hundred thousand."

"There's no need to give so much. I still might need boat fare at some point."

"Hey, hey, don't play dumb! We're not even halfway through this journey. Or do you still want to trudge along for the next week or ten days? Besides, don't forget that I'm a person of some means. I'm sure this goes without saying, but I don't want you to say anything about this. All right, enough already with this pointless conversation. Let me handle things."

Exactly! It's precisely this kind of conversation that will help clarify things. Thoughts of "patriots" and Korean floor heaters were watered down by the misfortune of having all his money taken from him, and the situation now became much more real. In his heart, therefore, Kyūzō had already agreed. Even though he knew that he was arguing merely for argument's sake, however, he could not remain silent since he wanted to see how Kō's words would further embellish his own dreams.

"But wouldn't it be better to hire a wagon?"

"Let me remind you that I'm Kō Sekitō. I've been involved in the political movement since I was young and am rather well known. Naturally, I have both enemies and allies. For better or worse, I stand out. For me, the towns where the two-legged beasts lurk are far more dangerous than the fields where the wolves roam. And that's especially true now that I'm carrying something valuable."

"You're thinking too much. We've already come close to dying so many times."

"No. These Nationalists have come all the way from the south, and they're easy to deal with. The fact is that I feel good about this. For better or worse, these men are strangers. If we just give them some money, they won't get in our way."

Kō continued talking despite the fact that he was so tired that he was forced to concentrate on each word so as to avoid tripping over his own tongue. From the start, Kyūzō knew that he was in no position to choose, and so there was no need for such pointless conversation, as Kō had said. But just as a heart patient cannot lie in bed keeping his eyes closed forever, so, too, the two men utterly lacked the courage to keep their mouths closed as a way of confirming their own sense of safety.

"Aren't we being tricked and they'll just take our money?"

"Other officers know that I've arrived here. Besides, that book will surely catch someone's eye. Naturally they'd know where I disappeared. They're not just nobodies, you know."

The two men continued their interminable discussion even as their voices grew hoarse and they rubbed their stiffened faces. Soon it grew dark.

They set off walking close together. With a stride that suggested they were rolling an invisible log, they didn't even glance back at the hut.

Martial law commenced at the same time as sunset. The sound of gunfire could sporadically be heard from the town. The town contained an inordinate number of gates. Gates could be found within gates, and within those gates there were even more gates. Sentries stood at each gate, yelling as they thrust out their guns from a distance. With a brief reply, Kō appeared to establish communication with them, and he and Kyūzō were immediately allowed to pass. The doors of the houses were shut tight, the town was darkly frozen, and the streets were choked of life. When they passed through several gates and finally arrived at the mansion with its courtyard that General Bai was occupying, even Kō had lost the energy to speak and was nearly shot. For some reason, his communication with the final sentry did not go well. Suddenly doubts about Bai's intentions flitted through Kyūzō's mind. In the next instant, however, the two men found themselves standing before a round smiling face, one that was shaven clean and white. The area smelled of acetylene torches and the air was hot and stuffy. There was also a Korean floor heater. The only thing that Kyūzō vaguely remembered thereafter was desperately sipping a bowl of hot water and then unconsciously putting up stiff resistance when an orderly tried to take their coats.

However, the floor heater fell short of expectations. It looked like some special torture device devised to persistently abuse them. The hunger and cold that had been unleashed for ten days exerted its last bit of strength, raging powerfully within them. Their bodies pounded and throbbed in agony, and their internal organs swelled to the point of bursting. As they writhed to escape the pain, the orderly who shared their room became so annoyed that he was forced to drag his blanket and flee to the next room.

At 3:30 a soldier came to wake them, turned on the lamp, and set down a washbowl filled with hot water. Kyūzō and Kō had crawled down from the floor heater and were sleeping on the earthen floor. Yet they were both dripping with sweat, and felt as if sticky machine oil had been poured between two pieces of skin. Their ears still ached, as did their fingertips and the area around their mouths. But what unbearable sleepiness!

In front of the building there echoed the sound of a car engine being started. Kō finally rose to his feet.

"Being at a dead end—that's the right expression." Crossing the earthen floor with bent knees and a strange gait, he suddenly plunged his face in the washbowl and began drinking the water.

Kyūzō pressed his fingers and face against the cool wall. It felt good. The skin on his lips had peeled; it had died and turned black. The sweat was irritating. It was a pity that his shirt had been stolen. At the very least, he wanted to strip down and wipe off his body. Kō, however, was absolutely against this. Finally reaching a compromise, Kō allowed Kyūzō to unbutton his shirt and air out the area under his vest.

He began to feel unbearably itchy from his shoulders to his belly. There had to be lice jumping about. When he scratched himself, a large clump of dirty skin fell down between his shirt and pants. If he were to roll this skin into a ball, he mused, there would really be quite a lot.

XXIV

The departure took place quietly but quickly. It seemed that there had been bad news. Kō referred to Bai as "general" while Bai called him "sir." The two engaged in eager consultations, but the language was from the south and Kyūzō understood little of it. Judging by the occasional use of Mandarin mixed in, however, it appeared that during the night flyers from the Eighth Route Army had been posted at important points around town, and that these contained messages hinting at danger.

Kō shaved—if somewhat roughly—dusted off his clothes, and brushed his hair with a comb that he borrowed from an orderly. If nothing else, his appearance was now more or less tidy, and yet he still suffered in comparison when standing next to Bai, who was tall, broad chested, and looked quite sharp in his uniform. Bai was also extremely pompous. His gray sideburns, gold-rimmed glasses, smooth skin, and strong double chin eminently suited his grave bearing and composed manner of speaking, and the sense of calm he displayed was in keeping with the name "general."

The two men treated one another with ridiculous courteousness. Ignoring the hurried activities of the soldiers, they appeared to be quite carefree, as if discussing the issue of poetry composition. As Kyūzō watched the faint smile that constantly hovered over Bai's lips as well as the large ring and long, polished nails on his fingers that moved before his mouth as if playing the koto, he felt unable to avoid the sense that reality was gradually slipping away. Kō held out the forty thousand yen as well as Kyūzō's watch. Holding the watch to his ear for a moment, Bai pocketed the object and then promptly counted out the roll of banknotes with a practiced hand.

Kō turned around and spoke. "We'll eat later, as it seems that we'll depart soon. And they say that they have something interesting to show us."

Kyūzō didn't respond. He was disappointed. He was sure that he had just heard, in the depths of his ears, the sound of dishes clanging together. To hell with something interesting! It's probably just another empty boasting of that "expert calligraphy" thing. For ten thousand yen and a wristwatch, they should really be entitled to ask for more. At the same time, however, he felt the desire to go to sleep as soon as possible. These two desires canceled each other out, and he wasn't concerned about anything else.

The truck was already waiting in the courtyard. It was a six-wheeler that had been used by the Japanese army, with a hood and high chassis. Outside the gateway several soldiers as well as two junior officers who were no longer young stood crowded around something. *That* was what was so interesting.

"It's him, right?"

An officer turned on a flashlight—one that was wrapped in cloth—and shone it at his feet. A man appeared, hands tied behind his back, painfully exhaling white plumes of breath as he was forced to kneel. His rubber raincoat looked familiar.

"Look up!"

A soldier pushed the man's chin up with the base of his gun. There was blood sticking around his swollen mouth. It was the young man who drove the wagon! His frightened features made him look extremely childlike. He might be around the same age as me, thought Kyūzō. Kō approached and suddenly kicked the youth in the shoulder. The young man looked down, clenching his teeth.

"I see. This is interesting," Kō said to Kyūzō before switching to Chinese and shouting at the young man. "Well then, do you understand now? Which soldiers did you think I'd prefer? You arrogant shithead!"

General Bai made some remark to Kō. Kō translated. It seemed that they couldn't find where the young man had hidden the bag and blanket.

"The soldiers took them. Not me!" The young man murmured weakly and mechanically. He surely had repeated these same words many times now. With each murmur, blood oozed from the corner of his lips.

Lowering his voice, Bai said something that appeared to be a joke, chuckling as he began walking toward the truck. Kō also laughed. While laughing, he again kicked the young man squarely in the face before staggering a bit. With a cry, the youth began spitting blood, and together with that blood a white tooth appeared dangling from the end of a red cord.

"You want a shot at him too?" Panting, Kō urged on Kyūzō. One of the soldiers kindly stepped on the young man's fingers to prevent him from moving. Quickly shaking his head, Kyūzō backed away.

General Bai called out to Kyūzō and Kō as the engine started. The young man began crying. The soldiers helped push the two men aboard the truck. In between the tightly packed baggage, near the driver's seat, lay bedding that had been prepared for the two men.

Bai occupied the driver's seat while an officer and four orderlies and soldiers secured positions by the back entrance. Preparations were finally completed with the packing of a light machine gun. The cloth-covered headlights were switched on and the gate door opened. Handing a canteen to the two men, an orderly whispered proudly, "Most of this baggage is the general's personal property."

The young man continued crying. As they pushed him around with their boot tips, the remaining soldiers turned toward the departing truck and simultaneously raised their hands in salute.

Chapter 4

Doors

XXV

The broken fountain was located in the center of the dried-up pond, which was approximately sixty meters wide, and from a distance appeared to be shaped like the gun turret of a battleship. The bulging part at the bottom had become hollow, and, apart from the inconvenience of having to keep one's head lowered, seemed to be a rather comfortable place to stay. The concrete walls were inlaid with many pieces of thick colored glass—long ago, no doubt, lightbulbs were placed on the inside so that the falling water would turn five different colors—and now functioned as a window. With the shifting sun, these colors would blend together as they announced the time by shining one after the other. The first color was blue, followed by red, green, and yellow before then changing to purple at dusk. The fountain was about five meters wide; and the floor, which was made of sand mixed with mud, was nonetheless quite dry.

Even more convenient was the fact that the entrance was indirect and so not easily visible from the outside. Also, the tower part served as both vent and a good lookout. In order to enter this den, one had to first climb up the platform before going down the manhole-like cavity and then pass from that compartment through the space between the platform and tower. Originally the passage was half submerged in water, which explained its structure. If one used stones to block up this space between the platform and tower, there would be no fear of discovery.

"Well, just go take a look," boasted Kō, using a pebble to draw a map on the ground as he told Kyūzō of the hiding place. General Bai had dropped them off a bit before town, and they were now resting at the first crossroads. "Right after the war ended, I got into some trouble and was forced to run. I found this hiding place by accident and used it for nearly two months without once being disturbed. When I finally left, I tightly sealed it up and dropped some shit into the hole. Well, it should be fine. Peacetime aside, people generally steer clear of parks at moments like this. But if you're worried, just throw a rock in to be sure. If someone is already occupying the area, go around to the other side where there used to be traces of kept animals. In any case, you just need to hold out for a day. I'm counting on you."

The two men parted. Kō turned east toward the old part of town while Kyūzō remained for a while walking around the fields before eventually arriving at the deserted factory district. There was hardly anyone about. Yet the area was part of the city. The streets were paved with asphalt. Like a Sunday morning, everything appeared to be glittering in fresh light. The hard echo of his footsteps seemed to make a show of human strength in having driven away nature. Kyūzō felt deeply proud that he was human. Passing over a girder bridge and entering the town, he felt a sense of hope and joy bubbling up inside him all the more intensely. It was wonderful to be alive! He wanted to quickly return to Japan to share this wonderful quality with other people. However, the fact that right at this moment he had no one with whom to speak also induced in him a lonely sadness. If the heavy, dangerous vest he wore were not restraining him from the inside, he would have smiled at anyone passing by. Yet the vest kept his exuberance in check, urging him forward.

Both the water tower and the antennae of the weather measurement station were landmarks. Kyūzō quickly recognized these, as the park was large with many trees. As instructed, he made a detour before entering at the south entrance, where there were hardly any people walking about.

It was precisely as Kō had described. The feces in the manhole were frozen black, while the space between the platform and tower was packed tightly with rocks. Although the park was in the middle of town, it was in any case quite large and there seemed to be no fear of disturbance. Moreover, the pond was located slightly to the north of the park's center at the bottom of a lowland area that was hollowed out in the shape of a mortar, thereby forming another world that was even further isolated from its surroundings. If it was only for a day, Kyūzō supposed, he should be able to get by.

Looking around, however, he spotted something odd. On the southern slope of the mortar there were scattered about the head and bones of some animal. Judging by the shape of the legs, it appeared to be a dog. And there were not just one or two dogs but rather quite a lot. At a glance, Kyūzō noticed that there was a trap right next to the fountain. A disgusting device had been set up there.

It might be where they killed the dogs after catching them. He had come to a terrible place. Deciding to change his location, he went off in search of the animal pen. The fallen leaves mixed together with snow gave off a watery sound, and the cuffs of Kyūzō's pants were soaked. Compared with the cold that had continued until yesterday, it was hard to believe. He had a premonition that something wonderful was going to happen.

He soon found the animal pen. It was on the slope of a small hill. Although called an animal pen, it was really just a simple, low tunnel-like structure made of stacked bricks. It was probably used as a place for deer to sleep. The town could be seen through the grove of trees atop the hill. Many similar red roofs were lined up alongside one another; this appeared to be the Japanese residential district from long ago. On the right soared a huge water tank.

Kyūzō looked around for a while when suddenly a Chinese boy appeared from inside the pen. Unhealthy looking, he seemed to be an urchin. The two stared intensely at one another for a moment. Feeling apprehensive, Kyūzō nevertheless feigned an innocent look, turned around, and passed on.

He felt troubled. It was probably best to return to the fountain. He deeply resented having to bear this burden of the vest with which Kō had entrusted him. If not for the vest, he could head straight off to town. He had merely passed through the town, but it was wonderful. Shops were on display, stagecoaches were running, and people busily walked about. After all, Shenyang was the largest city that Kyūzō had ever seen. It would have been fun just to look at the covered wagons with their rubber wheels or the crowd of rickshaws peddling by. If he wanted, he could find even more enjoyable things to do. He could even sell the Dania spoon and buy freshly steamed meat buns.

The vest, however, thrust its blades into him from the inside. At any rate, he should flee, for this was dangerous. It was less courage than fear that helped make up his mind.

It was just at the moment when the color of the glass was about to change from yellow to purple. Lining up alongside the wall the food and water-filled beer bottle that General Bai had shared with them upon parting, Kyūzō took out the pistol that Kō had left him just in case and placed it at his side. Of course it had no bullets. Still, it might come in handy to scare off that urchin.

I'll take a sip of water and then go to sleep. Kō should finish up his work in Shenyang by tomorrow and then come and get me with good news to report. Although I mostly slept in the truck, it wasn't a deep sleep. Hopefully tonight won't be so cold.

Kyūzō had felt that he could go to sleep immediately, but now discovered that he somehow could not. The final color of the glass faded, and now only the light from above the tower shone dimly. ("There was something worrying. What was it?") As time passed, he merely felt increasingly on edge. He heard the strange sound of a bugle from somewhere. A dog was barking in the distance. Was the work of catching and then killing the dogs done at night, or during the day? Someone with creaking footsteps was walking outside the fountain! No, that was the sound of the ground starting to freeze over. ("There was something worrying. What was it?") There appeared from the young wagon driver's mouth a dangling tooth with a red cord. "If I'm a man, then you're also a man." The mouse's burnt, swollen belly. Suddenly recalling the scene of the horrible lead ocean, Kyūzō experienced the acute sense that he was alive now, that he had lived to make it all the way here, and he felt so treasured that he wished to embrace himself. *Alas, halfway there, all of us, here.* He began to feel spasms of pain in his armpits and lower back. ("But what could possibly be so worrying?") Relax! Kō will bring good news tomorrow. ("Why sure! 'I won't harm you,' he had said. 'Let me handle things.'")

Kyūzō recalled something that one of the officers had told Kō in the truck while they were eating. Japanese smugglers, he said, often came to the port of Shacheng to buy saccharin and cooking oil. If that were true, then it was not at all impossible that Kō would have good news.

However, even this rationalization in no way reduced Kyūzō's anxiety. The light from above the tower had already disappeared. The cold was growing and he felt increasingly awake. Of course he had some idea about how to determine the true nature of his anxiety. Were he to act upon that, however, his suspicions would surely grow even stronger and his fixation all the more intense. That would be frightening.

Removing a small paper package from his pocket, he placed it in the palm of his hand and made as if to gauge its weight. There shouldn't be any weight. "You can't fall asleep if you're too tired. At such times, just a small taste of this will help. Just a bit, a tiny bit, about how much one could pick up with a match tip," Kō had said, handing him a bag of heroin when he left. But even this might be another one of his tricks, Kyūzō reflected.

He just couldn't understand what kind of work Kō was doing in Shenyang. What work involved entrusting to a complete stranger goods that were worth the equivalent of fifty foreign cars? Kō was a wanted man. Considered at its most basic level, the obvious answer was that Kyūzō was being used as a kind of hiding place for the goods. Of course he didn't care about that. It was all too clear. The problem was what came later, when his role came to an end when Kō's pursuers confirmed that Kō was not carrying the goods. Kyūzō would no longer be of any use to

Kō then. Would Kō still recognize the need to provide him with helpful information as well as his share of the money?

No chance, Kyūzō thought. It was far crazier to think that Kō considered him anything but a hiding place. Using him was not a means; it was doubtless the goal itself. Kō's attitude was entirely consistent here. Even Kō's mysterious ambiguity was in truth no ambiguity at all. Rather, everything was just a calculation based on his shrewd grasp of the psychological weaknesses of the person being used.

Maybe Kō had even predicted and taken into account that I'd be haunted by these doubts and constantly dwell on them tonight. And maybe this heroin is the result of his calculations. Maybe his plan was based on knowing that I'd worry, get anxious, and be unable to sleep, forcing me to take the drug. And then . . . and then he'll simply do what he must. He'll sneak in when I'm fast asleep, tear off the vest, take it, and leave. Then I'll become the butt of his jokes. "There was this idiot," he'll say.

No way! Where was the fool who understood so much and yet could still be so completely taken in? Where was the guard who tamely stood watch even as he knew that the man who entrusted him with something was also a thief who'd later come and take it? If it's clear that I'm going to be betrayed, then of course I'll betray him first! I'll just take the vest and disappear. That's not a bad idea at all! If the heroin is worth fifty foreign cars, then it definitely has to be good stuff. In any case, there's no need to feel guilty because Kō probably just stole it from somewhere. After all, he might not even be alive now if it weren't for me. No, he'd definitely be dead . . .

And yet Kyūzō also knew that he could not possibly escape. There was still a long journey to the coast, and then an even longer journey beyond that. He absolutely needed help. Besides, he had once heard a rumor about a nurse who had been killed—someone had gouged out her eyeballs with his fingers—simply because she was carrying ten grams of morphine. An amateur carrying drugs was as good as dead. But even more fundamental was the fact that, for all the workings of his imagination, this was all just hypothetical. He was fretting about things, but there was nothing he could do. No doubt Kō, aware of all his turmoil, had hired him as his guard dog for precisely this reason.

Stop it! Just going around in circles! I'm going crazy! Should I just go ahead and taste the stuff? But it's powerful, and I might die if I'm careless. When you take drugs, it's easy to freeze to death. I bet he'd be happy if I died. Right, that might be his aim. No way!

But what if I were to hold out until morning? I'd relax, become exhausted, and then drop off to sleep. Then Kō would sneak in. So it would be the same result! Even if I were able to hold out longer, it would still be easy for him to just take the vest from me if he wanted. He could use a loaded pistol or maybe just bring one of those dog-catching thugs, and the problem would be over at once.

So one falls into a trap in the very attempt to escape from it! There's no use even thinking about things. All that's left is for Kō to tell me frankly to leave the goods here and physically get out. So I'm still forced to give up the heroin money and any information and leave everything to him. Damn it, he's a sly bastard! He knows how to make use of guard dogs.

This stuff is really bitter! I wonder if I took too much.

XXVI

Kyūzō awoke to the sound of a dog yelping. He tried to drink some water but his body had grown numb, making it impossible to move freely. No matter how much the temperature had risen, it was still too much to sleep outdoors without a fire. Flapping his arms about like wings, he sought to restore some of his body warmth. The dog's yelping was horrible—had they already started to catch and kill the animals? Blue was just beginning to appear from the window. Yet the light from above was already quite bright.

He got up slowly, vigorously rubbing the area above his knees. Climbing up the tower, he peered out through the hole. This hole was part of the remains of the dismantled spout. The trap was choking the dog as it hung suspended in midair. The animal was filthy, with red fur and a thick neck. It stood on its hind legs as its forelegs flailed in the air, painfully licking its lips and barking. Its bark trailed off into a thin whine.

It's cold—I should eat. There are some flimsy pieces of floury dry bread, salted beans, and something I can't identify that seems like a kind of oily, sour candy. In order to save the food, he took a long time chewing slowly. I have to make sure that it lasts until tonight. I feel a bit sick. I wonder if it's because of the drug from last night. It didn't make me feel better at all. How could anyone get addicted to that stuff? Still, it worked. I went right to sleep.

The light from the window gradually changed from blue to red.

The dog stopped yelping. It was now making a low growl. Then it began barking wildly. There was a brief whistling sound mixed together with a menacing bark. Then Kyūzō heard a sound like sand being thrown, after which everything became quiet.

Climbing the tower and peering out, he saw that the dog had already been taken down from the trap and that blood was being pumped out of its slit throat. The animal's body had been placed on its side along a slope with its head facing down. Someone was pressing down upon the corpse with his knees, and red, creamy blood bubbled forth. It was the urchin from the animal pen whom he had seen yesterday!

Kyūzō felt sick as if he were almost smelling the stink, but he was relieved to know that the dogcatcher whom he had been so worried about was just a boy. The youth cut off the animal's tail and inserted the blade into its belly by its neck and legs, and proceeded to quickly skin it as if removing a shirt. Kyūzō was utterly impressed by the boy's skill and no longer regarded the act as particularly dirty. As the work progressed, the dog gradually began to look like meat, and Kyūzō even found himself wanting to taste it. However, this may have been less real appetite on his part than an indirect sign of his warm feelings for the urchin.

Kyūzō began to feel a strong temptation to speak to the youth. He felt that they could become very close friends. The youth's fingers were long and nimble. No doubt the warmth of the dog's blood helped keep away the cold. His face was thin and bony. By his nose, there was a deep crease etched into one side of his face, and this feature seemed to be awaiting the moment when he would suddenly burst out laughing.

The vest, however, held Kyūzō in check. Soon the youth got up and left, leaving behind the dog's head, legs, and internal organs. The rising steam shone white in the morning sunlight. Kyūzō somehow felt extremely irritated. He hungered for human contact in the same way that one's throat grows thirsty.

He took another small taste of the heroin. The sky clouded over and the wind picked up. He thought that he could hear the sounds of the town wafting in on the wind. I want to return to Japan soon, he thought. The inner walls of his face contracted tightly. In his mind, he repeated over and again the image of the youth's hands as they stripped off the dog's skin. In the same way, he reflected, I want to tear off that something which is holding me back. He rubbed both cheeks forcefully with the back of his hands. Something like dandruff fell to the ground. How in the world do I look?

His forehead felt smooth. The drug was beginning to take effect. He thought that Kō would certainly come with good news. Red was beginning to turn to green. But what could possibly be taking so long? he wondered. In any case ... He suddenly felt up for a fight. From the start, there was no need for me to be so weak! If he wants to hold me back, then I'll just hold him back too! As long as I keep the vest, he won't be able to leave me. Even he should know that. Right, if he wants to be so damn selfish, then there's no chance at all that I'm going to let go of the vest.

His navel area began to burn with itchiness. Turning over the band of his underwear, he saw a small white insect moving along the seam. He crushed it. It was unpleasant at first, but after a while he just couldn't stop. Because of the stiff vest, he was unable to bend freely and so just lowered his eyes, but this caused his head to hurt. Nevertheless, for a while he was able to forget that time was passing.

Green turned to yellow and then yellow turned to purple. But Kō didn't come. In the darkness, Kyūzō ate the last bit of food and drank the last drop of water. Yet this only made him feel unbearably thirsty. The anxiety from last night reared its head once again. Tasting the drug, he used the strength it gave him to boldly go outside, where he squeezed and drank the snow in the shade.

Someone approached from behind. Kyūzō thought that he felt something heavy on his neck. In fact, however, it was a sudden, powerful blow. He fell to his knees in a squat before gradually stretching out his arms and legs.

XXVII

Kyūzō was looking around for something somewhere. The air was considerably heavier than usual and the area around him was entirely reddish brown, like the color of rusted steel. One after another, things randomly appeared and then disappeared: a street corner, a playing field with banners, a scrap collector, a long earthen wall. Kyūzō knew that this was a dream and not reality. He was fighting with a dog inside a clay model of the wasteland while outside a man who appeared to be a teacher was explaining something to students. He felt tired and sleepy. This isn't real, he thought, so it should be all right to rest. Each time he tried to do so, however, the teacher scolded him. "Don't disturb class," he said. His mother stood behind the teacher on tiptoes, peering at him. She seemed to be pleading, "Please do as the teacher says and don't bring shame upon the dead." In a stern voice, the teacher asked, "Well, what's the matter then?" Then . . . Kyūzō summoned all his strength trying to remember. The sky was a dull red. Nearby there was a peeling brick wall with no ceiling. He had accepted the mummies' invitation. It was not especially pleasant, but he felt that it would have been wrong to refuse and so couldn't leave his seat. Suddenly mice sprang out of the mummies' faces. The rodents immediately grouped together, spreading throughout the space like a carpet of iron sand bristling on a magnet. Kyūzō fled. He climbed up a flagpole outside. The flagpole was weak, threatening to break at any moment. Suddenly

Kō rushed out from somewhere and began slashing at the base of the pole with a knife. Kyūzō fell and woke up. He found himself again back in the classroom. "Don't sleep!" the teacher screamed, raising his hands as he approached. "Please forgive me, but I'm so sleepy!" Kyūzō exclaimed as he now actually woke up.

He heard some kind of sad, weak yelping. It was still dark out. Shuddering, he tried to get up but was unable to move freely. His neck felt heavy and slack, as if it had been gouged out. The yelp faded and turned into a hacking bark. Right, I guess another stray dog has fallen into the trap . . . An obscure, black shadow suddenly came into focus and began to take form. ("I was trying to lick some snow. Someone approached and suddenly hit me from behind.") I might be dying, Kyūzō thought, and at that moment fear helped him summon his last bit of strength. Clawing at the ground for a long time, he finally placed his arms on the stone pedestal of the fountain and sat up. He was close to losing nearly all sensation in his limbs. Fighting off sleep, he pressed his arms to his side and tried desperately to shake them. In an effort to drive away sleep, he tried to target something—getting angry seemed best. He concentrated on Kō.

Intense pain began in his right ear before coursing through his entire body. This was a sign that, despite the crushing pain, he was gradually regaining sensation in his limbs. With open hands, he noisily slapped the area above his knees. His overcoat slipped from his shoulders and fell to the ground. His arms were not in the sleeves. Why not? He suddenly realized that his coat had also been unbuttoned. The overcoat had been cut from top to bottom all the way to the jacket.

The vest had been stolen!

With that, Kyūzō nearly fell asleep again. Perhaps he even did sleep for a bit. He dreamt of the Sea of Japan. It was only about the size of a brook. On the far shore there was a mountain, in the folds of which appeared a town. The town was identical to Baharin, which had abandoned him and driven him out. It even seemed as if Baharin had moved while remaining as it was. That might even have been possible if the sea were so narrow. Kyūzō's heart ached with the desire to reach the town. However, the gap was slightly too wide to jump across. He shook his fists and bared his teeth as he shouted in frustration.

He shouted in his dream, but also shouted in reality. The dog began yelping again. Without knowing what was wrong with what parts of his body, he forced himself to his feet on the basis of the sharp pain in his knees and his vague sense of up and down. As soon as he thought that gravity had disappeared, he again fell flat on his face. However, these efforts were useful. His heart regained its vitality while the muscles throughout his body roused themselves at the sense of danger.

Kyūzō still needed warmth. If he could not create this warmth from inside, then he had no choice but to seek it from the outside. He got on all fours and began moving. Circling the fountain, he headed south. The dog was growling furiously. Clambering up the slope, Kyūzō crawled into a pile of fallen leaves. He gathered them together and then took out a match. His fingers wouldn't move. Grasping four or five matches together in his hand, he tried to strike them against his shoe when he realized that his right shoe was missing. In the shoe was concealed the certificate that Alexandrov had signed for him. The dog continued growling. Kyūzō growled back no less loudly. At the same time, he felt around to discover that his knife and the Dania spoon were also gone. Holding the matches, he struck them against his left shoe. An orange flame flared up. When he set the flame to the leaves, however, it emitted only a thin steam before vanishing all too quickly.

Kyūzō once again began crawling south. His last hope now lay with the animal pen where the urchin stayed. Still, how awful the forest was! How long the distance! He nearly got lost among the complex uphills and downhills. He braced himself by stirring up the hatred within him. Damn it, it had to have been Kō! If not, then who else could have known about that certificate in my shoe? If it were just any thief, then he would have stripped me of everything, from my shoes and clothes. The fact that only one shoe was removed was proof that he was intentionally looking for the certificate. It had to have been Kō! Damn it, Kō that bastard! For some reason, however, Kyūzō felt sadness rather than hatred welling up inside him. The sadness was smooth and silky; it felt good. I might die now, he felt at last, as if referring to someone else. Suddenly he collapsed, his face plunging into the fallen leaves.

XXVIII

Faint smoke hung in the air all around him. Beyond the smoke shimmered the dazzling afternoon light. Right above his head there was the sound of someone blowing their nose with their fingers. The urchin was using a wooden spatula to scrape the fat off a dog's hide. Kyūzō found himself in the animal pen. Lumps of meat and threaded strands of garlic hung down alongside one another from the ceiling.

Their eyes met.

"So you're a Jap demon!" uttered the dog-catching youth, extending his foot and kicking Kyūzō in the head. Kyūzō was shocked, as he had been wondering how to thank the youth for his kindness. Yet he felt no animosity. The sense of something like friendship that began when he peered at the urchin from the tower continued unabated. He wanted to believe that this was rather a quarrel between friends over some minor misunderstanding.

Kyūzō tried to raise his head, but, as if stuck to the floor, could not budge. He tried to smile back at the urchin, but could only manage to slightly twitch the edge of his lips. He tried to speak, but his vocal chords were numb and utterly unresponsive.

"Where did you go and what were you doing after you were spying here the day before yesterday?" Sticking out his lower lip, the youth brandished the spatula he was holding before Kyūzō's eyes as if demanding an answer. There was a strong sense of wariness and aggression about him.

"Shui," Kyūzō barely replied, using the Chinese word for water.

Scowling, the youth spat. Gesturing with the spatula that he would slit Kyūzō's throat, the youth ladled some water into an empty can and roughly poured it into Kyūzō's mouth. Upon drinking the water, Kyūzō suddenly felt exhausted again. He closed his eyes. He wanted to sleep just as he was. However, the youth refused to let him. Kicking Kyūzō in the head, he again pressed for an explanation. Kyūzō felt absolutely no need to hide things. But he didn't understand what the youth wanted and so had no idea what to say that would satisfy him. He began speaking haphazardly. The explanation should have been simple. Once he began speaking, however, he discovered that this simplicity was extremely difficult to explain. Besides, he was not yet fully conscious.

Kyūzō nearly dropped off to sleep several times in the course of his explanation, but was immediately poked in the head. Gradually, however, this poking became softer until finally he was struck not in the head but in the shoulders. Eventually he again found himself asleep without remembering what or how much he had spoken.

On one occasion, he remembered getting up to urinate when the youth fed him something. It was dark. A dull, purplish light from a handmade lamp hovered about the ceiling. In addition to the youth, Kyūzō sensed that there were two or three other men nearby. He seemed to recall exchanging words with them about something, but his memory wasn't clear.

He fully awoke only in the afternoon of the following day. No one was there. He got up and drank some water. Moving about, Kyūzō felt as if his body were not his own. He was buoyant and felt good. Although he had no appetite, he felt a strong urge to eat something. He plucked some garlic from the ceiling and put it in his mouth; it was completely tasteless. Yet he immediately began to feel terrible stomach pains. Thrusting his head between the folds of the woven mat, he vomited up the water he had just drunk. A warm, exhilarating wind brushed past his face. "I survived!" he realized, and immediately felt the back of his nose become moist. However, he couldn't tell whether this was from his tears or his vomit.

"Want to eat something?" Kyūzō raised his head to find the youth standing there. He entered silently, took out a stale steamed bun from an inner wooden box, salted it, and handed it to Kyūzō. He then gave Kyūzō a small piece of meat. It had to be dog meat. The youth was expressionless, but his animosity from yesterday seemed to be gone. Kyūzō devoured the food. The thing called appetite awoke, and he felt as if he might faint from the desire to eat more. His teeth began to chatter as he gnawed them. His mouth filled with saliva, which dripped down his chin. "It's like I've become a dog," he thought.

"I'll take you to the Japanese people's place," the youth said, jerking his chin.

Kyūzō couldn't believe his ears. It was all too sudden.

"The Japanese people's place," the youth repeated, furrowing his brow in annoyance.

However, Kyūzō still could not believe it. That Japan could suddenly appear so close by—no, that's impossible. I'm dreaming now. If not, then all the pain and fear I've suffered have been a dream ... Kyūzo waited breathlessly for what the youth would say next. He suspected that the youth would soon begin laughing maliciously: It's just a joke! Serves you right! I bet you were excited! But the youth did not laugh. Instead, he took from the shadow of the inner wooden box Kyūzō's right shoe that had been removed and then forgotten by the fountain. He shook it enviously two or three times before silently throwing it at Kyūzō's feet. Nevertheless, Kyūzō was still half doubtful. He couldn't help feeling that some cruel trick was being played on him. He even wondered if the youth didn't plan to take him somewhere—for example, out to the slope where he had set the trap—and kill him like a dog. Suddenly he recalled the pistol that should still be where he had left it inside the fountain. Had Kō taken it? There was a strong possibility that he had, but Kyūzō needed to check. If it were still there, then it would now be the sole property that he had left. No matter how much the urchin wanted his shoe, he shouldn't sell it. The shoe wouldn't quite fit his foot, which had grown swollen and stiff like papier-mâché.

"In exchange, I'll take this," the youth stated, rolling up the garment padded with thick cotton that he wore around his midriff. The pistol was thrust inside his bellyband.

Kyūzō's face hardened as if it had been smeared with glue. He heard the sound of his own blood flowing above his eardrums. It doesn't have bullets in it anyway. Besides, this guy is much smaller and thinner than I am. I won't lose if it turns into a fight . . .

Yet Kyūzō said nothing, merely nodding slightly. The youth's expression "in exchange" took the air out of his mounting agitation, calming his tension. Certainly what this dog-catching youth had given him was irreplaceable. His life, his overcoat, and his shoe—as well as the place for Japanese people that he had just mentioned. And the youth had taken out and shown him that thing which could have remained hidden.

Rising to his feet, Kyūzō again nodded slowly and deeply.

XXIX

Like wood that is beginning to dry out, Kyūzō's entire body gave off a splintering sound as he set off walking. As always, the sky was a heavy gray. The ground was melting, mixed with shards of ice underfoot, giving off a pliant sound.

They left through the western entrance, which was on the opposite side from where he had come. There was a neatly paved road with streetcar tracks, beyond which appeared a leaden two-storied building that looked like a pile of boxes and was completely shrouded in withered ivy branches. The Chinese Nationalist Party flag was half twisted around a flagpole, fluttering painfully. Behind the gatepost stood a sentry, who slowly walked around in small, continuous circles. The sentry cast a glance in their direction, but quickly ignored them and turned away. Kyūzō realized how shabby he looked. He was covered all over with cuts and bruises from frostbite, his face was haggard with fatigue, and his clothes were ragged with holes and dust. If I had a mirror, I'd like to see who looks dirtier, this urchin or myself. Twisting his shoulders around, he scratched his back.

They cut across the road with streetcar tracks and proceeded straight. As Kyūzō tripped on the sidewalk pavement, the heel of his left shoe fell off. He picked it up and placed it in his pocket. Suddenly he was struck by a sense of foreboding that his entire foot had been removed. However, it worked out well for him to limp along behind the youth since the latter had a strange way of walking. With his eyes fixed on the ground, the youth would kick away pebbles, abruptly jump up to snap off branches from roadside trees before hurling them over the street walls, or leap up randomly while humming. He couldn't stand still for an instant. Kyūzō felt somehow relieved as he watched the youth, and yet his chest tightened with a certain sense of inferiority, for he had to convince himself that it was strictly because of his broken heel that he couldn't act the same way.

The town was divided into a precise grid. They continued for some time along a quiet, old-fashioned residential district, with little pedestrian traffic. Then they suddenly came upon a bustling main street. Shops appeared on both sides, but most —with the exception of grocery stores— were closed. What created such bustle were rather the small sidewalk vendors who had set up their wares directly on the street. One layer after another, these vendors crowded together all the way to the roadway, shouting at the top of their lungs. Among them was even an old woman holding a single wrapping cloth for sale. Men and women dressed in solid black cotton-padded garments wound their way through the crowd, coming and going slowly. Occasionally wagons passed by. The merchants would then quickly carry their belongings off to the side, waiting until the wagons passed before immediately returning to their original places to begin selling again. Most of the passengers riding in the wagons were soldiers.

The street was everywhere filled with the smell of food. Even among all the congestion, the youth continued with his strange manner of walking. When he bumped into someone, he would glare at them swaggeringly, while the other person merely remained silent, pretending not to notice. Suddenly the youth leaned over and deftly scooped up a darkly shriveled dried pear from the stall of a confectionery vendor. Perhaps his erratic way of walking served as a kind of preparation for shoplifting. The youth bit into the stolen pear as he continued walking, and his mouth became smeared with the amber-colored sugary juice. Urged on by the stomachache that now seemed to force its way up all the way below his chin, Kyūzō also began to shoot darting glances around him. It appeared, however, that he needed considerably more time before he might actually reach out to take something.

After two blocks, they came upon another large road with streetcar tracks. Ahead lay a quiet residential district. Stopping, the youth spoke for the first time. "It's close by now. You go on alone. Once you go, don't come back to the park. If I find you wandering around there again, you'll pay for it! You'll be treated the same way as those dogs!" With an exaggerated gesture, he signaled with his hands that he would slit Kyūzō's throat.

"No, you've got it wrong—wrong." Kyūzō repeated to himself. The youth continued, "Go west from here and then south after two blocks, and you'll soon arrive at the place where the Japanese are. All right then, don't come back again!"

Pivoting on one foot, the youth turned around and quickly slipped in among the crowd of people. Kyūzō felt utterly distraught and close to tears. "Damn it, you Chink!" he said to himself, but these words in no way corresponded to his feelings then. "No, you've got it wrong—wrong," he repeated, dragging his feet along the route the youth had described. Soon, however, his bitterness was overcome by the hope of arriving at the place for Japanese people as well as his anxiety over whether such a place even existed.

He quickly figured out the place where the Japanese were. It occupied one section of what appeared to be company-owned housing, with barbed wire stretched high above the walls. Approximately ten identical-looking buildings were lined up alongside one another. The walls facing the main street were all kept tightly shut with stacks of railroad ties, and only one common gate behind the alley was open. A small wooden sign had been nailed to the alley entrance: "Residence of Overseas Japanese Retainers." His mouth agape, Kyūzō breathed roughly. It was even difficult to close his mouth when he swallowed. He felt absolutely no sense of reality. He could not even distinguish whether he felt happy or sad. Only his long journey

ran through his mind, as if it were someone else's story. He felt that his
escape from Alexandrov's room was an event that took place so long ago
that he could no longer recall it.

Inside the gate, a Nationalist Army soldier carrying a gun and bayonet
and a Japanese young man wearing an armband were standing around a
large stove laughing wearily about something. When the soldier noticed
Kyūzō, he clucked his tongue and raised his hands as if driving away a dog.
Kyūzō was actually panting like a dog.

"I'm Jap-an-ese!"

With a flustered expression, the young man looked at the soldier.

"Get out of here!" warned the soldier, indiscriminately grabbing hold of
his gun.

"But I'm . . . Japanese." Kyūzō began trembling so violently that he
could no longer stand up.

"You can't come in here without a certificate," the Japanese said, averting his eyes as if annoyed. He was the first Japanese person whom Kyūzō
had seen in three years. "This place is now under the direct control of the
army."

"I know the Nationalist Army officer named Bai. He gave me a ride
partway in his truck!"

"Then you should go talk with him."

"But I've become separated from the person who knows his
whereabouts."

"Then nothing can be done."

"I've walked all the way from Baharin." Kyūzō's eyes began to overflow with tears. "Please help me. I've walked such a long way without
food."

"But really, nothing can be done. It's not the same as before, you see."

"What should I do?" Kyūzō rubbed the tears around his filthy face.

"What to do? Many kids your age have already died. We don't even
know what will happen to us tomorrow. I feel bad for you, but we've got
absolutely no power to do anything. I know that sounds cold."

"But what should I do?"

"The detention camps are gone and there are no more repatriation ships. There's absolutely nothing that can be done. In town, though, there are people who'd gladly hire a Japanese kid."

"But I want to return to Japan. I've walked all the way from Baharin"

"Never heard of it."

"Now get moving!" the soldier yelled mockingly in a provincial southern accent.

Choked with tears, Kyūzō made a sound like a broken pump as he threw himself at the young man's knees. As the young man quickly pulled back, Kyūzō suddenly crashed against the ground.

"Don't get violent!" the young man muttered bitterly. With a gleeful yell, the soldier grabbed Kyūzō by the neck and shoved him toward the alley. Cowering at the bottom of the opposite wall, Kyūzō loudly burst into tears. The soldier approached and began poking him with his gunstock. Clinging to the wall, Kyūzō rose to his feet and staggered away. His tears stopped once he left the alley. In their place, he was left only with a whitish sense of emptiness, as if his body weight had disappeared.

For a long time, Kyūzō sat still by the roadside facing the enclosure. Two or three people regularly walked past, but no one even turned to look at him. The sun began to go down, and soon the roofs across the street crept all the way to his feet. Japanese people lived under these roofs! Stretching his legs, Kyūzō kicked out with all his strength. He was surprised to feel something hard move about in his pocket. It was his shoe heel, he recalled dejectedly. Beyond the wall there was the sound of a door opening. Then Kyūzō heard the shrill voices of small children playing together: "That's not right! It's because he did that! Look, look! This is good!" Without realizing it, Kyūzō got up and approached the wall as if drawn in. Stepping onto an area where the wall jutted out, he supported his weight with both hands and peered in. Two boys about ten years old were playing with some mud. Despite his sobbing, Kyūzō could not stop looking at them. He was just worried that they would return home. His hands began to hurt, but he clung there, unable to leave.

One of the boys suddenly looked up and yelled. "Hey, there's a beggar spying on us!"

With that, he threw a lump of mud at Kyūzō. Covering his face with his arms, Kyūzō yelled back. "I'm Japanese, you idiot. I'm Japanese!"

"There's a beggar!" cried out the other boy toward the house. "As if Japanese people would have such dark faces!"

From the window the face of someone who appeared to be the children's mother peered out and then vanished. Kyūzō continued shouting. The door opened, the children were called back in, and then the door closed with a bang. Heavy footsteps could now be heard racing through the alley. At the same time that Kyūzō slipped down from the wall, the soldier turned a corner and rushed toward him. This time he appeared truly angry. Springing up on one foot, Kyūzō quickly ran away. From behind, jeers and pebbles grazed his ears.

Dusk was near. Where should I go? I've been completely abandoned. This feeling of helplessness was just like that of a middle school student who couldn't enter class because he was late. Yet there were houses everywhere. If there were houses, then there had to be doors; and if there were doors, then they had to be tightly locked. There was a door right over there, but its inside was infinitely far away. In the end, this is no different from the wasteland that was completely empty of people. Or maybe it's worse. The wasteland refused to allow me to escape, whereas the town prevents me from approaching. Even those mummies in that roofless, deserted house ended up dying just before town. If only I had money . . . damn it, Kō, you bastard! That's right, it was all his fault from beginning to end! I wonder if there isn't some way I could track him down. But I remember learning something at school when we studied geography: "The city of Mukden is larger in size than London." I don't know how large London is, but it has to be pretty big. Besides, he took back the vest. There's no way he's still in town. Kyūzō suddenly recalled what Alexandrov used to say: "All the enemies of the Soviet Union are fascists, and all fascists are bad." Come to think of it, it was precisely people like Kō who were fascists. He kicked that young wagon driver so hard that his teeth broke.

Kyūzō idly sat down on some stone steps. His mouth felt gritty with sand. He spat, and the color of his saliva was stained yellow like muddy water. I wonder if it's all over now. Before that, though, I'd at least like a cup of water. If I ever see that bastard Kō again, I've got to kill him . . .

At the same time, however, exactly the opposite thought emerged in the depths of his heart. He had perhaps never relied so much on Kō as now. If Kō were to unexpectedly appear here, Kyūzō would no doubt have burst into tears from excess joy. Kō was perhaps an evil man, but he had the strength to press on toward his goals. And maybe he really wasn't so evil after all. For example, proof could be seen in the pistol that he had left behind in the fountain. He had to have been extremely rushed. But why was he so rushed? A dog had fallen into the trap just then, causing him to panic. He originally didn't want to hit Kyūzō, but knocked him down because he mistook him for a thief. Although he quickly realized his mistake, he was surprised by the sounds coming from the trap and had no time to help Kyūzō, so just took the vest and fled. Right, that's entirely possible. That's precisely why he didn't try to kill Kyūzō but instead even covered him with the overcoat that he had taken off. Kō had treated him roughly. Still, maybe such treatment was unavoidable for something worth fifty foreign cars. In that case, maybe I should go back to the fountain and wait for Kō. He's much more reliable than the Japanese people here.

"Idiot!" said another voice in strong contradiction. The fact is that he was a fascist. He just used you as a hiding place. And once your job was finished, you became useless. Right, that's the long and short of it. It wasn't the dog who fell into the trap; it was you!

It's all the same! I just want some water. Rising to his feet, Kyūzō again set off walking. The sun was beginning to set. Soon martial law would go into effect.

I've got to decide where to stay until then. But where should I go? Can't think of anyplace else. The only thing that comes to mind is to return to that park. I suppose that dog-catching youth will be angry. I wonder if he still wouldn't forgive me if I told him that I was driven away by Japanese people. Come to think of it, it seems that I never thanked him. Right, I should go and thank him. I could then take the chance to ask for help. "I'll help you with anything. It's all right if I can't return to Japan for a while. If we clear up some misunderstandings, then you and I would get along well." But what kind of misunderstandings? Kyūzō could not quite grasp what separated him and the youth. He also felt that it wasn't simply misunderstandings that separated them, that there were rather larger things at stake.

Suddenly he roughly kicked away a rock on the ground. That's right, I should go to that bustling town before the merchants close up their shops. And I'll snatch something! Of course it was hunger that partly influenced his decision, but he also felt that stealing something would bring him that much closer to the youth. Imitating the urchin's way of walking, Kyūzō began staggering erratically as he set off straight ahead to the shopping district.

XXX

Three times Kyūzō walked back and forth, from one end to the other of the busy part of town. Yet he had absolutely nothing to show for it. At the moment he was about to reach out his hand, he would suddenly lock eyes with the vendors. Each time he walked back and forth, the number of shops would decrease. He just became more flustered and weary. The evening mist was already beginning to set in. Although the wind had died down, the temperature had steadily dropped. This time I just have to succeed, he thought. I'll target that peanut vendor in the corner, the one right next to the lamp-fuel stand. I'll do it quickly and casually, just like the urchin . . .

However, Kyūzō was unsure whether he could really make up his mind at the right moment. What would happen if I got caught? he reflected. They'd all gang up and beat me and then toss me in the back alley. If that happened, I'd probably die. Someone would come and strip off my clothes. Then some stray dogs would approach. The dog that bit me would fall into the trap, and then that guy would turn it into meat and sell it . . . Kyūzō trembled. Just as his heart had become empty, so, too, had he lost all physical strength. And yet—or rather precisely because of this—he had to succeed. Swallowing his belly back down after it had thrust its way upward inside him like a hard fist, he moved toward the peanut vendor.

Suddenly a man appeared before Kyūzō. There were many men, but this one was different from the others. He was distinctive. His clothes were inconspicuous, but the virtually straight line of his shoulders, the way he swung his hands with strength in the joints, and particularly the way he walked with bent knees as well as the thickness of the base of his neck—he was Japanese! He wasn't Korean; he had to be Japanese. Kyūzō turned pale, the area around his lips grew numb, and a tiny bit of urine leaked out from him, wetting his underwear. Imploringly Kyūzō called out to the man from behind.

"Hey, you're Japanese, right? Mister, you're Japanese, right?"

The man turned his dark, pointed face around quickly. He was younger than expected. His eyes were open wide, and his yellow teeth could be glimpsed from partly open lips. Spotting Kyūzō, the man gave a sigh of relief, but he clearly looked angry and annoyed. Feigning ignorance, he tried to walk past. Yet Kyūzō was not to be denied. Walking right next to the man, he hopped along while peering at him as he continued speaking.

"Help me! I'm close to dying from starvation. Mister, you're Japanese, right? I know it. I know you understand what I'm saying."

All gazes were focused upon them. This seemed to upset the man.

"Stop it!" Turning his face straight ahead, he continued in a hushed voice, "So what if I understand? You're of no concern to me."

"You're heartless, mister."

"I'm busy!"

"I'll really do whatever you say."

"Idiot! I told you to stop! We'll be killed if people find out we're Japanese. You're chattering too loud."

They were in front of the peanut vendor. Yet snatching anything was now out of the question. Kyūzō was just desperately clinging to the man.

"Hey mister, I'm begging you."

"Get lost!"

"I can't. If you abandon me like this, I'll die. I've walked all the way from Baharin."

"Baharin?" The man was about to push Kyūzō away, but suddenly stopped raising his arm and asked suspiciously. "When did you come from there?"

"About two weeks ago."

"Really? Then do you know a man named Kuki?"

"That's me!" Shocked, Kyūzō suddenly raised his voice like a record that had fallen while turning.

The man, however, seemed even more in shock.

"What did you say?"

"I'm Kuki! But how would you know that?" He found his voice rippling with a presentiment of hope that had suddenly begun to open up. "I grew up in Baharin. My name is Kuki Kyūzō. My mom was the housemother of the pulp factory. But . . . Right, you must have heard it from Mr. Kita."

"No . . . Well, wait a moment." The man's lips twitched as he smiled vaguely. When he smiled, several short, deep wrinkles appeared by his thin nostrils. "But your story does seem rather odd and interesting."

"That's right. I'm really begging you. I'm famished. I thought I would snatch something here and then sleep inside the fountain in the park."

Waving his hand in front of his face as if silencing Kyūzō, the man appeared to be deep in thought.

"Well, I'll take you to my lodgings. Don't say anything more here."

"The house for retainers? I was turned away there."

"No. I told you to be quiet."

They were near the southern end of the busy part of town. The man bought Kyūzō something that he didn't recognize—a thick white and yellow rice cake with black jam inside. He was given some hot water and ate the cake while walking. He was so happy that he felt like flaunting a bit.

They turned east along the road with streetcar tracks, in the opposite direction of the house for retainers. This meant that they would approach the park. The water tank soared up diagonally to the left, breaking up the line of roofs. I wonder if we might run into that dogcatcher, Kyūzō reflected. If we see him, I should ask the man to let me thank him . . . Dusk was approaching. Far to the north, multiple gunshots could be heard one after the other. Then another gunshot rang out close by. That had to be the martial law signal.

As if it were his own home, the man silently passed through an eating house with a sign of red piping and came out onto a large courtyard, which was surrounded on all four sides by a long building that looked like a castle wall. It seemed that one had to pass through some shop in order to arrive there. In the center was a two-storied building that appeared to be an apartment. The man was lodging in one of the rooms. He must be pretty important to stay in a place like this, Kyūzō thought with encouragement.

It was a single room roughly fifteen square meters in size. However, tatami straw mats were laid down in the Japanese style. Inside there was only a rucksack as well as bedding that had been left out. The man appeared to have no other belongings. "You're probably crawling with lice," he said, sprinkling some white powder on Kyūzō's neck. The man then turned on an acetylene lamp and ordered some steamed meat buns, allowing Kyūzō to eat his fill. Kyūzō began choking on the eighth bun. Unable to stop, however, he tore the food into small pieces, incessantly placing them in his mouth. He continued eating until he naturally fell asleep while still clutching the last bun. In the end, he appeared to have eaten a total of twelve or thirteen of them.

Throughout Kyūzō continued speaking. He first asked about the man's name and profession. The man told him that his name was Ōkane Yasuo, but he was vague and evasive about his profession. Kyūzō then asked if the man knew some way to return to Japan. "But of course you saved my life, and I am extremely happy for all that you have done for me now," he added, awkwardly mixing in words of thanks. Yet the man again made no reply.

Kyūzō now began to speak about himself. He was anxious that everything might turn into a dream and vanish if he closed his mouth. Besides, this man Ōkane was listening quite intently. Ōkane seemed particularly interested in the subject of Kō's vest. Exhausted, Kyūzō did not find his interest especially suspicious, however, and proceeded to tell him everything as prompted.

Kyūzō awoke the next morning to the sound of Ōkane returning from somewhere. Gazing up at the sky from the window, Ōkane cursed for some reason, and then removed from his rucksack a safety razor, moistened it with saliva, and began shaving quickly.

"Last night you talked about a fellow named Kō. I just went to a friend's place to check your story and it seems that it's true."

"Did you find out where Kō is?"

"That's not what I said. I just heard about him. But it seems that this guy is a huge faker. It was a good idea to use you as a hiding place. He split the heroin with the guy who gave him information."

As Ōkane explained, the situation was more or less as follows. Two years ago, having received information about the location of some heroin as well as travel expenses from a crime boss, Kō entered the occupation zone of the Eighth Route Army together with two friends. Two years passed without any word from them before Kō suddenly returned three days ago. He was alone and empty-handed. Rather than talk about the drugs, he harped on and on about his bitter disappointment in failing to sell the freight car. Of course the client sent men over to check Kō's lodgings and also waylaid him to search his person. Yet it seemed that Kō was telling the truth. Rumors of the train incident had already become well known here. And Kō's reputation correspondingly increased in value. Apart from the disappearance of his two friends, his failure with the drugs naturally came to be overlooked. Besides, the men who disappeared were, in a word, unlucky. At this point, it was no longer important to speak about those unlucky men.

"So then where's Kō?"

Silently Ōkane patted his freshly shaven jaw, which was now covered with nicks and cuts, and looked closely at Kyūzō as if sizing him up. Approaching Kyūzō, he squeezed the base of his shoulder.

"You stink," Ōkane remarked, curling his upper lip. "Now then, you do feel like doing some work, right?"

"Yes, I'll do anything."

"All right. Then perhaps I'll take you along."

"To see Kō?"

"No, to a seaside town called Shacheng. You can board our ship there."

Shacheng . . . Shacheng. Right, that's the town where smugglers come that Kō and the soldier had been talking about in the truck . . . Smiling, Kyūzō grit his teeth and tried hard to control the feelings that were twitching inside him.

"Hurry up," urged Ōkane as he carefully wiped the razor blade on the cuff of his trousers before wrapping it in paper and placing it in his breast pocket. "Fold up the bedding now and return it to the neighbor."

XXXI

Near dusk, two wagons left the outskirts of Shenyang heading south. The wagon driver cracked his whip, urging on the horses. They had to leave the area under martial law before sunset.

Above the receding town, which was flat and gray, the top of the enormous water tower shone red in the evening sun. Kyūzō's thoughts dwelled on the dog-catching youth, who was no doubt under the water tower. Perhaps he didn't know what else to think about.

Gazing up at the sky, Ōkane continued to grumble. Their departure schedule had been moved up a day on account of the weather. A heavy, strangely lukewarm wind had been blowing since morning. There were fears that the ice upstream would melt, causing the river to overflow. Because of this, it seemed that Ōkane had failed to procure some important goods.

In one group, there was a total of six people apart from the wagon driver. Ōkane, Kyūzō, and a whitish, small-eyed Chinese man named Zhao sat in the rear wagon; Zhao's younger brother and two burly employees rode in the front. Zhao's Japanese was poor, as was Ōkane's Chinese, so Kyūzō was forced at times to interpret for them.

From the conversation of the two men, Kyūzō was able to learn that the wagon cargo included such things as oil, sugar, cotton fabric, and medicinal alcohol, and that the Zhao brothers were major brokers in Shenyang who were close business associates of Ōkane's. Yet Zhao didn't seem to have any good feelings regarding Ōkane's present visit to Shenyang. "Because if you have control of the sea, then I have control of the land," he remarked, smiling pleasantly. However, even Kyūzō could immediately see that Zhao was not genuinely pleased. "Then it's your turn now to come aboard the *Tōkōmaru*," Ōkane replied in an attempt at casual evasion. "No, I don't like ships," Zhao declared without compromise.

Kyūzō was growing all the more nervous. Looking for a break in their conversation, he quickly cut in.

"What is Japan like now?"

Ōkane looked relieved to escape Zhao's displeasure. "Let me see . . ." he began. Removing his glove, he adjusted the large, name-engraved ring on his middle finger. "In short, it's entirely burned up. When I left, the prime minister was, I think, Katayama. But he might have already quit . . . Well, there will be Japanese newspapers on board the ship. Lots of things are written there."

"I suppose the cherry trees have all burned down too."

"Cherry trees? Who cares about cherry trees?"

"I've never seen one yet!"

"Who cares about such things? You're a strange one."

Ōkane blew his nose as he smiled. Rather than use his fingers, he took out a handkerchief and blew into it.

Zhao began talking about the market price of fountain pens and penicillin as Kyūzō grew sleepy. He dreamt. As always, he dreamt of Baharin.

The next morning, everyone alighted when they stopped at a small mountain village by a brook. Hiring three coolies, Zhao took out some pistols from beneath the wagon and distributed them to everyone except the coolies and Kyūzō. He then divided up the cargo so that each person carried packages on their shoulders. Kyūzō felt dejected when he realized that the trip was not going to be an easy one. Nevertheless, it seemed that last night they had safely passed through the battle line between the Nationalists and Eighth Route Army, which was the most difficult part of the journey.

The party boarded a train in a town at the bottom of the mountain. The single passenger car was full. Kyūzō climbed up on the roof together with Zhao's brother. The dirty smoke and soot were annoying, but the train moved slowly and so was not dangerous. After three hours, the sea appeared far off on the right, shining a milky white. Zhao's brother told Kyūzō that that was Liaodong Bay. He grinned broadly, his cheeks naturally relaxing. However, that was not the sea where they were heading. They traveled another two hours before getting off at a small station called Pingshui.

They stayed overnight at a small inn located in front of the station. Kyūzō slept together with the coolies atop a woven mat spread out on the earthen floor. The group would now finally cross the Liaodong Peninsula, which seemed to be the final part of the journey. Kyūzō was too excited to sleep. As a result, the mountain crossing the next day felt even more painful than all the suffering he had previously endured. They departed at 5:00 A.M. Visibility was poor on the mountain, which contained an unusually large number of trees. Zhao had to put down his packages midway. Ōkane began limping. The back part of Kyūzō's right shoe completely tore apart, and his foot rubbed directly against the ground. When they arrived at the base of the mountain, it was already near evening.

There they hired another wagon. The backs of each of the horses were adorned with red banners. Everyone was too exhausted to really speak. They were stopped for questioning late at night. Zhao produced what appeared to be a certificate and uttered the name of some long, incomprehensible union, explaining that the goods were to be brought there. They were quickly allowed to pass. The soldier was extremely quiet and mild mannered. Sound asleep, Kyūzō didn't remember anything else.

Shaken awake, he noticed a strange smell in the air. It was the smell of fish. He thought that he heard the rustling of bushes, but it was the sound of waves. However, he could see nothing. The night was so dark that he had to grope about just to stand still.

The beam of the flashlight slipped on the bellies of the panting horses, circled about, fell to the ground before quickly rebounding, and then jumped to Kyūzō's face.

"We're at the sea," Ōkane announced.

Shivering, Kyūzō nodded in silence.

"You cold?"

Kyūzō shook his head with a toothy smile, but continued shivering.

In front of a long, gentle slope lay a small, rotting dock, and a large, wide barge sat level next to it. Hurried footsteps soon made their way back and forth. Low, sharp rallying cries were exchanged, weaving their way through the darkness. Wet, heavy footsteps treading on the wooden floor of the barge. Slapping waves blocked by the gunwale. Packages were piled atop packages. Wooden boxes, jute bags, and woven baskets that could only be packages for moving. It was incredible that they had carried so much stuff! Kyūzō lost his footing, and one of his feet plunged into the sea. He instinctively screamed out at the cold, but this scream turned to laughter. Roughly dragging him back up, Ōkane struck him on the ear with the back of his glove. "No playing around!" he yelled.

XXXII

The ship should be waiting on the other side of the island, about one hour away. Kyūzō no longer knew which direction was east or west. Soon a dark, flat silhouette appeared in front of them: that might be an island. A small yellow light suddenly flashed to the right. Turning around,

Kyūzō thought that he faintly heard the sharp rhythm of an engine. In both directions, there appeared a gap in the clouds that was somewhat higher than the horizon. The gap was a dark gray inside, around which could be seen a faint tinge of red. That was probably east.

A gentle wind blew in spurts. The gap in the clouds gradually expanded, increasing the reddish tinge, and as the darkness settled and grew in color, it came to be absorbed within the shape of things. Suddenly, Kyūzō realized, the sea surrounded them on all four sides. Its color had become even darker, and only the crest of the waves took on the same gray as the gap in the clouds. It was not unlike dawn in the wasteland. However, the waves of the wasteland were the claws of wild beasts. In comparison, the waves of the sea were like a woman's hair. In the wasteland there was not enough air; here, however, there was more than enough. Kyūzō felt so unsettled that he wanted to scream, to sleep, to laugh uncontrollably.

The ship came into sight. It was obviously small and insubstantial. "What is its tonnage?" "A bit over one hundred tons" came the reply, but Kyūzō didn't understand what that meant. Yet he was concerned that the steamboat of his fantasies was far too flimsy and tarnished with a corrosive agent. Nevertheless, he settled down by telling himself that such a ship was perfectly suited to him.

"Hey!" hailed a voice from the ship.

"Hey!" Ōkane called back as loudly as possible.

"Everything all right?"

"Hey! Has the cargo arrived from the first delivery?"

"Yes."

"Here's the rope!"

"Hey, lower the water pipe!"

The sound of the winch engaging the chain, the sound of the ship planks banging together, the light of the square hand lantern illuminating the ship's side, the filthy gray surface of the ship that appeared not to have been repainted in years, the shouting, the rhythm of the engine as it accelerated in spurts, the sound of whistling . . . The zeal for work reappeared, overwhelming the listless slapping of the waves. Kyūzō ambled about, wondering what he might do to help. Yet everyone's actions were linked together like a machine that was interconnected by joints, and he had no idea how he might contribute. Besides, if possible, he probably wanted to remain still. He wanted to stay right where he was and savor the wonderful taste of being alive.

The gangway was lowered.

"You're fine. Come on," Ōkane urged, grabbing Kyūzō by the arm. At the top of the ramp he turned to Kyūzō. "Take one step up and you'll be in Japanese territory. Still . . ."

Kyūzō couldn't make out what Ōkane said after that. Yet he felt quite somber. He set down his right foot, the one without a shoe heel. I'll never forget this moment, he thought to himself.

"Good work," greeted a large, hunchbacked man, leaning against the wall of the bridge. He spoke in an extremely deep, shapeless voice. He appeared quite unenthusiastic, which was ill suited to such a place.

"Hello, doctor," Ōkane replied in a lively voice, approaching the hunchback and whispering something in his ear. It was probably about Kyūzō, as the man peered at him from behind Ōkane's shoulder.

"Good work!" sang out someone who looked like a sailor, running in between the two men.

("How about it? Look! Everyone's Japanese!")

From the stern came angry shouts like the spewing of gathered spit. "Turn it more slowly!" "Idiot, the draft in front is too low!" "Remove the pipe, and turn that large one to two. Two!" "Idiot!"

"Hey, captain." Ōkane called out to that voice. "I brought an interesting guest."

"Save it for later."

The hunchback snickered. As the captain was about to pass by, Ōkane used his weight to push him back, quickly whispering something. The captain shone his flashlight in Kyūzō's face for an instant before turning it off. "It's bright enough now that you don't need to do that," thought

Kyūzō disagreeably. In fact, he could see the captain's face quite clearly. He was a young man, thirty-two or -three years old, small, with no distinguishing features. The only things that stood out were his dark-blue uniform with gold stripes and his regulation cap, which he wore so slanted that one of his ears was bent. Kyūzō somehow found himself deep in thought as he gazed at the way the captain wore his cap. That's right, the war's over, he reflected. The captain, too, appeared quite curious. "That's fine," he remarked. Making no reply to Kyūzō's bow, however, he impatiently fidgeted, banged his hand abruptly against the wall of the bridge, peered at the ship's side, and, as if recalling something, walked off toward the stern. "But make sure that the stranger doesn't come on deck when we're working!" he warned.

"That's why I'm now going to . . ." Ōkane began to say, but the captain had already left. Ōkane and the doctor looked at each other with a smile.

As Ōkane opened the door of the bridge, the hum of the engine suddenly shot up. The sticky smell of fuel oil and paint mixed together, penetrating all the way to the back of one's eyes. As the two men descended the narrow iron ladder, a heavy echo resounded throughout the surrounding walls, appearing to bounce back from several kilometers ahead. A drowsy yellow lamp. Heat that was so sticky that it could not be properly absorbed.

"Is that person a real doctor?"

"You could say that."

"When is the ship leaving?"

Making no reply, Ōkane peered into the engine room and seemed about to say something when he suddenly closed his mouth in surprise. In the middle of the room, which was covered with oil, surrounded by machinery, and had a low ceiling, a man stood motionless, a shirt wrapped around his head and a cigarette in his mouth.

"You looking at this?" Stopping the engine, the man waved the cigarette between his fingers. There was the trace of a cruel smile on his lower lip. "I plan to blow up this ship."

"Stop joking."

"I'm the one who decides things here. Hurry up and call the southern barbarian. Is there no one in the bridge?"

"In any case, I'll tell the captain."

"About what?"

"About the southern barbarian," Ōkane replied with a contemptuous snort. "In any case, will you look after this kid until we weigh anchor? He's a pretty interesting guest."

The man said nothing. Gazing idly at Kyūzō, he merely thrust out his lower lip.

"I'm counting on you," Ōkane reminded the man before turning to Kyūzō. "Don't be so eager to ask questions. The chief engineer isn't one for chatting."

As soon as Ōkane left, the man pinched the lit end of his cigarette, carefully stubbing it out as he collected the sparks in his palm so that they wouldn't scatter. Kyūzō waited for the man to begin speaking to him. However, the man placed his hand inside a tangle of pipes, loosened some valve, and listened closely to the hiss of the released air. He repeated this action, never bothering to turn around. Kyūzō removed his coat but, still unable to bear the heat, undid the buttons of his jacket. Unconsciously he thrust his fingers into his pants and began scratching the area around his hipbone, which was now completely covered in scabs. Damn it, he said to himself, doesn't this man realize how happy I am? It would have been nice if he had listened more carefully to Ōkane. Look, didn't Ōkane say that I'm an interesting guest? If you knew all the things I've been through, then you'd realize how lucky you are now . . . "Stand by!" The bell rang, and the captain's irritated voice could be heard through the speaking tube. "Hey!" Casting a quick glance around the machinery, the man shouted back, "The southern barbarian hasn't come yet!" He opened a spigot, removed a valve, closed the right handle, adjusted the left handle, pushed a button, and then spun the flywheel. The entire room began to shake as the engine started. Slowly turning the handle, the man reduced the engine speed. Kyūzō gasped, his forehead dripping with sweat.

XXXIII

Thirty minutes after the ship began moving, Ōkane came to call on Kyūzō. The captain and "doctor" were waiting on deck. As if by common consent, the three men tried hard to affect a nonchalant manner, but their focus was elsewhere. Kyūzō didn't particularly care, however, as he was relieved to have been allowed out of the engine room and now found himself engrossed in the brilliance of the sea that he was looking at for the first time.

"It really is very blue, isn't it?"

"It's called the Yellow Sea because it's yellow," the doctor replied laughing.

Surrounding Kyūzō, the three men walked toward the stern. "We've got something interesting to show you." ("Right. Didn't General Bai also say something like that? He was referring then to that bloodied wagon driver.") "What is it?" "Come and see." Gray birds were circling above the mast. The sky was blue. I suppose that the sea is really not all that blue. Perhaps it's more blue-green. Kyūzō peered at the side of the ship. Countless bubbles emerged from beneath the light cobalt-colored water. Just like cider, he thought, suddenly feeling thirsty.

Below the ladder leading up to the lookout in the stern there was a low side door. Inside was a dark tunnel. On each side there was a single door. Knocking on the door on the right, Ōkane called out.

"Are you resting now, sir?"

"Oh, please come in."

A hoarse, phlegm-ridden voice replied from inside. At that moment, Kyūzō had a strange feeling that he had experienced exactly this same moment a long time ago. Turning the knob, Ōkane quickly looked at Kyūzō, then nodded to no one in particular. The small, elongated room was unfinished and approximately five square meters in size with a low ceiling. There was a filthy round window. Below the window stood a crude and narrow wooden bed. On the bed was a man with thinning hair and khaki-colored clothes hunched over a newspaper.

The man slowly raised his head. He knit his eyebrows and tilted his head. It was Kō Sekitō!

No one spoke. It was as if the flow of time were being held back by the monotone hum of the engine. A cockroach as large as a man's palm dropped noisily from the ceiling. Someone breathed a heavy sigh.

"So I wonder which one of you is the real Mr. Kuki Kyūzō."

As Ōkane uttered this remark, Kō rose to his feet at the same time.

"Hello there! So you're safe!"

Kyūzō closed his eyes. He felt like he wanted to fill his entire body with a smile, and yet he also wished to turn his body into a clenched fist and strike Kō. Caught between these two contradictory, fervent emotions, Kyūzō merely felt an unbearable sense of fatigue. He felt ill. Perhaps it was seasickness.

"Seems like you couldn't get away with it," the captain said hurriedly, rubbing his hands together.

"I'd like to speak to Kuki alone for a bit."

"But I thought you were Kuki," replied Ōkane with a smile.

"I guess you're out of luck," the doctor groaned.

The newspaper that Kō held in his hands was shaking. His wide-open artificial eye glared at the ceiling. Only Kyūzō noticed, however, that his half-open seeing eye was peering closely at the door.

"I'd like to speak alone . . ."

As Kō rubbed his face, pieces of thin, frostbitten skin peeled off and fell to the floor. His entire face was mottled like a map. I'm sure my face looks the same way, thought Kyūzō.

"He says he wants to speak to you," Ōkane stated, looking solemnly at Kyūzō. Kyūzō's lips moved slightly, but he was unable to speak. "It's too late," whispered the doctor. "Well, let's settle things over there," said the captain, jerking his chin as he took a step forward.

The newspaper left Kō's hands and slipped across the floor. At the same time, he thrust the captain aside and rushed toward the door. There he collided with Ōkane, and the two fell in a heap. Blood began to flow from between the captain's fingers as he covered his face. Kō screamed as he grabbed Ōkane's face, while Ōkane screamed as he pressed his fingers into Kō's neck. Straddling the two men on the floor, the doctor pinned Kō's arms behind his back. Kō kicked his legs up in the air from behind. Adjusting his cap as he held his right hand to his bloody nose, the captain pressed his left arm against Kō's right elbow. Ōkane stood up, brushed the dirt from his clothes, and with a roar wrapped his arm around Kō's left elbow. The doctor lifted up Kō's clothes in the back and patted the vest. "You can't move freely with something so heavy attached to you." "Let me go! I'm not like you bastards!" "That's obvious," shouted the captain, plugging up his nose.

"You stay here," Ōkane ordered when Kyūzō tried to follow them.

"That's right. After all, this room is rented out to Kuki Kyūzō," chimed in the doctor, nodding.

Entangled together, the men left the room. For a moment, Kō looked back over his shoulder. Kyūzō could not understand the meaning of his gaze. However, he vaguely remembered the eyes of something he had seen at the bank of the marsh.

Kyūzō felt nauseous. The entire cabin creaked as it began to list. He stumbled to the middle of the bed. Kō's body odor still covered the stiff blanket. Kyūzō pulled in his arms and legs like a threatened spider, and his heart also recoiled like a threatened spider. He felt as if he were in a room whose four sides were stretched by a mirror, such that front and back were indistinguishable. He was sure that he had walked on and on for a long time through the wide world, but now he even felt as if everything were just an internal event. What is Kō doing here now? he wondered. Serves him right! You reap what you sow! Still, those guys are really violent. They didn't need to be so rough with him. But I wonder if I should have let him speak with me alone, as he said. We have so many things to talk about. He owes me a lot of money. But those guys wouldn't . . .

As the cabin creaked like an old chair, the horizon slipped from the window and crept up toward the sky, shone white, and then tumbled down. An ominous thought weighed on Kyūzō: Those guys wouldn't . . . Once that unpleasant thought came to him, however, it revealed itself to be far more convincing. Could those guys really be so angry simply because Kō had falsely used Kyūzō's name? No chance! They had to be after Kō's vest. What were they planning to do with him now? Of course it's not my fault, it's punishment. But they wouldn't possibly kill him. We're now in Japan, after all . . .

Ōkane returned carrying a kettle of water and a steamed potato wrapped in paper.

"There's a food shortage in Japan. What, are you feeling sick? It's because the wind has picked up a bit. Well, get some sleep until you're used to it."

"How about Mr. Kō?"

"Huh? Oh, him? Don't worry about that. Just pretend he never existed. The only guest on this ship should be Kuki Kyūzō. Hah!"

"But there's something I'd like to talk to him about."

"You can't talk with someone who's not here. Don't worry about that. Forget about it. It's for your own good. Now then, there are only four people in the world who know what just happened here. Besides, that guy isn't really Japanese."

Kyūzō closed his eyes. We still haven't arrived in Japan, he thought. Ōkane removed something from his pocket and placed it on Kyūzō's pillow. "You can play this if you get bored," he said consolingly.

It was a rusted, peeling harmonica.

XXXIV

SHIP LOG OF THE *TŌKŌMARU*

(February 22, 1948)

Time: noon

Nautical miles traveled: 384.6

Course: S 75 E

Deviation: 6–22 W

Wind direction: S 20 E

Wind speed: 15 knots

Weather: b (fair)

Air pressure: 1,015 mb

Report: In accordance with Article 27 of Seafarer Law, we have taken appropriate steps regarding the passenger Kō Sekitō, who assumed the name "Kuki Kyūzō," for committing assault. The real Kuki Kyūzō regained his health yesterday evening. After being sprayed thoroughly with DDT, he was ordered this morning to assist the cook as a steward. He raised various objections with regard to the fake Kuki's illegal belongings, creating a nuisance. He still must be convinced. At 3:00, we arrived at a coastal area and anchored off K Island. We waited until sunset, changed course to S 10 E while watching the O Lighthouse off the starboard bow, and should now arrive in P Harbor in approximately two hours. No additional items are to be noted.

XXXV

Kyūzō was desperate to find out Kō's whereabouts. He was driven neither by mere sympathy nor desire. Rather, the emotion was akin to a bestial lust for revenge.

Having been assigned to help with the cooking, Kyūzō brought food for the first time to Ōkane and the two others below the map room. Upon seeing the captain proudly toying with the Mongolian knife and Dania spoon, he asked for these back and was promptly struck so hard on the wrist with the knife handle that it left a mark. This treatment brought out a clear sense of defiance in him. Another major reason for his frustration was because they steadfastly refused to tell him the name of the town where they would enter port. It was essentially useless to ask the sailors on board. It seemed that these sailors had already received certain instructions, and they appeared to even avoid speaking with him.

"No need to be in such a rush," remarked the captain, who seemed to even find amusement in Kyūzō's impatience. "Things won't be so good once you leave the ship. You'll wind up an urchin, wandering about scrounging in garbage. Best to spend a bit more time enjoying yourself here."

"Urchin! But I've got money. I've got the share that Mr. Kō will pay me. Please give that money back to me!"

"Kō? Let me see, I've never heard of anyone by that name."

Damn it, me an urchin! Kō clearly promised that he'd give me five hundred thousand yen. From beginning to end, I've been abandoned over and again. Now when I'm finally about to reach the last door, I'm still treated like this! I should be fairly compensated for all my suffering. Beside himself with furious anger, Kyūzō was barely able to control himself until they reached port.

On the very day that they were heading into port in the evening, Kyūzō became convinced that Kō was still alive somewhere on board the ship. While washing the empty pot after they had finished the last meal, he suddenly noticed Baldy, the cook, filling an empty can with leftovers. There had been no sign whatsoever of anyone keeping pets on board. No question about it, thought Kyūzō.

"What are you doing with that?"

"How would I know?" The cook tried to hide his discomfort with his shrill laugh, but he clearly looked flustered.

"You're bringing that to Mr. Kō, right?"

"I don't know, I don't know. I'm just delivering this because Mr. Ōkane, the purser, asked me to."

"Please tell me where Mr. Kō is. Please, I'm begging you."

"I said I don't know. I've got no idea what you're talking about."

Kō is alive! It has to be Kō! If this is the kind of food they're giving him, then he must really be treated badly. Kyūzō began trying to persuade the cook. After all the pain and suffering he had been through, he now had a right to know where Kō was. If the cook told him, then Kyūzō would of course do what he could for him.

"Shh!" The cook appeared to play the fool as he looked around exaggeratedly, the flab on his neck shaking. "Now then, I didn't hear anything you just said. You've really got a loose tongue! You're forgetting that you're with a group of reckless men who've got no fear of death. Knock on wood, I didn't hear anything. If you insist, just go ahead and take these leftovers from me and bring them to the purser yourself. Then you can ask the boss in person. At any rate, you might want to remember this one thing: to have no fear of death means to have no fear of someone else's death. It doesn't mean your own life, for these men value their own lives twice as much as they do anyone else's. Look at this." Removing a bottle from below the cooking counter, the cook filled an aluminum cup about halfway, added a pinch of salt and some water, skillfully waved it about, and then gulped it down, coughing. "That is undiluted medicinal alcohol. Now look at this one," he said, taking out another bottle, uncorking it, and then pouring about the same amount gently down the sink. The line of its flow shook like a pendulum along with the ship's rocking. "Understand? I got this second bottle from the doctor. It was among the cargo that we picked up the day before yesterday. No one knows exactly what it is. Maybe a bit of methyl is mixed in with it. No matter how much of an addict I might be, I wouldn't be able to take it. That's why I pretend to drink it and put it in a place that's easy to see. But no, you shouldn't think that the doctor is a bad man. He's probably the kindest man on the ship. It's just that he has no fear of death. And I'm the same way. I pretend to drink it and then leave the bottle out. Well, he's probably known all along that I don't drink it. So if you plan to join up with these men who have no fear of death, you need to take better care of your own life. As long as we know this about each other, we can feel calm and at ease being with men who've got no fear of death."

With a heavy sigh, the cook looked quite pleased with this talk as he wiped his tomato-red brow with the sleeve of his work clothes. He pushed the empty can toward Kyūzō. "Well now, bring it to him. Take it from me. But just remember that I didn't hear anything."

Cracking his knuckles, Ōkane gave Kyūzō a wry smile. He then told him Kō's whereabouts in a surprisingly matter-of-fact manner.

"I guess you're pretty perceptive. You can just bring him the food yourself, if you won't regret it. Was it Baldy who told you?"

"No, I figured it out myself. Where is he?"

"In the hold."

It wasn't exactly the hold, however. When Kyūzō opened what appeared to be a storeroom door in the left-hand corner of the engine room, he found a low side opening—Kō was locked up in the back there. It was a narrow, rectangular gap surrounded by the wall of the hold in the front, the wall of the engine room in the back, the cistern on the right, and the side of the ship on the left. The curve of the ship's side was directly connected to the wall of the cistern, so the room was actually floorless. Probably the same gap could be found on the starboard side as well. The ventilation was good, but the rumbling and heat of the engine were horrible. Kō's ankle was shackled to a hole in the iron plate that formed part of the seam in the wall. His body was beaten and his clothes were torn up. With his feet propped against the vertical wall and his back held against the curved wall, he gazed up at the ceiling, which extended all the way to the deck. A large, dark blotch appeared below his artificial eye. Light leaked in from somewhere, faintly illuminating the oxide-red walls.

Kō's mind appeared to be as shredded as his clothes. He didn't even glance at the can that Kyūzō held out to him.

"Mr. Kō!" Kyūzō tried calling into his ear. "Are you all right? It's me, Kuki."

"Aah!" Kō's handcuffs rattled as he shrank back in fear. Slowly turning his seeing eye, he stared at Kyūzō's face. With his swollen lips partly open, however, he showed no emotion whatsoever.

"What happened? They stole the vest, right?"

Kō coughed and spat loudly. He then began to murmur something under his breath. Kyūzō leaned forward, straining to hear. Opening his arms, Kō grabbed Kyūzō by the shoulders as if embracing him.

"Actually, there's something I've wanted to discuss with you. Listen, it's an important secret. I bought this ship. But as you know, I'm actually on an important mission. That's why I've got to hide like this. But thank you for visiting me."

Kyūzō felt spooked. Instinctively he tried to pull back but was restrained by Kō's strong arms. Kō continued in a monotone, as if singing.

"Wait. The thing that I wanted to tell you. No one's listening, right? Actually, I've been charged with the task of establishing the central government in exile of the Republic of Manchuria. But the situation seems to be pressing, and I'm thinking about holding the presidential inauguration ceremony now. This is top secret, of course. Now I'd like you to attend. Understand? I've been charged with this task. This is top secret, and I can tell only Japanese people, but the fact is that I'm really Japanese. My name is Kuki Kyūzō. But Manchuria and Japan must become allies. My name is Kuki Kyūzō and I'm really Japanese. It's been officially recognized as the central government in exile of the Republic of Manchuria. And secretly . . ."

The rumbling of the engine that seemed about to strike one, the heat that appeared to take on color, Kō's stinging bad breath, and his slow, pressing repetition . . . Kyūzō could no longer stand it and forcefully pushed Kō away. Kō fell over on his side uttering inanities: Ho, ho, ho! Leaving the can at his feet, Kyūzō banged into things left and right as he desperately escaped.

"What's wrong, sir? Good riddance, right?" The chief engineer greeted him with a cruel smile. "I'm sure your room is better than this one."

"Nonsense!" exclaimed Ōkane with a forced laugh as he locked the side opening.

"In any case, I think your room used to be a morgue. I was worried, you know."

"That's ridiculous! It was just a storage room," Ōkane remarked flippantly, joining in on the joke.

A young sailor raced toward them yelling.

"We've spotted land. Land!"

Kyūzō passed the sailor as he went out. He ran up the stairs, pretending to appear on deck. Kō's fate could no longer be someone else's problem. He had to settle this somehow before they arrived in port. Everything depended now simply on whether or not he could grab the stuff. If only he could lay his hands on the stuff, then he was in control. He could threaten to rip the bag and scatter the drugs to the wind or maybe throw the bag into the sea. Nobody would be able to interfere then. If the stuff was anywhere, then it had to be in the room of those three men below the map room. The captain was probably in the map room while Ōkane was still down below. If anyone remained in the room, it would just be the doctor. Surely he's asleep drunk, as always. Even if he's awake, a man like him would surely understand. After all, it's my legitimate right...

But Kyūzō was unlucky. At exactly the same time he finished climbing the stairs, the door opened and the captain appeared. Kyūzō tried to go back but Ōkane was climbing the stairs from below. There was no time to hesitate. With his head bowed, Kyūzō lunged forward.

He was just a moment too late, however. At the instant he launched himself forward, the ship listed, pulling him back. As the captain dodged out of the way, Kyūzō tripped and stumbled into the room. In front of him sat the doctor, facing him. Turning around, Kyūzō saw that the captain and Ōkane stood alongside each other blocking his path from behind. He suddenly rushed to the bed on the left, pushed aside the blanket cover, and began randomly groping about.

"What the hell are you doing?" exclaimed the captain, throwing himself upon Kyūzō. Ōkane then grabbed his leg, dragging him down. The doctor merely gazed at them in silence.

"Give it back! Half is mine!" No, I guess it wasn't half, he admitted to himself. But half wouldn't be bad. I've got a right to that much. Really, I've got a right to all of it!

"I said give it back! Kō and I have an agreement!"

"Idiot!" said the captain, grabbing Kyūzō by his growing hair and rubbing his face on the floor.

"That's no thing for a child to have," added the doctor in a blank voice.

"But half of it's mine. It would be too hard for me to arrive in Japan penniless."

"What the hell are you talking about? We've already arrived. This right here is officially Japan!" laughed Ōkane.

"No, I mean the land!"

"Don't worry," shrieked the captain. "In any case, you needn't fear that we'll let you off the ship."

"Really, you might be better off here than going ashore and becoming an urchin," muttered the doctor as if remembering.

"That's why I'm asking you to give it back to me!"

"You won't need it if you're not going ashore," said the captain, baring his teeth.

"But that's not what you promised!"

"Promise?" Ōkane replied, playing innocent. "I don't remember making such a promise. Besides, this right here is officially Japan."

"Oh, and even the sea below is Japan."

Kyūzō stopped going against them. The stuff was no longer important. In any case, he had to somehow think of a way to escape. He gingerly rose to his feet, rubbing his body.

"Hey, it's time to head to the bridge," said the captain. "We have to put this boy to sleep somewhere. Does that room have a lock on the outside?"

"It will if we put one there," answered Ōkane, rubbing his face.

The ship again listed heavily. The momentum caused the door to open of itself. Kyūzō suddenly made a dash for it. In the next instant, however, he found his body afloat. The doctor had grabbed his wrist, twisting him up. Still twisting him, the doctor handed Kyūzō over to the captain. The captain, in turn, handed him to Ōkane. "What a stupid boy! I'll take this back," remarked Ōkane pitifully as he took the harmonica from Kyūzō's pocket.

With his wrist still twisted up, Kyūzō was brought back along the path from where he had just come. From the stairs to the passageway, then from the passageway to the engine room. As a young sailor helped him, the chief engineer smiled cynically at Kyūzō while shouting in amusement. "I'll give you lots of attention once you safely get out!" From the engine room to the side opening, then from the side opening to the gap with the oxidered walls.

One part of the handcuffs was removed from the iron plate and placed around Kyūzō's ankle. He and Kō were now bound together by a single handcuff. The chief engineer shouted something. The door of the side opening was closed and locked from the outside.

Screaming, Kyūzō crawled toward the side opening. Kō angrily tried to push him aside. In the small room their legs became entangled, and each movement caused the ring of the handcuffs to clamp down even more tightly. Kyūzō finally gave up and grew quiet.

Kō still showed no sign of emotion. Kyūzō clenched his teeth and tightly shut his eyes, trying to think and feel nothing. The more he tried, however, the more his eyes opened and his mouth sagged. This can't be true, he thought. They have to be playing a prank. Making a joke for their own amusement . . . Without realizing it, he began to cry.

He awoke to the changing sound of the engine. It seemed that he had fallen asleep at some point. It had become completely quiet. The sound of the winch echoed from the deck. Does that mean we're now in port? If that's true, Kyūzō thought in spite of himself, then this stupid situation can't be real . . . As if remembering, he began screaming again. He soon tried to stand up but was promptly yanked back by Kō. "Hey, I'm Kuki. I'm really Kuki. Kuki Kyūzō." Suddenly a sound echoed forth—inconspicuous, dull, large, and penetrating. It was the quay! "I'm Kuki. Kuki Kyūzō. No mistake . . ."

"Mr. Kō!" Kyūzō grabbed him by the shoulders, shaking him. "We've arrived! We've arrived in Japan!"

Another, even larger sound echoed forth heavily. Rattling the handcuffs, Kō abruptly stood up. Peering at the middle of the wall as if looking right through it, he exclaimed, "What? Could that be the sound of a cannon?" "I said that we've arrived in Japan!" "No, it's a cannon. I guess the war has begun. Like I said, America and the Soviet Union have begun fighting. Ha-ha! My name is Kuki Kyūzō. Actually, let me tell you . . .

Actually, I'm the chief president. Understand? I'm president of the government in exile."

There was repeated several times a dull echo like a tree being cut down. That had to be the sound of the hatch being removed. "It's war!" Kō yelled out, clinging to the wall. Ignoring the twisting in his ankle, Kyūzō grasped the wall of the ship's side with both arms, drawing his cheek close to it and pressing his chest against it. Damn it! Japan is just a few centimeters on the other side!

"Speaking of Kuki Kyūzō, I'm rather well known," Kō continued, banging his forehead hard against the iron plate. Suddenly he began singing, "Young lady!" "Idiot!" snapped Kyūzō, instinctively hitting him before sitting down exhausted on the ship bottom. "All right. So war is like weeds, and all you need is the right land for many to grow. I suppose that there's land suited to war. I guess it's a man's purpose in life . . . Lieutenant Yoshino was a man . . ."

Kyūzō caressed the gritty, red iron plate. Damn it, those bastards! To think that Japan is just on the other side! Still, did I really want to come here? I wonder if I didn't want to go somewhere else. What's worse, I'm still together with Kō! Perhaps it's all been just a dream. Maybe I'm still sleeping out in the wasteland somewhere, about to get frostbite . . .

Someone passed above deck dragging something heavy.

"It's war!" Kō shouted, his voice twitching.

Damn it, it seems that I've just been circling around the same place. No matter how far I go, I can't take a single step out of the wasteland. Perhaps Japan doesn't exist anywhere. With every step I take, the wasteland walks together with me. Japan just flees further away . . . For an instant, Kyūzō dreamt a sparklike dream. He dreamt of Baharin when he was very little. His mother was doing laundry behind a high wall. Crouching at her side, he played with the bubbles from the washbasin, popping them with his fingers one after another. No matter how many bubbles he popped, the infinite sky and sun whirled around in radiant gold. From over the wall, another Kyūzō, this one exhausted, peeped timidly in at the sight of them. He was utterly unable to cross over. Why must I spend my whole life wandering outside the wall? Outside the wall people are lonely, forced to bare their teeth like apes in order to live. They can only live like beasts, just as Baldy said. "Ha ha ha," Kō inanely burst out laughing, like an idiot . . . Right, perhaps I took the wrong road from the very beginning. "It's war! Ha-ha! War! Ha! I'm the chief president. Ha!" From the time I first set out, surely I began walking in the opposite direction. It's probably because of that that I keep getting lost in the wasteland . . .

Suddenly, however, Kyūzō made a fist, raised it, and began striking the oxide-red iron plate. He became a beast, roaring as the skin of his hand peeled and blood oozed out, and yet pounding with all his strength.

WEATHERHEAD BOOKS ON ASIA

WEATHERHEAD EAST ASIAN INSTITUTE,

COLUMBIA UNIVERSITY

Kim Sŏk-pŏm, *The Curious Tale of Mandogi's Ghost*, translated by Cindi Textor (2010)
The Columbia Anthology of Modern Chinese Drama, edited by Xiaomei Chen (2011)
Qian Zhongshu, *Humans, Beasts, and Ghosts: Stories and Essays*, edited by Christopher
G. Rea, translated by Dennis T. Hu, Nathan K. Mao, Yiran Mao, Christopher G. Rea,
and Philip F. Williams (2011)
Dung Kai-cheung, *Atlas: The Archaeology of an Imaginary City*, translated by Dung
Kai-cheung, Anders Hansson, and Bonnie S. McDougall (2012)
O Chŏnghŭi, *River of Fire and Other Stories*, translated by Bruce Fulton and Ju-Chan
Fulton (2012)
Endō Shūsaku, *Kiku's Prayer: A Novel*, translated by Van Gessel (2013)
Li Rui, *Trees Without Wind: A Novel*, translated by John Balcom (2013)
Zhu Wen, *The Matchmaker, the Apprentice, and the Football Fan: More Stories of China*,
translated by Julia Lovell (2013)
The Columbia Anthology of Modern Chinese Drama, Abridged Edition, edited by Xiaomei
Chen (2013)
Natsume Sōseki, *Light and Dark*, translated by John Nathan (2013)
Seirai Yūichi, *Ground Zero, Nagasaki: Stories*, translated by Paul Warham (2015)
Hideo Furukawa, *Horses, Horses, in the End the Light Remains Pure: A Tale That Begins
with Fukushima* (2016)

History, Society, and Culture

CAROL GLUCK, EDITOR

Takeuchi Yoshimi, *What Is Modernity? Writings of Takeuchi Yoshimi*, edited and
translated, with an introduction, by Richard F. Calichman (2005)
Contemporary Japanese Thought, edited and translated by Richard F. Calichman (2005)
Overcoming Modernity, edited and translated by Richard F. Calichman (2008)
Natsume Sōseki, *Theory of Literature and Other Critical Writings*, edited and translated by
Michael Bourdaghs, Atsuko Ueda, and Joseph A. Murphy (2009)
Kojin Karatani, *History and Repetition*, edited by Seiji M. Lippit (2012)
The Birth of Chinese Feminism: Essential Texts in Transnational Theory, edited by Lydia
H. Liu, Rebecca E. Karl, and Dorothy Ko (2013)
Yoshiaki Yoshimi, *Grassroots Fascism: The War Experience of the Japanese People*, translated
by Ethan Mark